HUNTING
the
WOLF

Denis Bright

Cover design by: The Tin Studio

Inspired by Australian artist Eric Smith

ISBN: 978-0-6450407-1-5

DEDICATION

TO MY WIFE VICKI

AND DAUGHTERS MARAYA AND JILLIAN

A dream itself is but a shadow

William Shakespeare

The neighbourhood is empty.
In the dim grey light,
The occasional street lamp
Barely reveals the creature.
The wolf is running close to the gutter.
Its stride is even paced,
Its disposition unnerving.
There is no vicious snarl, no growl.
The face is expressionless.
In the solitude and darkness, the boy awakes,
Immersed in soul-sinking dread.
He knows it is coming.
The wolf will not be deterred.
One night it will arrive.

Denis Bright

1

Ambushed

The drive through Sydney went smoothly and Sebastian Darcy would be on time for a rendezvous with his mate, Joe. With just a flicker of life from the leaves atop the Moreton Bay figs lining Anzac Parade, the sky to the east was clearing and it looked like being another hot one.

He passed through Kingsford without having to stop at a single set of traffic lights. What were the odds of that? It had to be a good sign, he thought to himself.

With the rifle range in the distance, Sebastian made a left turn towards the water. Beams of sunshine burst through the clouds, glistening in patterns, lighting up the tar road like a stage. Across the bay were fishermen with their rods, chancing their luck on the rocky outcrops near the water's edge.

Sebastian drove into the golf-club car park and got his first surprise of the day. Joe's Falcon was already there. One of Joe's less endearing traits was that he was rarely on time, let alone early.

Sebastian unloaded his clubs, securing them to his fold-up buggy. Making his way along the pathway adjoining the clubhouse, the pungent smell of salt and seaweed was as familiar as it was soothing.

He saw Joe up ahead, standing outside the pro shop, talking with his son Matt.

Joe was tall with broad shoulders. He was wearing a red and green polo top featuring the emblem of the South Sydney Rabbitohs, his beloved NRL team. Joe had a long scar above his chin and a silver earring dangling from his right ear. With his hound-dog eyes, long black hair, and dark complexion, it wasn't surprising that some of his mates referred to Joe De Gabriel as 'The Pirate'. It was ironic because Joe was not fond of boats. According to Joe, a dislike of deep water was in his gene memory, the result of a horrific boat journey back in the 1800s when his ancestors migrated from Sicily.

Matt waved when he saw Sebastian. As far as looks go, the apple didn't fall far from the tree. Matt, with his short cropped hair and brand-name clothing, might have been plucked from the streets of L.A. Sebastian was surprised he had come along.

Joe greeted Sebastian with his customary thumbs entwined handshake, a habit he had adopted after his stint in prison. The two hugged enthusiastically. After they had exchanged pleasantries, Joe indicated towards the water. He spoke in a gentle, whimsical tone.

'Hey Seb, remember that year the Christmas tides were huge? Tame Malabar had the best surf on the coast. We sat over there on the cliff above the pool with our guitars, writing a song. Do you remember the song we wrote?'

'*Surf Rider*,' replied Sebastian without hesitation.

'It's a good name for a song,' said Matt. I can remember you playing it years ago, Dad.'

'You would have been only four or five,' said Joe. He lightly clapped his hands. 'Ok, Seb. This one will test you. It was Boxing Day, and we were out at La Perouse. We were watching the yachts in the Sydney to Hobart yacht race sail past. What was the song we wrote that day?'

Sebastian looked Joe in the eyes as he thought. Joe smiled, enjoying the fact that Sebastian was struggling to remember.

'*Noise Complaints*? replied Seb, with a questioning upwards intonation.

'No, that was later, when you were living at Surry Hills with Des,' said Joe, waiting a beat before coming out with it. '*Botany Bay*... I've been mucking around with it on guitar. Taken it up to E so I can use open strings.' Joe began singing the melody.

Down and out in ole London town,

Scratching for survival.

'Your idea, Sebastian,' said Joe, in a tone that was full of praise. 'You'd just listened to an interview on the radio. Somebody had traced their ancestors back to the eighteenth century and discovered they were related to an early convict. Some poor dude stole a loaf of bread, or did something equally petty, and got transported to the colony.'

'I can't believe you can still remember all that, Joe.'

'Tell you what it is, Sebastian. It's being out this way again. Call me sentimental, but there are so many memories around here. It must be the same for you?'

Sebastian agreed. 'It's where we grew up, Joe.'

Joe tapped the top of his golf bag. 'It's great we could get a game in, Seb. Been practicing for this one,' he said in a serious tone.

Matt smirked. 'I wouldn't be too worried if I were you, Seb. Dad's idea of practice is hitting fucking acorns in the backyard. He's way too much of a scrooge to go to the driving range.'

Joe was unperturbed. 'You don't need a driving range. All you need is a golden elm in your yard. I'm telling you, it works. You can tell if it's a good shot by the feel of the acorn as it leaves the club.'

Sebastian spoke in a deadpan manner. 'Maybe you should market the idea as Joe's Golden Elm Method – GEM. That's it... your catch phrase, GEM.'

Matt laughed. 'How about, "Don't go wasting your time with those silly white things called golf balls. Purchase a packet of Ole Joe's GEMs".'

'The proof will be in the pudding,' said Joe, adamant.

Sebastian turned towards Matt. 'So Matt, are you going to have a hit with us?' he asked, knowing that it was highly unlikely.

His enquiry was met by a sour grimace. 'Golf... you are joking.' He patted the bag that was slung across his shoulder. 'I'm going pillin'. Found nearly fifty balls last time,' he said with pride.

'When we were kids, your dad and I used to get heaps from the gulley near the third hole. Kept us in pocket money, eh Joe?'

'I bet I know what Dad spent his money on!' said Matt, lightheartedly.

'Isn't he funny?' said Joe. 'Be doing standup soon if he keeps it up.'

When Joe wanted to show Sebastian his new putter, Matt knew it was his cue to leave them to it.

'Have a good one,' he said affectionately before trotting off with purpose along the path parallel to the first fairway.

'Matt was lucky with that court business,' said Sebastian, once Matt was out of earshot. 'Yeah. Got him a topnotch barrister. The same fella who helped me out once.'

'He must have been good, alright. Up my way they give out custodial sentences for similar charges.'

'I didn't want to talk too much on the phone, but he got the charges reduced from supplying to possession. And we got him a reference and put a case together about Matt having prospects of employment as a DJ.' At that point Joe became more animated. 'There's this fella, Greg Santos, played some first grade for the Roosters a few years back. You might have heard of him?'

Sebastian shrugged his shoulders, 'Rings a bell.'

'Well, he's part owner of a couple of clubs and pubs in town. Heard Matt in some club and said he'd give him some DJ work.'

'Great... nothing like getting out and doing a few gigs.'

'Music keeps him occupied. That's part of Matt's problem, I reckon, not enough interests.'

Sebastian refrained from saying what he was thinking. Part of Matt's problem was that when he was a kid, Joe had been off his face most of the time. And Matt certainly found plenty of interests, albeit dubious ones. But Sebastian did marvel at the way Joe just seemed to take things in his stride. He would have been beside himself if he had a son in the type of trouble Matt had been in.

Sebastian nodded in the direction of the car park where there were a couple of boys struggling to get their clubs and buggies out of the boot of their car.

'Let's get a move on, before those kids get in front of us.'

The two went into the pro shop to pay their green fees. The sullen attendant raised his head slowly from the timesheet and a smile formed on his face. This was Rabbitoh territory, and it was soon clear that he too was a South Sydney supporter.

'Hey… go the Bunnies!' he said, with gusto.

Joe responded by giving a glowing account of the team's new signings and premiership prospects, while an amused Sebastian watched on. The two left the pro shop in a cheerful mood and made their way down to the first tee. There was a group of golfers still playing out the hole.

Sebastian took a club from his bag and had a practice swing.

Joe assumed a serious countenance as he observed Sebastian. He then stepped in close and spoke with authority.

'Hey mate. Something I just noticed, Seb. Your body is swaying. You'll be slicing the ball all over the place.' There was a pause as Sebastian began to consider what Joe was saying.

Joe had barely managed to suppress his laughter. Sebastian soon cottoned on, responding with a lighthearted, 'Fuck off!'

The two childhood friends talked about old times. 'Remember Brooksie, I ran into him at Maroubra Junction. Still lives around here. Got a concrete business.'

'Good on him. He used to hit his driver a mile,' said Sebastian. 'We used to joke that it had springs in it.'

'He used to hit golf balls at the boats fishing in the bay,' said Joe.

'Lucky for them he didn't shoot straight,' said Sebastian, adding a beat later, 'You two were dangerous together.'

'While I think of it, Seb, thanks for letting Matt and I stay at your mum's place. Really appreciate it.'

'That's cool, Joe. Happy to have somebody living in the place while things are being sorted out.'

'It's given me a chance to get my head together. Been good for Matt, too. Got him away from the dickheads he was hanging with.'

Joe's demeanor changed and he became almost solemn.

'Seb… I have a proposition for you.'

Sebastian was curious. 'Yeah… go on.'

'I've been playing guitar and singing a lot again and I want to get back into it, seriously. I was thinking, you and I, we know so many great songs between us. What do you think about putting a few sets together? Hit the pubs and clubs. Do something we love and make some money. Good money if we have a bit of luck and are smart about it.'

Sebastian's first reaction to the proposal was one of ambivalence. The idea of playing music live again was alluring but it seemed like such a stretch in his present frame of mind. Lately he felt jaded and unmotivated. Just getting out of bed in the morning was arduous.

He stared back at Joe with a blank expression, trying to find the words to respond. But Joe wasn't going to be deterred by Sebastian's initial lack of enthusiasm.

Joe spoke with conviction. He told Sebastian that he'd dropped in on a few venues lately, and that much of their old material was as relevant as ever. And because they had played together before they would be able to build a repertoire quickly.

He then reminded Sebastian that he owned a powerful Bose PA with speakers that could handle a large venue, a state-of-the-art mixer and Shure 58 mikes. That would save them the cost of hiring gear and he didn't want a cent from Sebastian. Joe went on to say he'd been playing with downloaded drum and bass tracks. They could play with a drummer and bass player for large venues and use the backup tracks for smaller, mid-week gigs. Joe finished off his pitch by rolling off the names of a few people they knew who still worked in the industry. Sebastian agreed they would be useful contacts.

'I'm impressed, Joe. You have been busy.'

He began to consider the idea seriously. Joe had a great voice and over the years had developed into a more than competent guitarist. And maybe a change like this was just what his life needed. It might be just the thing to shake himself out of the rut he was in. He would have to check with his wife, Astrid, but it might also provide the spark their relationship needed. And he could afford to give it a go. In that sense the timing was perfect. He and his sister Kate had inherited their mother's house. Even though it wasn't renovated, it was still worth nearly two million.

Before long Sebastian and Joe were suggesting possible songs. By the time the players ahead had putted out, they had already agreed on twenty or so.

They hit their tee shots, grabbed their buggies, and ambled off along the fairway. A slight breeze was coming up off the ocean; the impending southerly introducing itself. Sebastian glanced to the south-east where a bank of clouds was leisurely gathering. For a brief moment he could make out the shape of a wolf's face in the ever-changing shades of misty white and grey.

As they approached the green Joe screwed up his face, waving his hand in front of his nose. The ground had been top-dressed recently and the astringent stench of fertiliser was overpowering.

Joe won the first hole, playing a freakish bunker shot that hit the flag hard and dropped in for a birdie.

Sebastian won the second when Joe hit a nine iron through the back of the green.

On the third, Joe went one up after sinking a long putt.

Joe was ecstatic. 'Never looked like missing,' he boasted, ruffling Sebastian's hair playfully.

'Aren't you chirpy and full of beans when you're in front,' quipped Sebastian.

Joe didn't overdo it. He knew only too well how fickle the golfing gods could be.

The group in front were still playing the hole and they had to wait on the fourth tee. Joe pulled out a spiff and lighter from his trouser pocket, cupped his hands and lit up.

Sebastian pointed towards the water where a couple of fishermen were coming up from the rocks.

'Joe!' he blurted, in a sharp, reprimanding tone.

'Come on, Seb. They won't give a fuck. Probably stink of fish so much they can't smell anything anyway.'

'They could be off-duty cops for all you know.'

'Relax, mate, you'll give yourself high blood pressure. Walk through Bondi or Manly on a Saturday night, you'll smell bongs from every second house.'

After taking a few tokes he offered it to Sebastian.

Sebastian dismissed his offer with a brush of the hand.

'I'm only smoking two or three a day,' said Joe proudly. 'Given up tobacco completely.'

Typical Joe, boasting about his abstemious ways while indulging, thought Sebastian. Joe had another puff, stubbed out the spiff and placed the butt into a green tin box that he tucked away in his golf bag.

'Got to have some fun. You used to like a bit of weed yourself, back in the day. I can't drink alcohol 'cause of the liver. You still have a drink, don't you?'

Joe's comment hit the mark, making Sebastian feel like a killjoy. Who was he to talk? Lately he had been devouring at least a bottle of wine a night; more on weekends. And then there were the cigarettes. Despite his prolific use of weed, Joe was probably doing far less damage to his body than he was.

After the smoke Joe was in a garrulous mood, displaying childlike delight recalling a practical joke he had played on the assistant professional, Craig Heath. Craig had hit his tee shot onto the green up ahead, where a hump in the middle of the fairway made it impossible to see the green from the tee. Joe was on the green, having just putted out. Egged on by his playing partner, another junior, he'd placed Craig's ball into the hole.

'I can remember something about that,' said Sebastian. 'Did you tell Heathy?'

'Nah,' replied Joe. 'He was so pleased with himself I didn't have the heart. We used to get up to some mischief, eh? What about the time we wrote those names, R. Soule and Ally Gator, on the starting sheet. Heathy actually called them over the microphone.'

'Seriously? I don't remember that!'

'It's true, Seb. We got in the shit over it.'

Joe could narrate an entertaining story, although Sebastian had no doubt he used a fair degree of poetic licence. When he claimed the woman who used to live in a cave along the rocks nearby had pushed her husband off a cliff to his death, Sebastian was again skeptical.

'I know people used to say that, but she would have been locked up if she had killed her husband.'

Sebastian thought about the woman and how they had regarded her as a freak, sneaking into the cave when she wasn't there for amusement. The poor woman most probably had a mental illness or was homeless, or both; back then he'd had no understanding of such things.

Joe pointed across the bay to the headland where the *Malabar* had run aground in the 1930s. 'I took Matt out there the other day, Seb. You can still see remnants of the hull.'

'It must have been big news in sleepy old Malabar back then.'

'Big enough to change the name of the suburb from Long Bay. My ma caught the tram out from Surry Hills to see the wreck. Boxes of fruit and meat floated up onto the beach. Some of the cargo drifted as far north as Newcastle. They reckon the *Malabar* was used to import opium.'

Joe started talking about the notorious Chinese crime gangs that operated in Sydney back in the early nineteen hundreds. After a while Sebastian was only half listening. He'd heard it all before. Probably the last time Joe was in an exuberant mood after a joint he thought, disparagingly.

Sebastian began to have second thoughts, weighing up the practicalities of playing with Joe again. Perhaps it was merely a pipedream. Did Joe really have it in him to get back up on stage or would his lifestyle suck the drive out of him? Could he work with somebody who was stoned most of the time? Getting a band together wouldn't be easy. Was either of them up to the task? Neither of them had played professionally for years. Then Joe made a statement that had him willing to suspend his doubts.

'I'm doing a few songs with a band tonight.'

'Tonight?'

'Yeah, the Bondi Hotel. Come along if you like.'

'What time are you going on?' asked Sebastian, enthusiastically.

'About eight... it's just a bit of fun, ya know... I want to get the feel of getting up in front of a crowd again.'

Sebastian didn't want to miss it. It would mean getting home late but he could drive straight back to Newcastle from the gig. And besides, would Astrid, his wife, really care if he came home late? Things had been so frosty between them lately; she would probably appreciate the respite. The anticipation of seeing Joe on stage singing with a band had him excited. Perhaps he'd underestimated Joe's determination and commitment.

'Ok, I'll come,' said Sebastian. 'When they hear you sing, they might want to keep you in their band.'

Joe scoffed at the comment, but Sebastian could remember bands in earlier times attempting to poach Joe after hearing him sing.

They both hit their tee shots short and to the left of the distant green. As they strode along the fairway, they could see Matt up ahead, trudging through the thick heath, head down, golf balls bulging from his carry bag. Sebastian and Joe were in their own worlds, but unbeknown to either, there was a synchronicity to their thoughts. Both were thinking about an incident that had happened up ahead near the green, many years earlier. They'd come over the hill to see a man, one of a group of three, lying on the ground. His friends had rung 000 but were unsure what to do next. Sebastian assessed the situation and decided the man had suffered a heart attack. He performed CPR, and the man began breathing again. Sebastian had saved the man's life. The ambos said as much when they arrived on the scene twenty minutes later. The fortunate man had sought Sebastian out, weeks later, to thank him.

As Sebastian and Joe approached the green, Matt emerged from the rough. He stood nearby, juggling golf balls in his hands as he waited for them to play their shots. Joe was furthest from the green and first to play. He took his stance and was about to start his back swing.

Out of the blue a distant crack and a high-pitched whirring sound split the air.

Almost immediately, a sharp whack sent fragments of rock splintering from a sandstone boulder just metres away from where they were standing, giving them the scare of their lives.

'Get down!' shouted Joe, and the three of them scrambled for cover behind the embankment at the back of the green, as a second bullet hit into the same boulder.

'What the fuck is going on?' screeched Matt.

'Some clown is shooting at us,' replied Joe with consternation.

Staying low to the ground, the three huddled together, their thumping heartbeats punching through the stillness like bass drums as they waited anxiously to see if more bullets were coming their way.

Sebastian was beside himself; thoughts of maniacs and massacres occupying his thoughts. He turned to Matt, his voice pleading, desperate.

'Have you got your phone with you?'

Sebastian and Joe had a longstanding agreement. They didn't bring their phones with them when they played golf; they were too much of a distraction.

'Left it in the car,' replied Matt.

'Fuck!' said Sebastian, with disappointment.

'My idea. I told him to,' said Joe.

Nothing happened for half a minute or so and Joe began moving higher up the hump. When he tentatively stuck his head out into the open, Sebastian was furious.

'Get back down you fucking idiot! Are you crazy?' shrieked Sebastian, fearful for Joe's safety.

'Sebastian... calm down, mate. If he didn't hit us when we were out in the open, he's unlikely to get me now. I need to know what this dude is up to. What if he's coming after us?'

Joe's reasoning did nothing to assuage Sebastian's anxiety. They would be sitting ducks if the gunman came marching down the fairway. Joe raised his golf club and pointed towards the plateau above.

'I'm pretty sure it came from up there.'

Matt tried to put on a brave front. 'It's probably just some feral kids.'

Joe shook his head. 'I don't think so. Whoever it was… they knew what they were doing.'

'You don't know that, Dad.'

Joe's gaze shifted to where the bullets had struck the boulder. 'Both bullets hit almost the identical spot.'

'Maybe it was just two bad misses,' said Sebastian, sweat streaming from his brow.

'Maybe,' replied Joe, unconvinced.

'What a fucking idiot! I'll kill the bastard if I get my hands on him,' said Matt.

They were on the most secluded part of the course, close to the southern headland, with cliffs and water all around; the perfect spot for an ambush. A short time later, Joe slapped Sebastian across the shoulder.

'I'd say the joker has pissed off. Come on, let's fuck off out of here.'

They collected their gear and darted towards the path at the back of the green that led to the next tee. They walked up the winding path in silence, rounding the last bend on edge, half expecting to come face to face with the gunman. But all was as normal when they reached the higher section of the course. They could see golfers up ahead, but they were playing their shots oblivious to what had occurred in the ravine below.

The three of them made the long trek back to the clubhouse, still wary but feeling as though they'd weathered the storm. The consensus was that the shooter had left the scene. Even so, when they reached the clubhouse, they approached the building with caution. Nothing seemed askew and there was certainly no sign of a crazy gunman running amok. They went straight to the carpark to put their clubs away.

Joe and Matt diligently went over the Falcon, spending a good ten minutes underneath, checking every nook and cranny to ensure it hadn't been tampered with.

Sebastian watched on, confident he had nothing to worry about.

When Joe and Matt were finished, Sebastian said, 'Let's go into the clubhouse and tell the manager. Then we can drop by the police station and file a report.'

Joe let Sebastian's words hang in the air for a beat before he replied.

'Seb... there's no point. We can't even give them a fucking description. And besides, nobody was hurt.'

'Somebody just fired two bullets at us! Are you fucking kidding me? Are you just going to do nothing?'

'Of course, I'll do something. I'll make some enquires.'

Matt chuckled. 'The cops... ha... they won't do anything. Even if they did believe us, they'd keep us there for hours asking stupid fucking questions. Then they'd probably arrest us.'

Sebastian was in a quandary. If he did report the incident off his own bat, he couldn't do so without mentioning Joe and Matt. He felt stymied. Do the right thing and betray your friend, or do nothing?

They agreed to meet up at a coffee shop up on Anzac Parade.

Sebastian followed Joe along Bay Parade past the skids. There were still no signs of anything unusual, and gradually Sebastian's fear abated. He mulled over the seriousness of what had just happened and felt increasingly guilty for not having reported the incident to the police immediately. That's what someone in his position should do. Sebastian brought up the matter again when they were sitting in the coffee shop, sipping their drinks.

'What if the lunatic is out there picking targets?

Joe shook his head and laughed it off. 'Come on, Seb. We would have heard sirens and there would be cops all over the place. And it's true what Matt said before. When they look at Matt's or my record, we'll be the ones in trouble.'

After finishing their drinks, Joe said that he wanted to put on a few bets at the TAB. Sebastian stared at Joe.

'So, you're just going to carry on as usual, as if nothing has happened?'

'I'm not saying it wasn't serious. What I am saying is that involving the cops is not an option for me and Matt. And over the years I've gotten into the habit of handling my own problems. I'll see you back at the house in a couple of hours. There's nothing for you to worry about, Seb. I'll sort it.'

2

Napier Street

As Sebastian made his way to Napier Street, he tried to make sense of what had happened out on the golf course. What Joe had said about the intentions of the shooter was the most likely explanation – two deliberate misses. That he hadn't reported the incident to the police still bugged him. He both admired and detested Joe's cavalier attitude. Joe had always been fearless, thought Sebastian, as he recalled a not so cheerful memory of how the two had first met. It had happened just up ahead, in Napier Street, not long after Sebastian had moved to the seaside suburb from Newtown when he was eight.

Playing around at the top of the Napier Street hill on an old penny-farthing, he had lost control and found himself careering down Napier Street hill towards the water. It had been harrowing because the fixed-wheel bike was impossible to stop. It had been potluck whether something was coming the other way as he flew past the last of the side streets towards a fifteen-metre drop onto jagged rocks. Joe was at the bottom of the hill and in an act of extreme bravery – that's how Sebastian saw it – leapt out in front of the bike and saved Sebastian's skin. For Joe, who had lived just up the road, it had been an instinctive act.

Now, Sebastian approached the house and saw Kate out the front checking the letterbox. Kate was a slim attractive woman of medium height. She had a sharp dainty chin, long dark hair and large hypnotic brown eyes. Sebastian was surprised to see her in a dress and wearing make-up. Kate waited while Sebastian reversed his car onto the narrow strip of grass out the front of the house.

When Sebastian got out of the car Kate gave her brother a massive hug, hamming it up for the benefit of the nosey neighbour peeking out from behind venetian blinds across the road.

'You didn't have to get all dolled up for me, Sis,' said Sebastian.

They went inside and Kate made a pot of tea. Sebastian was still reeling from the shock of being shot at on the golf course. Kate became anxious when Sebastian told her what had occurred. Her concern was appeased after Sebastian assured her that neither himself, Joe or Matt had been injured.

At first Kate was adamant that they should have reported the matter to the police. But when Sebastian told her about Joe's objection, and the reasons for it, she became ambivalent, saying she could understand where Joe was coming from.

'So now you agree with Joe,' said Sebastian, unimpressed.

'The main thing is, nobody was hurt,' replied Kate, not wanting to argue.

Kate talked about how much she missed her mother. She went on to thank Sebastian for helping her out with her two children, Jake and Darren, during their mother's illness.

'I think we're really lucky we get on, Seb. I've got a friend at work, Lucinda, who told me a horrific story about her own family. Her brothers squabbled over possessions and spent tens of thousands of dollars in legal fees; all over a few pieces of furniture. Can you imagine how Mum would feel if she thought we were arguing over her stuff?'

'Sibling rivalry,' said Sebastian. 'With some families it festers for years. Anyway, we were brought up to behave better than that,' he said self-mockingly.'

'Lucinda said her parents would be turning in their graves seeing the way her brothers carried on.'

Eventually the two felt sufficiently braced to deal with their mother's wardrobes. They got to their feet and made their way towards the back of the house.

'Joe's still bloody messy,' Sebastian remarked, as they passed the bedroom where Joe had been staying.

'A bit messy, sure, but the place is clean. And did you notice what he's done with the gardens? Smell those beautiful Italian herbs... yummy. What is it Sebastian... oregano? basil?'

Kate inhaled the aroma with delight. Sebastian observed his sister's ebullient behaviour with interest. Sure, Joe had put some work into the gardens (probably preparing the ground for a marijuana crop, thought Sebastian facetiously) but there was something else going on. He had had an inkling, but now he was almost certain. It had all the hallmarks. Kate dressed up like a million dollars. Kate changing her mind, after hearing Joe's objection to Sebastian reporting the shooting incident to the police.

The two were soon immersed in a surreal time warp, the past being conjured up from old papers, clippings and photos, some dating back to the early nineteen hundreds, long before either of them were born. Occasionally they discovered a real gem.

'Kate, check this out.' The faded photo of their mother was tagged, *Irene Starting Work*. Neither of them had seen it before.

'The spitting image of Jenna,' said Kate.

'I know what you mean, Sis. Jenna definitely has Mum's eyes and bone structure. And look at the hair. I can't remember seeing Mum with her hair that short. But doesn't she look proud, all dressed up? How old do you reckon she was?'

'She would have been fourteen, younger than Jenna. Nan told me the story. Mum heard that a factory somewhere in Alexandria was employing women to sew clothes. She walked all the way over there from Kingsford, all by herself, and scored a job.'

'There's no way I'd let Jenna go off to work in a factory at that age.'

'Nan didn't want mum to work. She was really annoyed because mum had just won a scholarship to Sydney Girls High. Nan wanted her to stay at school. To get an education. But it was during The Great Depression, the 1930s, and Grandad had died by then. Her brothers couldn't find work. At the time, Mum's wage was the only reliable income they had.'

'So typical of mum. To put other people first. She was like that even when she went into the nursing home. Didn't want us worrying about her.' said Sebastian.

'They loved her at the nursing home.'

'Ken Number Two certainly loved her.'

'Ken Number Two,' said Kate with a chuckle.

'Not the dead one.' said Sebastian.

This was enough to send them both into hysterics. It was an in-joke the siblings shared. Their father's name was Ken, and amongst themselves they had always referred to their mother's nursing home companion, as Ken Number Two. When they had been introduced to him, he had said, 'Hi. I'm Ken. Not the dead one.'

They were never sure whether he had a dry sense of humour, or genuinely didn't want to be confused with their father.

When the two had stopped laughing, Kate spoke in a wistful tone.

'Wasn't it great that Mum found romance in the latter years of her life?'

'Wasn't it strange when they called us to the nursing home to tell us Mum and Ken were sleeping together in the same bed?'

'I suppose they have to tell the family what's going on. At first, I thought Mum liked him because he had the same name as Dad. But he really was kind to her. Used to look after her and make her laugh.'

A look of pure terror had crossed Kate's face. Her gaze became fixed on the window where a large spider crawled out of the woodwork. She moved swiftly, grabbing a can of Mortein Plus sitting on the table and letting loose with a prolonged attack.

Sebastian responded with an exaggerated cough. 'What the hell, Kate! It's only a huntsman!'

'It's still a bloody spider!'

The insect curled up and fell to the floor in its death throes.

Sebastian looked at his watch. 'I thought Joe would be here by now. Did you know he was playing at The Bondi tonight?'

'He said something about it the other day.'

Sebastian believed Kate was being purposely vague. It occurred to Sebastian that if there was something going on between Kate and Joe, could it be the inheritance that had sparked Joe's interest in his sister? After all, in the past Joe had had a way of endearing himself to well-heeled women. Sebastian felt a pang of guilt for having had the disparaging thought.

The two continued sorting their mother's belongings in silence for five minutes or so. Kate then looked across at Sebastian, as though she had just remembered something important. Sebastian raised his eyebrows, expectantly.

'What's up?'

'Astrid rang me the other day.'

'What? Astrid rang you?' asked Sebastian. 'Well, I'm glad she'll talk to someone because she ain't saying much to me.'

'You need to talk to her, Seb.'

'It's not that easy. The truth is, and I know it sounds like a cliché, but we seem to antagonise each other every time we speak.'

'She thinks you're having an affair.'

'An affair! Really?'

Despite feeling ambushed by Kate's statement, Sebastian's face remained impassive.

'She told me you've been screwing some woman from work.'

Sebastian felt a surge of emotion as he struggled to process the information. Not only did Astrid know about Frances, but she had spoken about her with Kate. He certainly had no intention of trying to explain his lascivious desires to his sister. How could he? He couldn't even justify them to himself.

'By the way, Sis, I'm not having an affair. Nor am I screwing anybody.' He felt like a Judas as soon as he'd enunciated the words. But could one night really be classified as an affair?

Kate raised her eyebrows as though she considered his response to be less than honest. 'She'd better be something Seb, this other woman, because if you stuff up things with Astrid for a quick roll in the hay, then you're totally bloody insane.'

Sebastian knew that Kate's motives were coming from a good place.

She had suffered through a difficult divorce herself, and she really liked Astrid. Still, it wasn't as though Kate didn't have secrets of her own.

This matter was best left for him to deal with. He was not one who supported the adage, "a problem shared is a problem halved". It was complicated enough without having his sister's involvement. 'Thanks for that vote of confidence, Sis, but there is no other woman. And I love Astrid. We'll work things out.'

Eventually the wardrobes were sorted. While Kate was flicking through a pile of photos, Sebastian walked over to the old piano sitting against the inside wall near the door. He sat on the stool and, after staring at it for a second or two, lifted the fallboard and began tapping away on the keys. He'd learnt to play on the old Paling Upright.

He started to play a few bars from some of their mother's favourites. Ones that he had learnt as a kid and pulled out again to play at the nursing home: *When Irish Eyes Are Smiling*, *Moon River*, and *Alley Cat* with a left-hand vamp.

'Hey Seb... play us that song you made up for Mum's funeral.'

Sebastian decreased the tempo and began singing a slow-moving melody.

Someone so near, someone so dear,
Words can't explain.
We laugh, we cry, we laugh, we cry.
You know, crying is okay
When someone you love passes away.

Kate was teary. She applauded, whistled and cheered, mimicking a crowd. Soon after, Kate had to leave to do some shopping but her departing words were still reverberating through Sebastian's head ten minutes later.

'Just remember, Seb. Astrid gave up a lot to leave Holland and come to Australia with you.'

What Kate said was true and Sebastian sat there in the back room, feeling like a fiend. But the passion and excitement of those early years seemed a lifetime away. His thoughts turned to the first time he'd set eyes on Astrid. The chance encounter in Ireland all those years ago.

Sebastian had spent two days in Limerick, intending to go south to Cork. He'd stood at the intersection with his backpack and guitar for over an hour on that cold, foggy morning, before a car had finally pulled over. When the driver said he wasn't going to Cork but taking the turnoff to Tralee, Sebastian took the ride anyway. In doing so, he'd made a split-second decision that changed the course of his life.

What a strange day it had been. The second ride took him off the main drag, along the scenic route to Tralee. He got dropped off in a village where he had fish with chips and potato in the pub. On the outskirts of the village, he was picked up by a bemused local farmer on a tractor, who happily transported him back onto the main road.

It was four in the afternoon when he arrived at the youth hostel on the outskirts of Tralee. Gloomy clouds were gathering to the west as he joined a few fellow travellers waiting for the caretaker to arrive and open up the place for the night. According to the sign, that would not be until five o'clock. Half an hour passed; an old bus jerked to a stop out the front of the hostel. A small group of backpackers disembarked. One of the new arrivals, an attractive woman with a European accent, expressed her displeasure at having to wait in the cold. She and her friend began exploring alternatives. Sebastian watched on with amusement, as the charismatic woman in the blue boots and maroon beanie circled the building determined to find a way to get inside. It wasn't long before she found an unlocked window, pried it open with a penknife, got a leg up from her friend and climbed inside. Seconds later, she appeared at the front door.

'Come on in,' she implored, arms outstretched. A grandiose gesture that suggested she was indeed the lady of the manor, welcoming her friends for dinner.

'It's too cold out there,' she added, shivering to emphasis the point.

The group ignored her offer, with the exception of the woman's travelling companion and Sebastian.

Following the girls inside, Sebastian was blown away by the audacity of the two. Not content just to be out of the cold, they explored the kitchen and found a teapot and jug. Then out from one of their backpacks came a calico bag containing tea and biscuits. Once the girls spotted the kindle and logs near the fireplace, they didn't hesitate. The three travellers then sat around the fire in comfort, sipping tea and exchanging tales. Astrid and Gertrude were students living in Amsterdam.

By the time the caretaker arrived, it was well after five o'clock. Despite his initial surprise at the sight of the intruders sitting snugly by the fire, he appeared to take it in his stride. He gratefully accepted Astrid's offer of a cup of tea, and it was soon apparent that he too was somewhat captivated by her beauty and charm.

Later that night, Sebastian went looking for the girl in the blue boots and maroon beanie and found her lingering in the kitchen. She wasn't with her friend. He pulled a chair up beside her and the two began chatting.

Astrid had been to Australia and even managed a plausible, if humorous, Aussie accent. She told him she had relatives living in Cairns and, embarrassingly for Sebastian, had seen more of the country than he had. She even had an understanding of antipodean politics.

The two were still chatting seven hours later, when their intimacy was abruptly interrupted by a young German man unable to come to grips with the fact he wasn't first to arise. The man's reaction to their presence in the kitchen was bizarre. He tried to interrogate them, wanting to know how they had managed to get out of bed and into the kitchen before him. When he accused them of cheating, Sebastian and Astrid burst out laughing. They were love struck, and the pent-up emotions each had been suppressing blew like a fuse. The German man stood inert, shaking his head as though they were the ones who were crazy. The hysterics continued until someone in a room nearby called for them to "put a lid on it".

The hiker incident become a longstanding joke between Sebastian and Astrid. It would inevitably come up when people asked how they met. Their initial connection had been magnetic and powerful. Neither had made any attempt to make it a one-night stand, something neither of them were exactly averse to at that stage of their lives.

Astrid and her friend had to leave Tralee soon after breakfast, to meet up with friends in Cork. Before leaving, Astrid invited Sebastian to come and stay at her place in Amsterdam. He felt Lady Luck had truly smiled on him that day.

Sebastian was snapped out of his reverie by the distant sound of a car door being slammed shut. He thought it was Joe, but when he went out to the front of the house it was somebody across the road. He returned to the back room and began fiddling around on the piano. The longer he played, however, the more frustrated he became. Almost all the lower keys were sticking, and some were not responding at all. He decided to take a look inside; maybe he could loosen the hammers, do some quick repairs.

At first the lid wouldn't budge. This wasn't surprising considering the piano had hardly been touched since Sebastian was given an electric keyboard for Christmas in his early teens. He tugged with increased vigour, harder and harder until the lid sprung open, almost crushing his fingers. Peering inside, he could make out something wrapped in masking tape, nestled up against the strings. For a moment he thought he'd come across one of Joe's hiding places – he did have a reputation for stashing jewelry and cash – but as soon as he got a closer look, it dawned on him.

What a blast from the past!

It was the old claw hammer he'd filched from the shed for protection against the wolf. As a child he'd tape it to the inside of the piano during the day so he could take it out at night without his parents to knowing. He'd hide it under his pillow, to protect himself against the wolf, which in his dreams was coming for him.

Once he'd stopped having the wolf dreams and the fear of the wolf arriving had subsided, he'd forgotten the hammer was there. Over time, the tape must have lost its grip and the hammer fallen into the strings.

He removed the tape from the hammer and jiggled the object in his hands for a few seconds, contemplating the chances of discovering the old hammer and musing on those mysterious childhood dreams.

He placed the hammer on the windowsill. It might come in handy if they decided to break up the wooden boxes in the shed.

Another half hour passed before Joe and Matt pulled up outside. Matt poured himself a glass of water and disappeared into his bedroom, from where the muffled sound of a drumbeat and bass could be heard a short time later.

As Joe made a pot of coffee, he and Sebastian proposed various theories as to why someone would want to take a couple of pot shots at them. Why had there been two shots? Was that significant? Was it a lone gunman? If, as Joe was truly convinced, it wasn't a random event, who had the gunman been trying to scare, and why?

Sebastian assumed it had something to do with Joe's or Matt's dealings. 'Par for the course, Joe, in your line of work,' he said.

'You are a funny bastard,' said Joe. 'The thing is, I've cut right back on business. I only deal with people I've known for years. And hardly anyone knows I'm staying out this way.'

Their postulating was brought to an end when the house telephone rang. Joe was closest and he picked it up.

'Seb, for you... Astrid.'

Sebastian felt uneasy as he took the phone from Joe. After his conversation earlier with Kate, he had been half dreading this moment. Astrid went straight to the point, her tone detached and impersonal.

'Greg Wright called from Aboriginal and Torres Strait Legal Services. He wants you to ring him back as soon as possible. There was an armed robbery at a Newcastle beach last night. It's been on the news up here.'

Sebastian was thinking about what Kate had told him earlier, and relieved the call had nothing to do with his conjugal indiscretions.

'Yeah... I heard something about that on the radio.'

'Well, it appears that Deon was involved. He has been taken into custody.'

Sebastian felt a rush of irritation. 'What! Deon? An armed robbery? You're kidding me!'

The family knew Deon. It seemed so out of character. He'd always been so relaxed and easygoing.

'Hey, don't get annoyed at me,' Astrid fired back. 'I'm just passing on the information.' She spat out the number.

Before Sebastian had a chance to speak again, the line went dead.

His first thought was to ring her back to apologise and attempt to sort things out. But he knew it would be useless to try and reason with Astrid while she was in her present mood. He decided to wait, to talk to her face-to-face in the morning.

'What's up?' Joe asked, sensing something wasn't right.

'It's to do with work. A kid I know is in a bit of trouble. Nothing new about that with my job.'

But he was concerned. Deon's future was looking really promising. His dance troupe was riding a wave of success. And these charges were serious.

Joe wanted to talk music, but Sebastian's heart wasn't in it. He had a few things he wanted to do while in Sydney, including dropping in on his uncle Bert, his mother's younger brother. He left the house after telling Joe he would catch up with him later that night at The Bondi.

3

On the Trail

Soon after Seb left, Matt started nagging Joe to return to the golf course.

'What's there to lose, Dad? We might find the bullets or the shell casings. The casings might even have fingerprints on them.'

Matt began rambling on about how he could calculate the shooter's position from the angle that the bullets hit the rock. Joe retorted that he thought Matt had been watching too many episodes of C.S.I. Still, thought Joe, if they could determine the weapon the shooter used, they would have somewhere to start. And at least it would satisfy the boy's curiosity and stop his pestering.

They parked in Prince Edward Street, entering the course from a gravel laneway near the thirteenth green, where the few remaining trees stood like question marks amongst scattered pockets of shrub. The lack of vegetation meant they had an expansive view of the top part of the course. In the distance, the two boys who had been playing behind them earlier in the day could be seen moseying along the sixteenth fairway.

They waited until the two had putted out before casually strolling over. Joe did the talking, while Matt stayed in the background. He asked them whether they had heard two loud bangs earlier in the day.

The older of the two, a freckle-faced boy, was quick to respond.

'We'd been down in the gully looking for a ball and were coming back up to the green. Thought it was firecrackers going off. There was nobody around when we came back up, just a couple of fishermen walking along the fairway.'

'The two fishermen…' said Joe. 'What were they carrying?'

'Just rods and bags. I think.'

'Which way were they going?'

'They were walking towards the rocks.'

Joe probed, trying to elicit more information, but the boys had taken little interest in the fishermen. They had no idea whether they were old or young and couldn't even say for certain whether they were male or female.

Joe was about to thank the two boys for their help when Matt stepped forward. He had a devilish twinkle in his eye.

'You two don't seem to know much. You don't have a gun hidden in one of your golf bags, do you?'

Matt's comment left both boys bamboozled.

Joe was really annoyed, raising his hand, just managing to restrain himself from delivering a swift backhander in Matt's direction.

'Sorry fellas, he's being an idiot. Just ignore him. Thanks for your help. Have a good one,' Joe added, as the boys ambled off to the next tee.

Joe glowered at Matt. 'Jees you are stupid sometimes.'

'Was only mucking about,' Matt replied, with a self-satisfied grin on his face.

Joe and Matt strode off towards the fourth green. When they reached the sandstone boulders, Matt studied the dents the bullets had made in the rock with the intensity of a forensic scientist at a crime scene. He took photos with his phone from a variety of angles.

They searched for the bullets, long and hard, but found nothing. Matt became frustrated, losing his cool.

'What sort of idiot shoots at people on a golf course? Fucking kids,' he thundered. 'The idiot could have killed one of us.'

Joe shook his head. 'Like I said before, Matt. It wasn't a kid. The shooter, or shooters, knew what they were doing. From that distance, even with modern rifles, you need skill to put two bullets on almost the identical spot.'

'Come on, Dad, what the fuck do you know? Like, you're an expert!'

Joe maintained a measured, paternalistic calm. 'I'm just being realistic, Son.'

Then Matt saw it, glistening in the waning afternoon light. From his reaction one would have thought he had found a million-dollar nugget. He was ecstatic. Little Sherlock had made the breakthrough.

'Great work, Son,' said Joe, praising Matt for his diligence.

'I'll check it out on the internet when I get home,' said Matt with gusto. He pointed to the west, to a cluster of small trees in amongst the rocks parallel with the second tee.

'Dad... I'll tell you something. I reckon that's where the shooter was, behind those rocks.'

Joe bit his lip and laughed to himself. It was the same place he had pointed to with his putter shortly after the incident had occurred. 'Seems feasible, Son.'

'Maybe we'll find the shell casing,' said Matt optimistically.

'Maybe,' replied Joe.

With a spring in his step, Matt hurried off along the fairway, his talisman tight in his grasp. Now and then he would hold the bullet up to the light and study it, as though it held a secret that was yet to be revealed.

When they arrived at the shooter's hypothetical position, they split up and began assiduously combing the clusters of dense shrubs. Now and then, Matt would turn and stare in the direction of the distant fourth green, to check if the angle seemed plausible.

All of a sudden Joe stopped searching, adopting a pensive countenance. 'You know what, Matt? What if those two people the boys saw walking down the fairway were the shooters?'

'But the boys said they were fishermen,' replied Matt curtly, while continuing to search for the shell casings.

'Just hear me out for a second. If the shooter, or shooters, had any sense they would take off in the opposite direction from where they fired the shots. They wouldn't go anywhere near the clubhouse because they would have been seen.'

'They might have had a boat.'

'There's nowhere to moor it safely.'

'Maybe they had a helicopter.'

'Ha, ha. Very funny. You know there is a way to avoid the golf course and clubhouse. You end up near the ocean baths. Seb and I used to go that way sometimes when we were kids. I think we should check it out.'

'Dad, they're bound to be long gone.'

'Humour me, Son. Keen fishermen and sun-lovers hang by the water for hours on days like this. There's always a chance that someone might have seen something.'

Matt dismissed Joe's idea with a flick of the hand.

'It's worth a try, Matt.'

Joe began making his way down to the flat ground below. Matt kept searching, then let out a vociferous growl before giving up and following Joe.

The route near the rocks that Joe took was more a watercourse than a track. It wound around clumps of weeds and shrub. A gecko darted off into the saltbush up ahead. Joe could remember coming across red-bellies, and even brown snakes, sunning themselves in the open. Joe's phone rang and he told the caller he'd be busy for an hour or so.

It wasn't long before they reached a ledge that overlooked the ocean baths.

'We used to dive from the rocks there into the water,' said Joe, as they climbed down to the rock platform below.

Nearby was a popular fishing spot, but the rocks were deserted. The tide mustn't have been right. Joe had been hoping to be able to ask the fishermen a question or two. They stepped across the rocks, through shallow water, and onto the pool wall.

'The council has fucked up again,' said Joe.

'What are you talking about?'

'It used to be shallow near the edge of the pool, gradually getting deeper as you went further out. Look at it now! It's been dug out and is at least a metre deep all the way around.'

'Probably did it so people can swim laps.'

'Well, now the kids have nowhere to swim. And there used to be a small sandy beach where the little tots could play.'

'Shit happens. There's still Malabar beach,' retorted Matt.

'Yep, there's still the beach,' agreed Joe.

They walked around the perimeter of the pool. There were five or six people swimming or sunbaking. A young mum in a bikini watched two children play on the steps. With her bronzed tan, umbrella and esky, she seemed settled in for the day.

'Wait here a second, Matt,' instructed Joe.

Joe ambled over to where the young woman was sitting.

'Sorry to disturb you, mam. It's a great spot, isn't it? I used to play here as a kid. I'm searching for a couple of people who may have come along the rocks a couple of hours back.'

While Joe had been speaking, the woman had been sizing him up. From her body language it was clear she regarded him as another desperado on the make. Joe's friendly pirate smile did nothing to lessen her suspicion.

'Look mister... I mind my own business. I suggest you do the same.' She brushed a sandfly away from her face and returned her attention to the children.

'I'm really sorry to have bothered you... it's just that my son and I had our fishing gear stolen. You have a great day, mam.'

As Joe turned to leave, the woman seemed to have a change of heart. Or perhaps she only just remembered.

'Just a moment. You had gear stolen?'

'Yes,' said Joe, hopefully.

'There was this bloke and a chick. I had only just got here. They had rods and bags. They didn't seem like fishermen to me. They were racing around the rocks, swearing and carrying on. They went up the steps.' She gestured to the parking bay above the pool. 'I kept my eye on them because my car is parked up there.'

'Did they get into a car?'

'They drove off in a white Toyota van.'

'You didn't get the numberplate by any chance?'

She gave him an incredulous look, which told him not to push his luck.

'Thanks,' said Joe. 'You've been a great help.'

When Joe and Matt moved out of earshot, Joe turned eagerly to Matt. 'Did you hear that?'

'She probably made up the story so you'd stop pestering her. She didn't say nothin' 'bout a gun.'

'I'd say it was the shooters for certain. It's easy to hide a gun. Mmm… a white Toyota van,' he mused.

They walked towards the steps and Matt pointed to a signpost.

'You'd be crazy to swim here, Dad.'

Joe looked up at the sign.

Blue-ringed octopuses have been found in this area.

'Never heard of it… you'd have to be unlucky. I didn't think they were found this far down the coast. Have to run that one by Seb.'

They were both in a buoyant mood as they climbed the steps up to the car park. Matt had his bullet, and Joe's thoughts were focused on the white Toyota van. Joe was wondering how he could find out more about the vehicle or, more to the point, discover who the owner was.

'Hey, Dad… didn't you write a song about some bloke you saw fall from the clifftop around here?'

'No, not over there, out at Little Bay. It reminded me of what happened to my old man.'

'I thought Pop got swept off the rocks?'

'The thing is, Son, no-one knows what really happened to Pop. The song was a bit about both.'

'I reckon I could turn it into a cool rap. Do you remember the lyrics?'

'Think so. Most of them anyway.'

Riding past on my bike,

I saw a car with the door ajar.

Matt repeated the two lines Joe had sung, increasing the tempo and delivering them in a less melodic, more rhythmic style.

'That could work,' said Joe, impressed with Matt's spontaneous interpretation.

Matt was now eager to get back to the house. There was a beat he had in his head that might just fit with the lyrics. He wanted to record it while it was still fresh in his mind.

'Can you remember the rest, Dad?'

Joe called out the lyrics as they walked along.

I saw a man from afar,

He looked my way, quite bizarre.

Was about to call out,

'Is that your car?'

That was when I saw him,

That was when I saw him jump.

Lying there on the ground,

A toothpaste container,

A faded green jacket,

An old tennis racket.

Then I saw the note of estimations, valuations,

Calculations, manipulations,

Physicians, psychologists,

Resignation, castigation,

Lost job, lost house,

Wife went next, took the kids.

Life went into a skid,

'Didn't get a proper look,' is what I said.

That's what I told the cop with the book.

How could I tell, did he slip, or did he jump?

I think he fell, yeah... slipped and fell most likely.

4

Rivers to Cross

Sebastian parked his car a few blocks away from Bondi Hotel. As he walked along the footpath, he could hear the penetrating throb of a bass guitar. It was dark, and he became uneasy as he passed a group of boisterous half-tanked lads out on the town. He crossed the road, saying hello to an elderly woman who was out walking her dog.

The prospect of seeing Joe on stage had Sebastian in an elevated mood. But when he heard Joe's distinctive voice floating on the breeze long before he'd entered the hotel, he was confused. It was only seven thirty, yet Joe had said he wasn't going on until eight.

He entered the room to see Joe strumming a guitar and hamming it up with the lead guitarist, who was playing a solo. They were in the final strains of the Eric Clapton song, *Layla*. Joe was wearing an embroidered white cotton top, a pair of tight Levi jeans, a black urban Akubra hat, and a trendy light-blue jacket. The earring and gold chain dangling from his neck glistened in a wash of multicoloured lights.

After getting himself a beer, Sebastian walked up to the front of the room. Joe saw him and gave him a wave. There was a dark-haired woman sitting at the band's table, playing with her phone.

'With Joe,' said Sebastian, as he took a seat facing the stage. He asked the woman how long Joe had been up there and was disappointed to know he'd already done four songs. Bloody Joe, he mused. He could've sent a text.

Joe did an impressive version of the Springsteen classic, *Born to Run*. After receiving a thunderous applause for an old James Brown number,

Joe began playing a guitar riff that Sebastian knew well. This was impromptu Joe, and he called out the chords to *Surf Rider* for the other musicians who were quick enough to pick it up. The beat was easy enough for the drummer and Joe kept the arrangement simple, leaving out the time signature changes and complex chords.

Just as the song finished, Sebastian became aware of a commotion near the entrance to the bar. The security guard was the first to surrender, ducking to the side for his own protection as a gang of men wielding baseball bats burst into the room. The leader of the group, a solid man with cropped blonde hair, snapped his fingers and his associates began to search the place. The crowd of about sixty or so huddled together, anxiously watching the intruders, wondering if things might turn nasty.

It soon became apparent that whoever the gang was looking for wasn't on the premises. The sense of collective relief was palpable, but the mood soon changed when one of the interlopers, a scrawny, heavily tattooed man, jumped up onto the stage. His eyes became fixated on the drum kit. Before he had even taken a step towards it, his intentions were clear. Joe stepped across his path. He spoke in a peremptory tone, making it clear it would be wise to obey.

'No-one touches the gear, mate.'

There was a momentary stand-off that seemed to last for an eternity before the fella made a clumsy (he was probably drunk) lunge in the direction of the drums. Joe deftly slipped out his right foot, causing the man to sprawl across the stage. As he scrambled to his feet, Joe adjusted his foot pedal then hit a chord on the guitar. A deafening mix of distortion, digital delay and chorus reverberated throughout the space.

The drummer decided to join in, thumping the bass drum with venom. Joe stepped up to the microphone to adlib, bobbing his head in a jovial manner as he sang. The tattooed man was unsure how to respond.

You've got a lot of nerve,
Hassling us on the job.
You'll be going for a ride, man,
If you keep behaving like a nob.

When the leader of the gang applauded, the heavily tattooed man was left embarrassed and irate, his face red with rage. But he wasn't brave enough to take on Joe, not without the support of his mates.

The gang hastily departed, and the relieved audience began applauding. Joe relished the attention and, not one to let a chance go by, stepped up to the microphone and amused them by repeating a few of the lines he'd made up.

Throughout the drama Sebastian hadn't moved. He was left feeling unsettled by the sense of powerlessness he'd felt. By contrast, Joe and the band seemed to take it in their stride.

'I thought there was a gentleman's agreement that the band was left alone during pub brawls,' Joe joked as they sat around the table.

The drummer had elevated Joe to hero status, and he thanked him for saving his skin and his skins.

Sebastian said he would have just let the idiot have a turn. This drew a negative response from everyone, and he wished he'd kept his mouth shut.

Sebastian left the hotel a little before ten. Cruising along the expressway, he considered Joe's frenetic lifestyle. Shot at in the morning – probably as payback due to some past deed. Later that same day, infused himself into a situation that could easily have turned violent, but managed to save the day, becoming a local hero along the way. After the set, Joe went out the back of the pub and shared a joint with the drummer, seemingly without a care in the world. Sebastian wished he had more of Joe's carefree nature. Perhaps he would sleep better and wake up with more energy.

He arrived home just before midnight. The house was unusually quiet; both Astrid and Jenna were already in bed. As usual, Sebastian was hyped-up after the drive. He pulled out a bottle of dry Hunter white from the fridge and filled a large crystal glass, gulping most of it down in one go before refilling it and walking through to the lounge room.

The Di'Giorgio was propped against the wall, and he picked it up and started strumming it gently with his fingers. He worked out the chords to *Rivers to Cross*, a song Joe wanted included in their repertoire.

Afterwards, he began playing around with an original piece he and Joe used to play. It was called *Life in the West*, and he was working on a technique using semitone intervals that mimicked a didgeridoo. It was a rocky, four-to-the-floor number with a powerful beat.

Northern rains, rivers rising,
This ain't no place for compromising.
The opals may sparkle out at the Ridge,
But her wails cry out from the Namoi bridge.

Now and then he'd rest the guitar against the lounge and down a mouthful or two of wine. Then he was back in the kitchen. It was habitual, and he considered taking the bottle into the lounge room but decided against it, reminding himself that he was in a race against time to get the guitar part right before the wine had its soporific effect. Sebastian thought about Astrid's abstemious ways compared to his own indulgent behaviour. He couldn't remember her having more than one or two glasses of alcohol on any occasion since she'd fallen pregnant with Jenna. Certainly nothing like those wild days in the Netherlands, drinking and partying into the early hours.

'I learnt my lesson when I was young,' Astrid was fond of saying.

Ten minutes later he was back in the kitchen. Don't bang the bottle on the fridge door, he said to himself. He paused. Somebody was on the move. Sebastian recognised the pitter-patter of Jenna's footsteps on the floorboards. Down the hallway, a light came on and soon afterwards the toilet flushed. Jenna was quick – the light went off, footsteps, the night was quiet again.

Sebastian decided to make the next drink his last for the night – to put the genie back in the bottle. Any more, and he'd be too pissed, and maudlin thoughts would threaten. Four wines would do the trick.

He gained fleeting contentment from the fact that he now had the gist of two more useful songs. *Many Rivers to Cross* was an interesting choice, and Joe was sure to do the song justice. The versatile classic would be suitable for a laidback, mid-week gig, as well as a full-on Saturday night when the song would showcase Joe's soaring voice.

Glancing across the table, Sebastian noticed a sheet of paper sitting on top of a book. It was the message, penned in Astrid's flawless handwriting, that Greg Wright from Juvenile Justice had left. What a contrast the precise lettering was to his own scribble.

As he placed his guitar against the wall and tiptoed off to the bathroom, Sebastian contemplated Deon's situation – how restless and alone he would be feeling behind bars. Again, he found it hard to believe that Deon had been involved in an armed robbery. The more he thought about it, the less he could imagine Deon being part of it.

In the stillness of the night, Sebastian slid into bed. Astrid was well and truly camped over on her side. He couldn't remember the last time they had touched, let alone made love.

5

Deon

The train was going flat-chat along a straight section of track, outpacing the cars and trucks heading towards the city along the New England Highway that ran parallel.

In the second carriage, under a sign that had been altered to read *Uninformed officers patrol this train,* sat Murph and Donny. They'd been on this journey before. Both were well-dressed in trendy jeans and black metalhead T-shirts. Headphones on, boots resting on the seat opposite, they exuded cool indifference.

Across the aisle from them sat Deon and Michaela. Deon was wearing baggy trousers and sporting his precious Nike T-shirt, a birthday present from his mum. He didn't usually hang with Murph and Donny. He was here for the girl. The pulchritudinous Michaela was Murph's sister.

Dressed in a blue-and-grey crop top, smart white jeans, boots and scarf, Michaela would have still looked stunning in a sack. She wasn't easy to impress. But when she liked, she liked big time, and she really liked Deon. He was sweet and fun to be around. Michaela smiled, gently placing her foot over Deon's ankle.

Deon smiled back. How lucky was he? Michaela was hot. She was easy to talk to and reminded him of the girls back home. Strong-minded yet unpretentious. Deon put his arm around her, drawing her closer to him. Michaela didn't resist. Her insouciant manner suggested anything was possible, and for Deon it probably was.

The train passed an old farmhouse littered with rusted-out car bodies. The terrain began to change. Rolling hills, then wetlands came into view.

The train stopped near the outskirts of the city. A few people got on.

Deon talked to Michaela about his dance troupe. He showed her a thirty-second clip that had gone viral on social media. Deon was on a high. Why wouldn't he be? Things seemed promising with Michaela and next week he'd be on stage with his mates at The Opera House. It occurred to him that he should contact the Youth Centre to find out whether Sebastian was still up for the drive to Sydney for the show.

The train slowed on its approach to Hamilton Station. Murph's eyes drifted up and down the platform. Unlike Deon and Michaela, he and Donny didn't have tickets. Murph wasn't too concerned. He was familiar with the routines of the railway inspectors and knew where and when to get off without being challenged. If there was a crackdown on fare evaders, or inspectors were on the route, he would expect a text from one of his mates tipping him off.

Murph lifted his headphones. When he caught Deon's attention he grinned. 'Do some rorting tonight, eh?'

Deon looked him in the eye and said sternly.

'Not me, man.'

He'd done his share of rorting and those days were well and truly in the past. Some of his cousins spent half their lives behind bars and he had no intention of doing the same. If things went as planned, he and Michaela would lose Murph and Donny once they got into town.

They jumped off the train at Wickham and hopped on the light rail. Minutes later they were in the heart of Newcastle. The group strode off down Hunter Street with Donny and Murph clowning around, the predatory Donny offering his version of sweet talk to a group of nubile women unfortunate enough to be coming the other way.

The four turned right at the Great Northern Hotel and headed up the hill past Saint Phillips Church.

The message on the parish noticeboard, *Discover God's Love*, went unnoticed.

As they made their way towards the beach, the breeze picked up noticeably. Deon and Michaela were now hanging behind the other two, hugging and kissing, becoming increasingly immersed in each other. The number of passers-by began to thin out. Donny and Murph were methodically evaluating prospective targets and risks. They knew the importance of being patient and were prepared to wait. They couldn't believe their luck, when a group of three young teenagers came bounding around the corner.

The eldest of the three was Jacob. He was sixteen. With him was his fourteen-year-old brother, Alex. Tagging along was Mitch, their neighbour. He was also fourteen. They were from East Maitland. Jacob and Alex had spent the past six months cooped up in Lismore with their father. They were out on the town seeking fun and a cheap night's entertainment. They had no chance of getting into the clubs and bars. The boys were hoping to run into a group of girls. That was wishful thinking.

The puppies, you could say, had strayed into pit-bull territory.

After checking to see there weren't police or security guards in the vicinity, Donny signaled Murph and the two gradually slowed their stride, ensuring their path crossed that of the three boys, near the tunnel that led onto the beach.

When the targets were just a few metres away, Donny casually stepped into their path, smiled at Jacob, who was smoking a cigarette, and spoke in an avuncular fashion.

'How's it going, bro? You wouldn't have a spare ciggy on you by any chance?'

Jacob nodded to Mitch, who had filched a packet of Winfield Blues from his mother's carton earlier in the day.

As Jacob blew a smoke ring, Mitch reached into the pocket of his jacket and pulled out a packet of Winfield Blues. He opened the packet with a slick flick of the wrist – how cool was that! – before shaking the packet until a few of the cigarettes nudged their way to the top.

Donny held Mitch's gaze, as he plucked one from the pack. Before Mitch had withdrawn his hand, Murph swooped like a magpie, snatching two more, catching the boy off guard and putting the younger boys on the backfoot.

'One for now... one for Ron... later on,' he joked.

'Got a lighter on ya, man?' asked Donny, with rapid fire delivery.

While Mitch fumbled for the lighter in his jacket, Murph cast his eye over the fancy Rolex watch Alex was wearing. Alex began to feel uneasy and started to back away, but Murph was too quick, his muscular forearm clamping onto Alex's wrist like a steel trap.

'Only want to look, my friend,' said Murph, taking offence, acting as though Alex was being unreasonable.

Alex had little choice but to comply, and there was a momentary truce as the charade began to play out. Jacob made a failed attempt to free Alex from Murph's grasp. He then became angry.

'Let go of him... I'm fuckin' warning you.'

Murph laughed off the threat, taunting him. 'Warning me... are you?'

A group of teenagers came around the corner, and the eyes of Murph turned. The group sensed something wasn't right and turned back. Jacob took a step back from the group. Donny smiled, thinking Jacob was backing down. In fact, he was about to lift the confrontation to another level.

From that point on it all happened fast. Jacob slipped his hand under his jacket. When it reappeared a moment later, he was brandishing a handgun. His voice was high-pitched and threatening.

'We're not putting up with this fuckin' shit. Let him go. Let go of him... now!'

Murph reacted to the demands by holding Alex's arm even tighter and twisting Alex's body, so it became a shield.

Donny didn't move. He displayed little emotion as he watched Jacob flailing the gun around like a possessed gunslinger.

'I'll shoot... let him go... I'm warning you... I will fuckin' shoot!'

The older boys stood their ground while Jacob continued making threats. The longer the stand-off lasted, the less effective Jacob's action became, his words sounding increasingly weaker until the battery finally ran out of charge.

Sensing the danger had passed, Murph pushed Alex aside, stepping forward and calling Jacob's bluff.

'Go on, shoot... shoot the fucking thing... shoot if you're gunna.'

Jacob was in a quandary. His body seemed to visibly wilt as it became clear he had overplayed his hand.

While Murph continued to mock the kid, holding his attention, Donny, with the alacrity of a matador going in for the kill, stepped forward and deftly swept the pistol from Jacob's grasp.

Donny's eyes darted about, checking to see if anyone had observed the encounter. He gave Murph the all-clear and, like lambs to the slaughter, the three boys were chivvied down the grassy slope, through the tunnel and onto the beach.

The sound of the water gently caressing the shoreline could be heard as Donny and Murph informed the boys of the dangers of non-cooperation, while helping themselves to the watch, three mobile phones, a couple of gold chains and the little cash the boys had on them, expressing their satisfaction with the quality of the booty, and maintaining a running commentary along the way.

Donny feigned concern, shaking his head as he pocketed the cigarettes. 'Not good for you, boys... bad for your health.'

Job complete, Donny and Murph thanked the boys for their cooperation and warned them about the perils of 'doggin' before telling them to fuck off.

Emboldened by their success, they were on a high as they passed around the spoils. Not a bad score was the consensus. The gun was a bonus.

Meanwhile, Deon and Michaela had found a private enclave and were disturbed from a passionate embrace by the raucous laughter of Donny and Murph, who had gone back to find them.

'Deon... come and 'ave a look at this,' called Murph.

It didn't take them long to confirm what they had suspected. The pistol was a replica. Still, it looked real enough.

Not that far away from there, the three younger boys were huddled in a corner feeling distraught. The younger two wanted to go home, but Jacob wasn't finished yet. He felt like a coward for not at least attempting to resist. He'd caved in badly. Some pride had to be salvaged from the ignominy he felt.

He did what any respectable and responsible citizen would do after being a victim of crime. He marched up the hill to Newcastle Police Station and, with Alex nodding agreement in the background, reported the robbery to the officer on duty.

Several facts, however, were carefully altered.

In his statement, he failed to mention the pistol was a replica. He also claimed the other boys had pulled the weapon on them.

The police responded with a code red.

Meanwhile, Donny and Murph were still in a jovial mood, skylarking about as they strolled past the ocean baths and along Bather's Way towards town. Deon had his arm around Michaela and was telling her a story about his infamous cousin.

'It was just before Christmas, eh, and Wayne goes bush for a couple of days with Langie. They get back into Bre and Wayne sees Santa on the street giving away bags of sweets. Man, they hadn't eaten all day and when Santa gives them each a lolly the boys say to him, "One lousy lolly, Santa... come on". Santa tells 'em to clear off or he'll call the cops. So, they grabbed his sack and pinched a couple of handfuls of sweets from his stash and ran off.'

'Did Santa report them?' asked Michaela.

'Yeah, that's the mad part. Ya gotta hear Wayne tell it, man. The next day the whole town knows 'cause it's made the front page of the *The Telegraph*. "The Boys Who Robbed Santa" it headlined, like they were the worst crims since Ned Kelly. All week Sydney radio and TV stations were ringin' up to find out about it, like it's the biggest thing happening in the whole country.'

Donny and Murph had dropped back to listen to Deon's story. The four were ambling along the side of the road, with the halogen lamp from Nobby's Lighthouse blinking ominously up ahead.

From that point things seemed to happen in fast forward. Four police cars, two from each direction, caught the group completely by surprise. With the steep cliff face reaching up to Fort Scratchley above and a five-metre drop to the rocks below, there was nowhere to run. Murph made a futile attempt to dispose of the handgun in the bitou bush by the side of the road and was lucky not to have been shot.

Weapons drawn, the police easily rounded up the four, bundling them into the paddy wagon, and taking them to Newcastle Police Station where they were interviewed and, later, with the exception of Michaela, charged. The three boys had sworn Michaela was not involved.

6

Tot Ziens

A slight breeze drifted into the room, gently nudging the venetian blinds. The morning light danced across the wall as Sebastian awoke in a lather of sweat. The earthy scent of the wolf from his dream was palpable and he could still feel its intimidating presence. Gripped by panic, he cast a wary eye around the room, half expecting to see the creature bracing to pounce from the foot of his bed.

That dream. He hadn't had a dream like it since he was a boy. And for just a moment, as he was waking up, he was still that boy. Emotions from the past had chillingly resurfaced. There was confusion and then a stark realisation; nearly thirty years had passed. In his mind he had to actually reaffirm the year. He lay there on the bed for a few minutes, lost in thought, disturbed and disorientated, unsettled by the dream's clarity and power. When he was a child, sometimes the wolf was at a distant location, and it was possible for him to recognise the actual street it was running down. And although the wolf was always getting closer, he had been able to console himself with the knowledge that it probably wouldn't make it all the way to his house that night. The thought had given him solace as he lay awake, anxiously awaiting the morning light.

But there were other times when he had been terrified. In an attempt to stay awake, he would spray his face with water from the plastic spray bottle his mother used for ironing. If he found himself drifting off, he would place matches cushioned with cotton pads between his eyebrows and cheekbones, something he'd seen somebody do in an old movie.

There was something about the dream that had evolved over time that he couldn't remember. He had no idea when the dreams stopped. Had he simply outgrown the fear? Were the memories too painful to retain?

Sebastian became aware of movement in the house, brisk movement. The bedroom door was closed, and Astrid was not beside him. He dragged himself out of bed, put on his dressing-gown and stumbled out into the kitchen.

He was shocked to see Astrid was already dressed. His eyes darted across to four large travel bags sitting in the hallway.

'We're getting the seven o'clock train to Sydney... going up to Cairns to stay with Laura,' said Astrid, shakily, trying to restrain her emotion.

Sebastian was baffled. Still half-asleep, he peered back at Astrid as though what she had told him was a preposterous proposition.

'To Cairns? You and Jenna?'

'We were lucky to get on a flight with the school holidays on.'

'You were going to just leave, without even waking me up? You can't be serious!'

'I can't believe you even care. You've hardly been here lately, anyway.' Her words were infused with anger. 'And when you have been here, your head's been somewhere else.' She shot him a scolding look as the back door squeaked open.

Jenna came into the room.

'Gidday, Dad,' she said, followed by an animated "Mum's really pissed off with you" frown as she decided to leave them to it and continue walking through to her bedroom.

Sebastian turned to Astrid. 'You know I've been busy at work. And caught up sorting my mother's things.'

'Bullshit, Sebastian... that's such bullshit. It's like you have been living in another world for a long time now. You're impossible to talk to. Ask Jenna... she feels it too... and I've had enough.'

'I thought the three of us could go away?' said Sebastian. But before he could finish Astrid cut in.

'Oh, and by the way, there was another call for you last night. What's her name? Oh yeah, Frances.'

The false charm in her delivery left Sebastian in no doubt as to what she thought.

'That's to do with work!'

'I'm sick of all the crap. I know from the way you've been behaving that something's going on. You treat me like I'm a fool.'

Astrid looked hurt and her tone changed. 'I've smelt her on your clothes.'

'I hugged her, so what? What's wrong with giving someone a hug? It must be so good being Miss Fucking Perfect. You seem to have a convenient memory.'

'What are you getting at? If you're going to say something Sebastian, then just say it. I haven't got time for your games.'

A car horn tooted twice out in the street.

'Oh, come on... you know who I mean... what was his name? Ambrose... yeah, that's it, Ambrose Bayer.'

The words sounded spiteful, harsher than he'd intended.

Astrid was genuinely shocked. 'I never thought that you would stoop that low. It's totally ridiculous and you know it. We weren't even living in the same country at the time.'

'So, you *do* admit something went on.'

'You think you can use my past as a bargaining chip? To validate your disgraceful actions? You've failed your wife and your daughter. You're pathetic, Sebastian, you really are.' Astrid paused, taking a deep breath. Her emotions were raw, but her mind was clear and focussed. 'Remember I asked you what a dickhead was when I first came to live in Australia? Well now I have a perfect definition. You... you are a dickhead.'

She looked at him with distain, despising the animus he had become. 'You lie and cheat and think you can justify your behaviour by attacking me. Fuck off! Come on Jenna, we have a plane to catch.'

Jenna came out of her room, gave her father a hug and kissed him goodbye. If the exchange between her parents came as a shock, it didn't show.

Sebastian stood there in his spotted pyjamas like a stunned mullet, as

Astrid and Jenna trudged off with the bags to the driveway where a taxi was waiting. The taxi driver unlatched the boot and helped with the bags. As the cab drove away, Jenna waved to Sebastian from the back seat, blowing him a kiss as they turned the corner and disappeared up Algona Road.

Sebastian felt dismal, like a clown who had scared his audience away. Charlie was barking now, a chorus of accusations.

'Fuck off,' he barked back, as tears welled in his eyes, and he felt even more miserable for getting angry with Charlie. How could he be so stupid as to not have seen this coming? Downcast, he went back inside and sat on the lounge.

Ten minutes later he went into the bedroom, changed into some old clothes and found Charlie's lead. He couldn't stay in the house. Had to do something. Maybe a walk would clear his head.

'Come on, Charlie. Let's get out of here.'

His mind was a mix of anger and distress as he collared a skittish Charlie. With Charlie pulling hard on the lead, he headed off up Algona Road. He shuddered as he thought about how badly he had handled the situation. What had possessed him to bring up something he had gotten over years ago? To insult her just to conceal his own guilty conscience. Sebastian felt like jumping off the nearest cliff as he and Charlie made their way around the block.

When he got back to the house he felt as flat as a tack. Astrid and Jenna would be on a train to Sydney. He noticed that Jenna's viola was still on top of the piano. That gave him some comfort.

Frances! Why had she rung him at home? He hated thinking about her because it inevitably led to yearnings and lascivious feelings he could barely keep at bay. They were laced with guilt and a good dose of self-loathing, which had only intensified in the aftermath of the AGM.

What an idiot, he thought. He should have heeded the warning signs the first time he had set eyes on Frances.

7

Seduction and Sedition (four weeks earlier)

Sebastian worked in an old two-storey brick structure near the edge of Hunter River. It was one of Maitland's oldest dwellings. From the top floor window, he could see a fair stretch of the Hunter River, and across the floodplain to Lorn.

Sebastian's day was not going well. He'd just been in conversation with Lindsay Burnside, a police sergeant at Maitland Police Station. Stephen Redman, who Sebastian was tutoring in guitar, had been arrested, accused of stealing a carton of Coke from a service station in Rutherford. Sebastian had spoken to the teenager and, according to Stephen, he'd bought the drinks at the supermarket and was on his way home.

The brusque sergeant informed Sebastian that Redman had been cautioned before and that this time he would be charged. Sebastian said he wasn't disputing the law, but that Redman claimed he had only confessed to the offence because the arresting officer told him he would be free to go if he did so.

Sergeant Burnside brushed aside Sebastian's comment, ensuring him correct procedure had been followed. Redman had admitted to the offence – end of story. Burnside then proceeded to lecture Sebastian on the benefits of zero-tolerance policing.

Sebastian held his tongue. One complaint a day was more than enough. After the call, he contacted Jessie Trapman, a court support-worker, on Stephen's behalf.

His thoughts returned to another matter. Earlier in the day he'd had another run in with Vanessa Hadley, the president of Maitland Community

Centre. Her attitude to the youth clientele was making his job increasingly difficult and it was starting to get to him.

Sebastian was shaken from his reverie by a metallic click. Somebody was opening the back door downstairs. Seconds later, the rhythmic clicking of heels could be heard on the stairwell. It didn't sound like Lorraine, his secretary, who was due to start work at one, in thirty minutes time.

Sebastian was surprised to see Frances, a woman he'd only recently met, poke her head through the doorway. She was clad in a revealing crop top and a pair of black leather pants that clung to her lithe body like a second skin.

On seeing Sebastian hunched over his desk, Frances became hesitant. 'I hope this isn't a bad time?'

'No, no, it's fine.'

Frances gazed at him with curiosity. 'Why the sad face?'

'Just work stuff.'

She threw Sebastian a disarming smile. 'You can talk to me about it. I'm on the committee after all. We should be supporting you, particularly if something is stressing you out.'

Sebastian had met Frances at a regional, youth inter-agency meeting three weeks before. After she'd shown interest in his programs, he encouraged her to join the youth committee. Their committee was short of numbers, and they were appreciative of anyone who would make the commitment to attend meetings.

There had been rumours about Frances. That she had to do community hours due to a court order. Maybe just small-town talk. It can happen when somebody new appears on the scene. Sebastian was grateful to get an opportunity to offload. Besides his secretary Lorraine, there was nobody else interested enough to listen to his concerns. At home, the story would have been over in seconds. Astrid had heard one too many of his work stories.

'I'll say it in one word – Hadley.'

'I've heard she can be difficult.'

'Difficult... try impossible. Today this boy, Justin, was downstairs, waiting for his mate to arrive. He'd just been up to see me about his regime and was making a bit of a racket on his skateboard. Vanessa stormed out of the downstairs office and in a condescending tone asked him if he had a home to go to!

'That's what Hadley actually said?'

'That's exactly what she said. The altercation did have its ironic side. Justin is actually staying in emergency accommodation and so he doesn't have a home to go to. When I told Hadley as much, she shrugged her shoulders, gazed at me as though I was from outer space, then walked away.'

Frances became curious. She wanted to know more about Hadley and what went on at the Community Centre. What Frances did next caught Sebastian by surprise. She grabbed a nearby stool and plonked it next to his desk. Sitting there perched above him, she continued on with the conversation, barely missing a beat.

'Can't you put in a complaint about Hadley for harassing the teenager?'

'She's already put in one against me.'

'What the hell for?'

'Hadley claims I called her a bitch.'

'Did you?'

'Nah... I actually called her a witch. But keep that to yourself.'

'That's probably worse,' Frances hooted. She then adopted a more serious disposition.

'But I don't understand. You seem like a capable man. Why do you let Hadley bother you so much? She's not your boss, is she?'

'No, she's not my boss. But she's president of the Trust. The Trust controls everything, including the rents on the office space and hiring out the back hall. I don't want to sound like a whinger, but my other beef with Hadley is that she will only allow me to hire the hall once a week. Meanwhile, it sits there empty all week until Friday, when she uses it for lunch and bingo.'

'But the Trust would be better off financially if they rented it out to us when it's not being used?'

Sebastian was thrown off kilter by Frances's use of the word, us. Her loyalty and comradery made him like her more.

'Hadley doesn't want the riffraff that youth programs attract. Not in her neck of the woods. And she doesn't do too badly out of the hall the way things are. Fridays are a money spinner. She charges the oldies a premium for the day. Buses them in from near and far, crams them into the hall and puts on a cheap lunch. After lunch they play bingo. Hadley gives out a few prizes from the two-dollar shop. Fridays provide numbers... gives the impression people use the place. And funding bodies love numbers.'

'Not allowing you to use the hall seems ridiculous. And there really should be more going on than lunch and friggin' bingo, right?'

'They've had a go at cooking classes. It was aptly named "Cooking for Survival" with the emphasis being on survival. But they forgot to remove the pile of newspapers beside the stove.'

'What... they actually started a fire?'

'Hadley managed to burn down half the kitchen.'

'But they'd have safety procedures in place, surely.'

'The fire extinguisher didn't work. Something Hadley tried to blame on one of the boys. I was upstairs... saw the smoke, raced down and rang the fire brigade.'

Frances lent forward and playfully nudged Sebastian's shoulder.

'Are you bullshitting me? Did this actually happen?'

'All true, honest to God. You should have seen it... two fire engines arrived with sirens blazing and Hadley's out there in the car park screaming at them to get a move on. I'll find a photo and show you.'

Sebastian reached into his bottom drawer and shuffled through a few papers. He felt a tinge of guilt for allowing Frances to flirt with him. He wondered whether Frances behaved in a similar fashion with other men. He thought back to when he'd met her previously and he couldn't remember her being so inquisitive and full of beans.

He pulled out a newspaper, opened it and held it up for Frances to see.

'There she is, Vanessa on page three of *The Mercury*... arms flapping.'

Frances found the photo amusing. Sebastian read out a few lines from the article. Afterwards he put it back in his drawer. Another laugh, at another time, perhaps.

Sebastian was on a roll, enjoying the conversation and showing off a little. He was becoming increasingly besotted by the lascivious woman sitting almost on top of him. He asked Frances about herself, and she told him she had worked as a photographer in Sydney and lived in the eastern suburbs. She had fled Sydney because of a jealous boyfriend.

Sebastian became instantly envious of this boyfriend, even though he didn't know him from a bar of soap. He was overcome by a powerful urge to be protective.

'This man, he isn't bothering you?'

'No, no... nothing like that. Thanks for your concern.'

Sebastian hoped the attraction he felt towards Frances wasn't too obvious.

Both sets of ears pricked up at the sound of the door opening downstairs.

'That'll be Lorraine,' said Sebastian.

Frances slid her chair away from Sebastian's desk. He was disappointed the intimacy they had been sharing was interrupted.

He had been fortunate nobody else was in the building while Frances was in his office. His attempts to impress her would have been bleeding obvious.

Lorraine came into the office and greeted them both in an affable manner. She had once been president of the Community Centre and her efforts had been instrumental in securing the building and the hall for the use of the community. These days, Lorraine's time was taken up caring for her aging mother. She was a genius on the computer and helped Sebastian out two days a week. Her official role was secretary, but she was really his co-worker. He told her about his latest altercation with Hadley while Frances listened on. When Sebastian had finished, Frances made a suggestion.

'Well, Seb, maybe you should get on the front foot. Have you considered moving?'

'We can't afford to move. We don't get enough funding. Besides, it's a great location. Near transport and close to the courts.'

Then he grinned, the first time Lorraine had seen him happy in weeks, before adding.

'And I love the view from the window. How good is that!' he said, pointing towards the river.

'And don't forget, we fought hard to get this facility for the community,' said Lorraine with venom.

It had been painful at times for Lorraine to watch Hadley cast aside programs that had taken her years to establish.

Frances spoke in a strident manner. 'Then something must be done about this.'

Sebastian was curious. 'What do you suggest?'

Frances shot Sebastian a cheeky grin, before turning her attention towards Lorraine. 'Well, seeing they have an AGM coming up, why don't we run for some of the positions?'

'Stack the meeting you mean?' questioned Lorraine, with a glint in her eye that suggested she was more than comfortable with Frances's seditious proposition.

'I'll happily stand for a position... if there is enough support,' said Frances.

Sebastian was surprised by Frances's revolutionary zeal. Lorraine was cautious. While she welcomed the idea, she barely knew Frances, and there was something about the woman that made her wary. Frances had certainly managed to endear herself to Sebastian. That aside, the AGM was a real opportunity to do something about Vanessa Hadley and Frances would be a useful ally.

A day later, Sebastian, Lorraine, Frances and a few others got together down at The Imperial. With the office crowd partying in the background, the newly formed cabal decided that, if they had to take on Hadley to get fairness and relevant services restored in the community, then that was what they would do. With the AGM only a week away, there was a lot of work to be done.

Secret meetings were planned, important phone calls were made. A battle plan was prepared.

Sebastian saw a lot of Frances during that time. If he wasn't around her, she was in his thoughts. Merely thinking of her sent his head into a spin. He kept telling himself that Frances wasn't that good looking. He searched for negatives about her personality, in an attempt to keep things in perspective, and allay his desires.

That she held some strange power over him, was something that bugged him incessantly.

One time after Frances had left, he'd felt like such a loser, having told her she was special. He chastised himself. What a stupid and, immature thing to say.

But then, Frances didn't seem to mind.

One week later, D Day or in Sebastian's mind, F Day, arrived. It was not the bizarre meeting but the after-party, and his encounter with Frances that would forever define that day for Sebastian.

As zero hour approached, some of the troops were lying in wait upstairs in Sebastian's office. Lainey Austin had taken charge of the tea and coffee. She lightheartedly reprimanded Tommy Milton for making excess demands on the limited sugar supply. A true-blue country girl, she had worked as a stablehand when she was young and was deceptively strong for her size. Lainey became a bit of a local hero at Belmore Hotel a few years back when she decked a rapacious sleazebag who wouldn't accept no for an answer. For the past month, Lainey had been drumming up support amongst her old schoolfriends.

Tommy Milton knew everyone in town. He had kept in contact with Lorraine ever since she saved him from the clutches of a loan shark many years ago. His daughter Sarah, who had a mild intellectual disability, was with him. Sebastian had been tutoring Sarah, and she was attempting to show off her spelling skills to Scary Steve, who was testing her by selecting increasingly difficult words from an Oxford dictionary he'd borrowed from Sebastian's desk.

Old Laurie Lorenzo might sleep rough, but he did have an accounting degree from Sydney University. He was at his obsessive best, familiarising himself with the various regulations and policies. Off the drink he was a formidable force.

Sebastian was downstairs. The sense of mischievousness in the air was palpable. Some people were in suits, others in singlets and thongs. Some came from their palaces, others crawled out of the woodwork. Princes and paupers alike, they paid their two dollars and joined the Community Centre. This was grassroots democracy at work. Even Dodgy Dave, who rarely came into town more than once a year, was there.

As the queue grew and the hall filled, it still didn't twig. Hadley was preoccupied. She had ushered the mayor and Robert "please don't call me Bob" Holmes into her office. Hadley was testing their patience, insisting they watch her PowerPoint presentation entitled Friday Lunch and Bingo.

Sylvia was holding the fort for Hadley. She was Vanessa Hadley's deputy-sheriff, and this was her first AGM. She had no idea what to expect. Besides, she had her hands full collecting the money and ingratiating herself to the more prominent members of the community. She had Max Shepard from council pinned. As head of the peak funding body, he was a man worth impressing, or at least pressing up against, as Sylvia in her none-too-subtle maneuvering was doing.

Max's uneasiness was growing, and it wasn't just because of Sylvia's unctuous behaviour. He was only too aware of the number of people who usually turned up to these things. When he caught Sebastian's eye, he shot him a filthy glare.

Sebastian was talking to Sid Ryder, a local farmer. He held up his glass in mock celebration. If he'd told him of the plan, it would have compromised Max's position. Sebastian would apologise to him later, but for now Max had more than enough to contend with. Sylvia was in his face again.

'Good numbers for last month,' Sylvia said, full of pride, anticipating a positive response.

'There are certainly good numbers here today,' replied Max, the sarcasm in his tone going undetected by Sylvia.

Lorraine was across the aisle from Sebastian, still canvassing votes.

Sid went over to say hello to Lorraine, and a youth worker from Cessnock, Belle Ryder, came over and spoke to Sebastian. She began complaining about the lack of funding and Sebastian stole a look in Frances's direction. Then Frances was on the move, her long, honey-blonde hair bouncing across her shoulders, as she weaved her way across the room and stood beside him. Sebastian introduced Frances to Belle.

'It's looking promising,' said Frances, her face beaming with pleasure, like a child at a carnival, waiting for the fun to start.

'I can't believe there are so many people here,' said Belle, as a hush came over the crowd.

Someone from the back of the hall with a sense of humour sang the opening line to *God Save the Queen*, as Vanessa Hadley and the esteemed guests entered the hall.

The Mayor looked distinctly uncomfortable as he acknowledged a few of the faces in the crowd with a perfunctory wave, whilst being ushered to his seat. He knew the signs and could sense a storm brewing. Robert Holmes examined the confluence before him with apprehension. It was his job to chair the meeting.

Hadley's eyes darted around the room. What was Sebastian doing here? And who was that woman he was with?

Frances nudged Sebastian. 'I think she's finally worked it out.'

When Hadley spotted Lorraine, and a few other people she'd had altercations with, she rushed over to where Sylvia was standing.

'Why didn't you tell me there were so many people here?' she hissed.

'Tell you? You said you didn't want to be disturbed! I... I thought you'd be pleased.'

'Pleased? You thought... you thought,' she mocked.

'We collected over eighty dollars,' proffered Sylvia, hoping to appease her boss.

Vanessa gazed back in horror. 'You actually let all these people join? Are you a complete moron?'

Vanessa pondered the situation for a few seconds, taking in a deep breath. With her aquiline nose held high, she strode out of the hall and into the seclusion of her office.

Sebastian and Frances attempted to calculate the number of supporters they had, and the numbers seemed more than promising. The crowd was growing noisier, and now and then Frances would turn towards Sebastian, cup her hand and speak into his ear. Sebastian delighted in the warmth of her breath. Once or twice her lips touched his ear. Even in the midst of such a fracas, the intimacy was like a balm for his soul.

When Vanessa returned to the hall just minutes later, she was holding a document in one hand, and her briefcase in the other. She made a beeline for Robert Holmes. 'Robert... Robert! There is something I must show you.'

Holmes looked at his watch. He was not one to tolerate dilatory behaviour, but he knew better than to argue with Hadley. The two went into serious discussion. Afterwards, Vanessa stepped up to the mike and addressed the crowd.

'Greetings all,' she said, with arms outstretched in a manner one might use to greet a group of aliens who had just landed on planet Earth. 'I would like to introduce a very important man. A man we are so very fortunate to have with us today. Without further ado, the Mayor of this wonderful city... the honourable Stephen Hodges. Please give Stephen, and I hope it's alright to call him Stephen, a big hand.'

Vanessa turned to catch the Mayor's eye, but he was already on his feet and striding with alacrity towards the front table.

He proceeded to deliver the shortest speech of his political career. As some in the audience applauded politely, he gave them a glimpse of his winning smile, before swiftly returning to the safety of his seat. Amidst muffled conversation, Vanessa presented the annual accounts and read the minutes of the previous year's AGM, before vacating the chair for Robert Holmes.

Holmesy,' someone called with affection from the back of the hall.

Holmes reciprocated with a stifled wave. With a tissue clasped tightly in his fist and sweat on his brow, it was obvious that the pressure was getting to him. This was not surprising considering the incendiary nature of the announcement he was about to make.

'Before I proceed with the election of officers, I must clarify a thing or two.' He coughed nervously, clearing his throat. 'Under Section 23, Subsection 7B, a person must have been a member for a minimum period of twelve months to be eligible to vote, or to hold a position on the Community Centre Committee.'

There were shouts from the back of the hall. 'Bullshit! This is outrageous!'

Hadley decided to reinforce Holmes' point, and she stepped back up to the microphone. Her delivery was akin to that of a medieval town crier reading a royal proclamation. 'There will be no voting rights granted to anyone who has not been a member for at least twelve months.'

Dodgy Dave rose to his feet. 'Who says I can't fucking vote? This is supposed to be a democracy, isn't it?'

'I want my two dollars back,' shouted another disgruntled patron.

Frances whispered something to Sebastian that he couldn't decipher before she sprung to her feet and raised her hand, gaining Holmes' attention. Holmes called for order and the crowd quietened. She looked directly at Hadley as she spoke.

'Vanessa, it seems like you have collected money from people knowing full well they would not be allowed to vote. That's a bit dishonest don't you think? If you took their money, they should be entitled to a vote.' Frances turned her attention to Robert Holmes. 'Isn't that what this is supposed to be about, Mr. Holmes, community participation? We, the community, want our say.'

Holmes grimaced.

Hadley got to her feet. 'Oh… it was a misunderstanding,'

Hadley attempted to blame the oversight on Sylvia's lack of experience but was drowned out by a tide of dissent. Someone had picked up on

Frances's comment and a vociferous minority began to chant, 'We, the community, want our say! We, the community, want our say!'

A group near the back scrunched up their sheets of paper detailing the agenda and hurled them towards the front of the hall. This was accompanied by shrieks of laughter and ugly jeering as the sonorous chant grew.

'We, the community, want our say! We, the community, want our say!'

Lorraine had used her time well, teaming up with Laurie Lorenzo. The two busily sorted through the assortment of documents and downloads, they had procured from a Community Centre insider, Cynthia Fox. When Laurie Lorenzo rose from his chair, Holmes did the only thing that would pacify the crowd; he gave Laurie the floor.

'I have the relevant part of the constitution you are referring to, Section 23, here in front of me. It clearly states that all paid-up members are eligible to vote. There is no mention of any waiting period,' said the burly man.

Hadley claimed it had been changed at the last monthly meeting. 'It merely put us in line with other community organisations. Robert has the relevant documentation, don't you Robert?' she asked, shooting a smile of complicity in Robert Holmes' direction.

This was met with more sneering and taunting.

Lorraine looked across at Sebastian. They had reached the same conclusion. Hadley most likely forged the document when she had made that frenetic dash to her office earlier. But Lorraine still had a card or two up her sleeve. Laurie Lorenzo passed her a document and she got to her feet and began waving it around. The crowd quietened.

'According to the Community Centre's constitution, there must be at least four members present to form a quorum. I have before me a copy of the attendance book from the meeting back on the fourteenth that Vanessa was referring to. There were only three people present. So even if this motion was passed then, it would be invalid.

'Nellie Moss voted by proxy,' called Hadley.

'By Poxy, you mean!' someone shouted.

8

Salt at the Core

Astrid and Jenna were on their way to Cairns, and Sebastian sat on the lounge inert, unmotivated and without an appetite. There was a photograph propped up against a book on Astrid's bedside table. She must have had a photo album out. What a blast from the past! Sebastian had his arm around Astrid, who was standing, lopsided, paintbrush raised, feigning to swipe him with the brush. They were both beaming – a happiness he could barely recognise now; clearly a couple in love. Sebastian remembered his sister Kate taking the shot shortly after they'd moved into their Charlestown home.

As painful as it was, Sebastian couldn't take his eyes away from the photo. Tears welled as he stared at Astrid's photogenic face with just a hint of a smile, and those curious brown eyes that could read him like a book.

They were in love back them. Where had it gone? Had it simply dissolved? Was there a day, a minute, or even a split second when it had ended? Was it a choice that he or Astrid had made? It had happened well before he met Frances, he told himself.

He drank more coffee. He couldn't shirk work; it was the busiest day of the week as well as his favourite day. More social than educational. If he didn't turn up, his clientele would be turned away. There was also the matter of Deon's arrest to deal with.

On the drive to Maitland, he fought the urge to speed but he was the proverbial lane-hopper, springing here to there like a grasshopper, darting in and out of traffic, blasting the horn of the Commodore at the slightest provocation. He was held up on the approach to East Maitland, got pissed off so turned down a side street, taking a shortcut that would shave only a minute off the trip. Eventually he came to his senses after a close encounter with a truck reversing out of a driveway.

He couldn't help but think about Astrid's hasty departure. Maybe she needed a break. She wouldn't leave him long term. No way: she wouldn't do that to Jenna.

Sebastian got to work and parked. When he got out of his car, he could hear hysterical laughter coming from the upstairs office. As he grew closer, he recognised the Scottish accent. Josie was a former work colleague of Lorraine's who worked in the disability sector. Lorraine had been telling her about the Community Centre AGM. As a former tenant, Josie also had been subject to the whims of Vanessa Hadley and wasn't unhappy to learn of her demise.

'Can you believe that when we first moved in here, after the police left, we had five organisations operating out of this building?'

'And don't forget our ghost,' said Lorraine.

Sebastian was amused. 'Come on Lorraine. Did you ever see this ghost?'

'I mightn't be the ghost-seeing type. Just because you can't see something doesn't mean it's not there.'

'They say it's the spirit of a blackfella who was killed here... an early death in custody,' said Josie.

'Probably just birds in the roof,' scoffed Sebastian.

'Jees, Sebastian, you're in a good mood today,' said Lorraine.

He put what was really on his mind to the back of his head.

'Try doing the drive from Newcastle. I swear the traffic is getting worse each day. It took me forever to get across from East Maitland.'

'Look on the bright side,' said Josie,' At least you can look at the cows in the pastures. It's a sight more pleasant than being stuck on Parramatta Road in Sydney.'

'I'm with you there, Josie,' Sebastian replied, making an effort to be more congenial. 'I can't believe there is farmland so close to the middle of the city.'

'Yeah, well it would be developed if it was worthwhile. Can't get flood insurance. That's why we got the building and the hall. Speaking of the hall, does Hadley still come here and do her lunch and bingo?' asked Josie.

'She hasn't been back since the meeting. I've sent her a couple of emails, telling her she can still have the hall on Fridays, but she hasn't replied. I know Council's offered her a bigger space near the mall at the same rent, so it's in her court,' said Lorraine. She glanced out the window facing the courts. 'Some of the gang are here already, Seb.'

Sebastian walked over to the window. Josie did likewise. A couple of the regulars were sitting on the fence, Coke in one hand and cigarette in the other. At least Sebastian didn't have to worry about Hadley racing out from the downstairs office and moving them on.

'I like this one-way glass. They have no idea we can see them, 'said Josie.

'It can be handy on court days. It's a leftover from when the police were here,' explained Lorraine.'

'Hey Sebastian, I saw that photo of you and a couple of the group in *The Mercury*,' said Josie.

'There're always happy to promote the programs.'

'Sebastian's going to get a band together with some of the older kids. The River Brats,' said Lorraine and they all laughed.

Sebastian looked at his watch. He took a piece of paper from his pocket and told them about Deon's arrest. Both already knew about it.

'Have either of you heard of a Greg Wright, from the Aboriginal and Torres Strait Legal Service?'

Neither had heard of him, but Josie was full of praise for the organisation. 'Deon's fortunate. He won't have to rely on the court solicitors. I'm not saying they're not good, but you should see how busy the poor bastards are. Like blue-arsed flies buzzing up and down the corridors on court days.'

Sebastian rang the number, announced himself and was put on hold. In the background, a recording of Christine Anu singing *My Island Home* was playing. He thought of the time he'd seen her perform in Maitland Park. She'd put on a great show. There was a short crackle before a voice came on the line at the other end.

'Sebastian! How are you going? Greg Wright here. Deon Murray gave your name as a contact. He's been charged with robbery in company, while armed with an offensive weapon. Serious charges,' he said in a solemn voice.

'It does sound serious, but it doesn't sound like Deon.'

'Yeah, well it turns out the weapon was a metal replica of a semiautomatic. And there's still some conjecture as to who the gun belonged to. They don't think it was Deon's.'

It was sounding better for Deon. Doing a long stretch in lock-up would do him in. Too much for his adventurous, fun-loving spirit to endure.

'Will he get out on bail?'

'That was one of the things I wanted to talk to you about. Do you know whether he has any family down here?'

'No-one I know of. Most of his family are in Brewarrina. I doubt Deon's mum could get down here. She has three young kids. Not sure about his dad… somewhere in Western Australia, I think.'

'The reason Deon was refused bail was because the address he had given the police was the same address one of the others accused. The one they call Donny. Apparently, it's Donny's aunt's place. The court won't allow Deon to go there, but they would have allowed his release if he'd had somewhere reliable to stay. He did mention you as a possibility.'

'Me?' said Sebastian, as though the idea was ludicrous.

There was silence while Sebastian deliberated. Deon was earning money teaching and performing. His troupe was gaining a reputation. He was supposed to be performing at the Sydney Opera House later in the week and that would be some gig. It would be a pity to see Deon miss out on that one. But, of course, one of the unspoken rules of youth work is that you should never get personally involved with clients. You never take them home. He'd broken the rules plenty of times, he decided, and this was a special case. How could he live with himself if he left Deon locked up? Astrid and Jenna liked him. Astrid would agree to let him stay; that's for certain.

'Look, I suppose he can stay at my place for the short-term, until something is sorted out.'

'Ok, that's great. I'll get in touch with the senior constable who's handling the case. Deon's fortunate to have somebody like you around. I'm pretty confident they'll be cool with bail if you go guarantor and let him stay at your place.'

Sebastian became apprehensive. 'What's this about going guarantor?'

'It's just a precaution in case he shoots through. I'll organise it so that there is no bond attached. You won't have to put up security.'

'The courts close at four, don't they?'

'Deon's being kept at Baxter, on the Central Coast. It's unlikely they'll bring him up today.'

The conversation finished with Sebastian making a mental note to ring around and find out more about the case. For the moment, he had his hands full. There was a din coming from down below. From the window facing the river he could see a group of teenagers mucking around on skateboards outside the hall. There were mostly familiar faces and a couple of new ones. He opened the window and called out. 'I'll be down in a sec.'

The few of them who had heard him waved back.

Most of the group had either dropped out of school or been kicked out. They were an amiable enough bunch, appreciative of having a place to hang out. If you could ignore their swearing, and you allowed them to disappear for a cigarette, you were unlikely to have problems. The best idea was to chill out, and that's what he intended to do.

Sebastian went downstairs and unlocked the hall. He gave Liam, a ginger-haired boy, the pool equipment. When Liam challenged him to a game, he couldn't resist. The game was over quickly after Sebastian potted the black.

There was still half an hour before it was time to start the comps. Sebastian went back upstairs, where he tried unsuccessfully to contact Astrid.

A little later, Kylie, one of the regulars, came racing up the stairs. She stuck her head in through the doorway. 'Hey Seb, can we have the card so we can do the shopping for the spag bol?'

'Thought we were doing Mexican today.'

'Nah… changed our minds. Oh, and Nikki wants to make a curry.'

'Who's going with you?'

'Paula and Chantelle.'

Sebastian opened his wallet, took out an IGA card, handing it to the girl.

'Don't forget the receipts, and don't buy the cheapest mince. It's full of fat,' he said, before adding under his breath, 'and it tastes like shit.'

From mid-morning until lunch the place was buzzing. Kylie sautéed the onions, garlic and mushrooms in olive oil before adding a blend of Italian spices. An amalgam of enticing spices wafted through the space, and Sebastian was reminded of what Kate had said as they were walking through the Napier Street house the previous day. In retrospect, he wondered whether he'd read too much into it, but at the time, her comment about smelling the beautiful Italian herbs had convinced him something was going on between Kate and Joe.

Sebastian's musings were interrupted by Nikki, who wanted his opinion on the vegetarian curry (pumpkin lentils and spinach) she was cooking up. She handed him a spoon and watched on eagerly as he tasted the concoction. Afterwards Sebastian was full of praise. Nikki hadn't held back on the chili, but no critical damage was done.

While Liam did the draw for the pool competition, some of the keen dart players were warming up down the far end of the hall. Darts was a recent addition to morning activities. Sebastian used the game as a maths teaching aid and some of the students had become first-rate players. Daryl, the Indigenous Welfare Officer, had come along for the day and was appointed adjudicator. Scores were hotly contested (they were playing for a double movie ticket) and the scorekeepers had to be on the ball.

Sebastian was standing near the pool table when he overheard Christie mention Deon's name.

'Have any of you seen Deon lately,' he asked?

Deon was popular with most of this crew. If anyone thought they could help him out they would.

'Seen the boys dance the other week,' said Chad, 'But I ain't seen Deon around much... not since he met that babe... Michaela. We heard he got arrested.'

'You know about it?' asked Sebastian, acting as though he didn't know as much as he did.

'I heard he was gunna be staying with you for a while, Seb,' said Hannah.

Sebastian was shocked that Hannah had found out so quickly. Country towns! Sometimes information seemed to simply diffuse like osmosis, he thought.

'Maybe. We'll see how things turn out. That fella Jacob who had the run-in with Deon and his mates... he was here for the pool competition once, wasn't he?'

'Yeah... I think so. He's such a fuckwit,' said Christie. 'I thought he'd gone to Brisbane or somewhere.'

'Nah... he's back,' replied Kylie.

'Do any of you know anything about Deon and his mates having a gun?'

'Nah, not Deon,' replied Kylie. 'Jacob's the one who had the gun. The other night he was flashing the thing about like he was some big shot. It was a fake anyway. He's a real try-hard.'

'He's into all that gangster shit,' said Geordie.

'Hey, his brother Alex is cute. Gunna be hot in a few years,' said Sarah.

'Did many people see Jacob with the fake gun?' asked Sebastian.

'Yeah... you ask Chris and Robbie when you see 'em. He pointed it at Robbie and Chris. Chris was going to punch the fuck out of him,' said Kylie, with a giggle.

Apart from some lettuce and a little pasta, all the food was eaten. The darts competition had been decided, and the pool competition was won by one the older boys, Kelvin, who walked away with a Silverchair CD.

Sebastian was wrapping it up for the day when he received a call from Greg Wright. As Wright had expected, the court would grant bail, providing Deon stayed with Sebastian. Corrective Services couldn't get him up to Newcastle until the next day. At least he had a night to get used to the idea. Before hanging up, Sebastian discussed with Wright the information he had obtained from Kylie regarding Jacob's possession of the weapon. Wright said he would bring it up with the police and get back to him.

Sebastian was on his way downstairs to lock up for the day, when he turned at the bottom of the stairway only to collide with Frances, who was exiting the front office.

He, having momentum as well as size in his favour, should have come off better but, in attempting to avoid knocking her over, he changed direction, lost balance and toppled down.

He got to his feet a little bruised and confused, and embarrassed.

'You alright, Sebastian? I was hoping to run into you, but not like this!'

'I'm, fine,' he said, dusting himself off. 'I'll be back up soon. I've just got to lock up the hall.'

'That's ok, I wanted to see Lorraine, actually. Community Centre stuff.'

'Yeah... well... Lorraine's upstairs.'

Sebastian wondered what Frances was doing in the front office. It had been closed, so she must have a key.

Frances got to the top of the stairs and greeted Lorraine like a long-lost friend. Lorraine paused, responding with a curt nod of the head.

'What are you after?'

She had heard a few things about Frances lately and it made her wary. In the aftermath of the Community Centre's AGM, most of the new brigade were content to enjoy the peace. But not Frances. Behind the scenes, she had been promoting herself about town and making new friends. To use Josie's words, she was attacking the sleepy world of community groups with the tenacity of a politician seeking pre-selection.

'I was after a copy of the Treasurer's report.'

Lorraine looked at her curiously. 'Do you want to check something?'

'No, no, I just wanted to be prepared for the next meeting.'

Lorraine wasn't going to be rushed. Not by Frances. 'I've got a couple of things to do first. I'll run off a copy afterwards if you can wait a few minutes.

Frances said she'd wait. She didn't seem at all bothered by Lorraine's less than friendly manner.

Lorraine returned her attention to the keyboard. It wasn't long before Sebastian came back up the stairs. Frances then got to her feet and began making her way out. When she got to the doorway, she turned and spoke.

'Oh, Seb... would you be a dear and drop off the report Lorraine's running off for me on your way home? Really appreciate it. I must run. Got an appointment.'

She threw Sebastian a playful smile that was full of promise. 'I'll be back home in a couple of hours.'

'No worries,' replied Sebastian, much to Lorraine's ire, as Frances darted off.

Lorraine wondered whether Frances's flirting was for her benefit. To show her how much power she had over Sebastian.

Once Frances had gone, Lorraine swung around in her chair and gazed at Sebastian. 'How stupid can men be?' she said, her words barely audible.

'What did you say?' asked Sebastian.

'Sebastian... maybe you don't know Frances as well as you think you do.

'What do you mean?'

'Just be aware that she shoots her mouth off to people.'

'She just says what she thinks,' he replied, becoming defensive.

Lorraine's face became stern. 'I don't want to sound like a hardnosed bitch, but there is more to her than meets the eye. If I were you, I wouldn't be telling her too much. By the way, how's Astrid doing?'

'She's gone up to Cairns with Jenna for a holiday.'

Lorraine knew straight away things were not right.

'I thought you were all going to go?' she questioned.

'So did I. Tell you about it later.'

Sebastian might have been quick to jump to Frances's defence, but he knew Lorraine well enough to know she wasn't one for fabrications. He didn't doubt there was some truth in what she had said. He must have seemed like a complete fool and it embarrassed him to think how readily he had agreed to drop the documents off at Frances's place. What was he? Her errand boy. Surely, nearing forty, he would be at a stage of life where he possessed the self-control and integrity to say no and resist such carnal urges?

There was no doubting the youthful exuberance he had felt, particularly in the early stages of his infatuation with Frances. He refused to think of it as love, more like a chimera etched into his consciousness. There was something unnerving about it all, an immaturity of spirit, because at the core, as Lorraine had reminded him, was his betrayal of Astrid.

Sebastian left work half an hour later and drove to Frances's house with the document she had asked for. The house appeared different to what he had remembered on his previous visit. Then it had been dark, and he hadn't noticed the relative seclusion of the place. It was a large block, probably a quarter of an acre. There was thick, pungent murraya screening the front, and at the back and sides grew tall gum trees. There was no sign of her car. As he had hoped, she was still in town.

As he drew closer, Sebastian could hear a guitar being strummed. The top E string was slightly out of tune, but he could tell the instrument was not a cheap one. He tapped on the door and the music abruptly stopped. He waited at the door for a while, but nobody came.

He was sure somebody was inside. The idea that someone else might be intimate with Frances brought pangs of jealousy to the fore. He chided himself. Another reminder of how pathetic he had become, and why he was doing what he was doing now. He hoped taking this action would restore some pride.

Sebastian was able to open the screen door. He took a folder from his bag and slipped it behind the screen. Enclosed with the Treasurer's report was a short note.

Dear Frances,

I think it might be better if we don't socialise outside of work. After all, I am a married man.

Wishing you all the best,

Sebastian.

He thought he'd been witty, using the married man phrase. It was a reference to something he had once heard Frances say. She'd remember and hopefully find it amusing. It felt cowardly, just leaving a note and not talking directly with her. But at least it was decisive and had a finality about it.

Leaving Frances's house, Sebastian felt some degree of gratification. He had finally righted a wrong. At least now he could talk with Astrid about his fling in all honesty. A mistake, it was. And he was sorry.

He felt lighter in spirit, as though a load had been lifted from his mind.

When Sebastian got home from work, he decided to clean up. He became curious and checked to see whether Astrid had taken her and Jenna's passports. He could only find his own, which was not good news. Then he found something that sent his head into a spin. It was a poem, a poem he'd written after that strange night with Frances. How did Astrid get a copy? Had she intended for him to find it?

I love, we love... all you need is love.

My lustful body knows no bounds,

I will follow your direction.

Your enticement dictates,

My desperation obeys.

Exposed are my imperfections,

But I follow your dictates.

A script to be adhered to,

I didn't ask for a reason.

You were too desirable for that,

Was I really that disappointing?

Was it something I said?
I hope I didn't go too early,
Did I prove to be an unworthy choice?
I know you have sweeter ones in the jar,
But did I really taste that bitter?
Yuk, tastes bad, spit it out,
Like a Dutch sweet with salt at the core.

He wondered whether Astrid had known it was about Frances. When he re-read the final line, he could see how she might misinterpret it. Astrid might see the words, "Dutch sweets", as being about her. But how would she interpret some of the other lines. What could he say to her if she asked?

'Oh Astrid, that part about sex games and lust was just my imagination?'

9

Ireland and Amsterdam

Sebastian had known Astrid was the love of his life after their chance meeting in Ireland. She had written her address and phone number on a green pub coaster. He had revered the coaster like a Dutch masterpiece. Back then, her departure had left him with that same empty, gut-wrenching feeling. It felt as though all of his strength had been sapped from him.

In Ireland, he had deluded himself into thinking it was because of travel fatigue or homesickness, as he had been away for over six months. The truth was that after meeting Astrid, backpacking through Ireland just wasn't the same. But he was resolute and kept to his travel plans, placating his restless spirit with the promise that he would visit Astrid in Amsterdam one day soon. He'd found her profile on social media but didn't want to spoil the magic by making contact. After all, he'd only known her for a night. And nothing physical had occurred. Best tactic, he thought, was to wait until he was in Amsterdam.

It was a grey overcast afternoon when Sebastian arrived in Amsterdam a month later; normal weather for that time year, according to an American tourist he met. He booked himself into a cheap student hostel in the middle of town, showered, and changed into his cleanest cotton shirt and blue jeans. He was upset when he rang her number and there was no reply. When he rang again an hour later and she still didn't pick up, he became impatient and decided to go to her flat. The hostel manager patiently drew a small map and wrote an accompanying set of directions showing Sebastian how to get to Amsterdam Oust.

It was close to four when he set out full of hope for a rendezvous with the woman he'd been fantasising about. The bus journey over quaint bridges and canals was enchanting, but a number of doubts began to creep up on him. Would he be intruding? She probably gave her address out to lots of people. Perhaps she had a boyfriend? With her looks and personality, she was bound to attract amorous attention.

Her block was located off a large square, where there were beautiful gardens. When he found her flat, he was overcome with shyness and trepidation. So much so that at first his feeble knock was barely audible. Pulling himself together he knocked again, this time more forcibly. There was still no sound or movement from inside and he felt a peculiar ambivalence – disappointment at not seeing Astrid, but joy that he had found his way to her door. There was still hope. It occurred to him that he didn't even know the phone number of the hotel where he was staying. He cursed himself for the oversight. Were his thoughts so scattered that he hadn't anticipated this possibility? At least he knew the name of the hotel.

After ripping up his first two attempts, he wrote a note which was simple and succinct. He signed it and dropped it into Astrid's mailbox.

I am staying at the Vandeburg Hotel. Would be great to catch up, Seb Darcy.

He caught the bus back into town, oblivious to the beauty of the city. He could only think of Astrid. When he arrived back at the hotel, he plonked himself in the foyer and informed the receptionist he was expecting a very important call. He then watched the woman's every reaction, in anticipation of a call from Astrid.

An hour later, Carlos, a friendly South American man whom he had met earlier, enquired about his plans for dinner and the two of them decided to go out for something to eat. Sebastian tried to be realistic; maybe Astrid was never going to call. She might have a lover living with her. Maybe that was why nothing sexual had happened during that long night together in Ireland.

Sebastian's fascination with new places and people was what propelled him as a lone traveller backpacking around the world. But it didn't mean he was going to like everybody. His propinquity with Carlos was short-lived. During the meal, Carlos revealed that he was a mercenary soldier just back from a stint in Africa. A smile came over the man's face as he boasted about how easy it was to shoot untrained black Africans because they closed their eyes when they fired their weapons.

After that insight into Carlos's mind, Sebastian decided to eat up quickly, finishing his drink and coming up with an excuse that he had to meet with somebody else.

The shorter than expected outing proved to be a blessing. There was a message from Astrid waiting when he returned to the hotel. She had been busy working at the university all day.

An hour later, the two met at a bar in town. Sebastian had learnt some functional Dutch, such as *een bier* and *een rose*, phrases he was to use many times in the future. After a couple of drinks and at Astrid's insistence, he collected his pack from the hostel and went with Astrid back to her flat.

Astrid's place had a large living area, a main bedroom, and a study. She had set up a spare bed in the study and they had a glass of hot chocolate before going to bed.

The next day, they caught a bus into town and spent the day strolling through the city. They couldn't get into the Van Gough Museum, but Sebastian was more than happy to leave it for another time. The attraction between the two was strong, but as it can be when two people feel something bigger than a brief fling might be on offer, neither was in a hurry to take the relationship to a physical level.

When Astrid eventually was ready, on the final night of his stay in Amsterdam, her actions were so convoluted and seemingly out of character with how Sebastian had perceived her to be, that he was slow to catch on.

As Astrid knew, Sebastian had prior arrangements to meet up with some Australian friends in Germany. He and Astrid had spent the night out on the town, with friends of Astrid.

It was around two in the morning when they finally staggered back into the flat. Astrid had been talking to somebody on the phone. Sebastian began yawning, and was thinking of crashing for the night, when Astrid came back into the lounge room with a forlorn expression on her face. At first Sebastian thought that something serious had happened. When Astrid spoke, he was relieved.

'Seb, will you change the light bulb in my bedroom? I can't quite reach it.'

'I'll have a look,' said Sebastian, surprised that such a simple matter could cause her such distress.

He followed Astrid into her bedroom where a stepladder was already in place. When he saw the dusty old globe, he hesitated, but Astrid assured him she would not let her new friend go up in smoke.

The light globe was easy enough to change. It was when Sebastian made his descent that sparks began to fly.

Sebastian initially felt uneasy. Did Astrid realise how close to the stepladder she was standing? How was he going to get down without falling on top of her?

When he got to the last rung, and she still hadn't moved, he was about to ask her to shift over when he noticed Astrid had her finger across her lip. The slightest of smiles came over her face, and it was at that moment when Sebastian gazed into her brazen brown eyes and realised she had been deliberately blocking his path.

With the lights dimmed and the aroma of burning incense hanging in the air, their lustful bodies were soon entwined. They continued to talk and make love into the early hours before drifting off to sleep, wrapped together in each other's warmth.

Leaving Amsterdam on an incredible high, Sebastian caught the train to Dusseldorf and met up with his friends.

They visited the majestic castles along the Rhine and camped and played music deep in the Black Forest. He travelled through Germany in a love-struck state. Wherever he went, Astrid was always at the forefront of his thoughts. Occasionally they would talk on the phone. They also exchanged letters. Astrid posted her letters to the next major city Sebastian was expected to visit. The moment he would arrived, he'd hot foot it to the central post office where hopefully a letter would be waiting.

I am lying in bed eating an apple that a friend gave me. I'm longing for a coffee, but I haven't any filters left. As I told you once before, I have problems writing letters because I don't like writing about what I am thinking or feeling without receiving a reaction immediately. In fact, I don't like writing letters at all, but I found out how it can feel to get a letter, so I had to write back of course.

Another problem for me is the language. I'm afraid I make a lot of mistakes in English, and it doesn't work easily for me because all the time I have to think about how to spell and the order to put the words.

I still have my "engagement bracelet" (however you write that) on my arm, but the string is getting thinner and thinner. It will surely break one of these days. Wilhelmina and Stephani are coming around tonight so I'll write to you again another time.

Tot Ziens,

Astrid.

Sebastian and his friends made iceblocks with raspberry cordial high in the Swiss Alps. At night they sat around the bars, drinking and having a yarn to the locals and fellow travellers. Seeking warmer weather, they fast tracked it down through the French Riviera, only slowing down once they crossed into Spain. By the time they reached Barcelona, Sebastian was longing to return to Amsterdam. But he was too proud to go running back to a woman he barely knew.

Two weeks later they were in Cadiz. The group was split on whether to cross to Tangier or travel up through Portugal. Sebastian had intended to go to Tangier, but a letter from Astrid changed his mind.

I have been so busy lately. My job at the university is taking more and more time. Last week I had meetings from 8 o'clock in the morning till 4 o'clock in the afternoon.

And then I had to get my work done and get up early again. But this weekend I was so tired that I slept most of the time.

I had a very strange experience with that on Sunday. I went to bed Saturday night at twelve and woke up at six. I thought it was still morning and I wanted to get something to drink because I was so thirsty, but when I went to the front room, I saw lots of lights on outside. It was already evening again.

With this crazy sleep I have been having strange dreams. I dreamt that you were lying beside me but when I turned to look it was someone I didn't know. It was freaky. Is that the expression?

By the way, my engagement bracelet broke, but it still did not make me think less of you. I got a message the other day that some friends from Ireland will be coming to Amsterdam in a week's time. They want me to go to Sweden with them. Any chance you will be in Amsterdam by then?

Tot Ziens (I hope you are still learning Dutch).

Love,

Astrid.

Sebastian left Cadiz the next day. After being painstakingly delayed in Barcelona because of a soccer match, he arrived in Amsterdam, once again in the afternoon.

The snowflakes were falling lightly, and he crossed the canals, feeling as though he had stepped into a fairytale. Astrid had returned from university early, anticipating his arrival. From their first moment together, it was apparent the magic was still there.

10

The Scene

Joe was cruising along Maroubra Bay Road in his Ford Falcon, heading towards the beach. There were more units, but the sleepy beachside suburb had maintained the laidback character it had been renowned for back in Joe's youth. He'd once driven along this road most days of the week. He'd owned a big old Falcon back then too. They were hard, cold, soulless times, when he was constantly on the lookout for an easy break-and-enter, something to trade for the quick fix his body achingly craved.

It had occurred to Joe that the shooting incident on the golf course could be linked to somebody from the old days. Perhaps they recognised him and figured they had a score to settle. A brother or a cousin maybe of someone he had wronged. Who knows, he thought, how many people his actions had impacted on, inadvertently or otherwise?

Joe took his foot off the accelerator. Up ahead was the block of units where he had once lived. He thought about the Bradley kid who'd overdosed upstairs. Only seventeen. There was nothing he could have done. Long gone by the time Joe found him, he'd rung an ambulance and left town for a week. He'd been paranoid about getting set up by the police. In the end nothing much happened. Barely made the news. Another junkie bites the dust. End of story.

Eventually Joe the junkie stepped up and became Joe the sleazy dealer. One of many whom the crooked detectives hounded or manipulated maliciously in order to secure their cut of the prolific trade.

Then there was a change of government. When the crooks got a whiff of the upcoming Crime Investigation Unit, they wanted to tie up loose ends. Joe was on their disposable list. He knew too much and was past his used-by-date. It was touch-and-go for a while, and Joe was jittery and dangerous. He went out bush for a few days, practised with his pistol and learnt how to use a semiautomatic. He didn't venture out without a loaded weapon. Those people were cruel bastards. If they were gunning for you, you had to prepare.

The scare hadn't been enough to get him off the gear though. He got close a few times. He traded some dope for a good guitar and went busking in the city. One day when he was busking at Martin Place, he was offered a job as the lead singer in a working band. He took it and for a time there he was clean and working five nights a week. For six months he had money and even managed to save. Then he was offered a hit one night after a show and found himself back at square one.

It was only later, after Matt was born, that he legalised his addiction by transferring to methadone. By the time Joe was accepted into the methadone program, he was in bad shape. He had hepatitis types B and C, plus other complications. Then a miracle happened. A new wonder drug. It was just a trial but for Joe it was lifesaving. His case was even documented in the prestigious medical journal *The Lancet*. One of the first in the country to successfully respond to Interferon. That was the beginning of his amazing recovery (doctors had previously given him only two years). His liver function returned close to normal, and he was cured of hepatitis. Joe knew how lucky he had been. Most of his junkie mates were either burnt out or dead.

With a block of land up the north coast and half a million buried in Sebastian's backyard, things were looking pretty good for Joe. Recently he'd donated a large sum of money to a drug rehab group. It lessened the guilt, and hopefully appeased the gods. He'd paid Sebastian back, at long last. And he'd apologised for hocking Sebastian's Maton twelve-string all those years ago. His mate had saved him a few times. Whenever he asked, actually, and once when he hadn't.

The cool, salty night breeze had an anodyne effect on his body and mind as he walked from his car to The Bay Hotel. According to the gig guide, it had live music during the week. He and Sebastian had played at The Bay when they were just out of school.

Joe stepped up to the bar and found a stool adjacent to the serving area. There were mostly men present, with a handful of older women. He nodded to a fella who turned to see who'd just come me.

The pub was once a venue for raging local rock bands, and it was not unusual to see the crowd spilling out onto the footpath. Tonight, it was quiet with barely a handful of people inside. In the far corner near the pool table an old fella was plugging away on a steel-string guitar. He was running his guitar and microphone through and old forty-watt amplifier. The vocals sounded muddy as a result. At least the bloke didn't have much to carry. If the venue was full, the sound would have died within a few metres of where he was playing.

Joe caught the barmaid's eye. She was young and voluptuous with long, sun-bleached blonde hair; one of the ubiquitous lissom beauties seen throughout the beach suburbs during the warmer months.

'A lemon squash, thanks love… it's pretty quiet tonight.'

'Yeah… a bit quieter than usual.'

'Do you always have live music?'

The young woman moved gracefully around the bar area, picking up glasses as she spoke. 'On and off. Now and then they put something on.'

'Is the manager in?'

'He's out the back. Is he expecting you?'

'I haven't got an appointment, but do you mind asking him if I can have a quick word? I'd really appreciate it. Joe De'Gabriel's the name.'

She gave him his drink and smiled. 'I'll duck out and see if he's available.'

The manager was a thickset man with the rough-and-ready demeanour of an ex-footballer.

'Jim Saunders,' he said, offering his hand.

The big man's crushing grip hurt Joe's fingers. Joe showed no pain and didn't react. Once he would have ripped Jim Sounder's thumb away quick smart, ensuring pain was felt.

Saunders listened with interest as Joe explained he played in a duo, mentioning some of the more popular artists they covered. He shot Saunders a line about being interested in finding an extra gig or two close to home.

The manager looked across at the solitary figure performing in the corner. 'We could do with a few changes around here. This bloke is ordinary. Sometimes I think he chases our customers away,' he said, sniggering at his own comment as he noisily tossed a few glasses into the dishwasher.

'My partner lined him up,' he added dryly, feeling the need to justify the performer's presence.

Joe morphed into salesman mode, mentioning the broad appeal of their repertoire and how this would bring in younger as well as middle-aged customers. He spoke about the mutual benefits of dealing directly with management rather than through an agent.

The manager continued to traduce the performer, dismissing him with a disdainful flick of the wrist after he played what Joe thought was a reasonable rendition of the old Beach Boys hit, *Surfer Girl*.

The girl at the bar clapped. Jimmy Saunders said, 'We could do with something a bit more upbeat around here, that's for sure. As you can see, we haven't got a big space. I'm happy to give you guys a go if the price is right. How much do you and your mate charge?'

Joe tried to keep the price down to what he thought was a reasonable figure. Setting the price was always tricky. It was the type of venue where they could build a local following and it could well be his and Sebastian's first gig. Don't go too high, Joe said to himself.

'For a three-hour gig… two–sixty,' he replied, knowing that it was half what an agent would charge for a duo.

The sour grimace on the face of Jim Saunders was painful to watch. The manager's lupine demeanour circled Joe with ill intent.

'Two-sixty? You are fucking joking!'

From Saunders' reaction, Joe may well have asked for two-sixty thousand with a new Mercedes thrown in for good measure. He laughed in Joe's face.

'Pull the other one, mate... Two-sixty? No freaking way!'

'Just "no thanks" would have done fine,' countered Joe sarcastically.

'Don't try it on with me, mate,' replied Saunders as he left Joe to serve a customer.

Joe decided Saunders was either having a bad day or was a complete dickhead. But he wasn't going anywhere until he'd finished his drink. He sat there, listening to the music and ignoring Saunders, who would occasionally fix his wolven stare on Joe, eyeing him like prey.

In a complete turnaround from his earlier betrayal, the manager applauded the country performer when he completed his set. There's a song in that, thought Joe.

A bald man sitting nearby had his face buried in the form guide. Attired in thongs and stubbies, and with the obligatory beer gut, he appeared to be a local with a lifetime lease on his spot by the bar. When the manager was out of earshot, he lifted his head and spoke.

'He's a real tightarse, mate. Don't waste ya time. The fella up there is only playing for drinks anyway and he still whinges about him.'

'Takes all types I suppose,' said Joe. 'Got any tips for tomorrow at Randwick?'

For the next few minutes, the two discussed the horses, the weather forecast, and the possibilities of a wet track, before Joe reminded himself of his mission for the night.

He said goodbye to his new friend and left the hotel. On the golf course with Sebastian, he'd been shooting his mouth off a bit, he thought to himself. He wondered whether he'd been underestimating the difficulty of finding work. Despite being keen to play, the reality was they still didn't have one gig. Maybe he'd have better luck at The Junction.

The Junction used to be your run-of-the-mill watering hole frequented by knock-about locals, tradesmen and labourers. Around closing time, it could get a bit hectic. There was a period in Joe's life when he would barely have gone a day without a visit. For business reasons mostly. Dubious business.

Joe parked in the middle of the main drag and approached the hotel. He entered the foyer where signs of renovation were apparent in the fancy décor and fresh stylish colours. He found his way around a small cordoned-off section of trestles and building materials and stepped into the main bar. A quick look around revealed a well-heeled clientele. He ordered a lime and soda water.

There was a table of eight celebrating nearby and a television in the corner blaring away to nobody in particular. Behind the noise, Joe could just make out the mellow sound of an electric piano emanating from somewhere. Was it a radio, or someone playing inside the pub? He listened intently. There was a familiarity about the style – the jazz-flavoured chord progressions, ninths and sixths in the left hand, accompanied by a lightning-fast right hand – but he couldn't put his finger on it.

Intrigued, Joe picked up his drink and walked out of the bar, determined to find the source of the music. It was coming from the beer garden, and when Joe stepped into the space his face broke into a grin. The man tickling the ivories was his old schoolfriend, Fernando Johnson. Joe listened from the back of the room as Johnno played a series of chords that ascended the keyboard chromatically, leading to a sudden five-four time signature switch culminating in a frantic sixteen-bar finale. There must have been fifty or sixty people there, many of them applauding generously in appreciation of the quality of musicianship on display.

Johnno cast his eyes around the audience and saw Joe waving back at him. He acknowledged Joe with a nod of the head before he leapt into the next number, the Dave Brubeck classic, *Take Five*. After he'd finished, Johnno thanked the audience and announced he would be taking a short break.

Joe walked up to the front of the room.

'Joe... Joe De'Gabriel... how are you, man? Great to see you,' enthused Johnno.

They greeted each other enthusiastically, both delighted at the chance encounter.

Johnno, Joe and Sebastian had played together in a band at school.

They'd all been capable musicians, but Johnno was the standout. He was the drummer. He'd played piano and sax up until then and had wanted to try a different instrument. Sebastian was the keyboard player and Joe the lead singer. Johnno could play jazz, blues, country and rock, and he could trot out a classical repertoire if the need arose. But that was the sideshow. His main game was composition.

For Joe, who had little training in music, Johnno had been an encyclopedia of information. Johnno was only twenty-two when The Sydney Symphony Orchestra first performed one of his works. He went on to write for many Australian and international orchestras and performance groups. Joe could still remember reading a five-star review in which Johnno's work was commended by *The Sydney Morning Herald* reviewer for its distinctive Australian flavour and originality of structure. Fernando Johnson had been acclaimed as being one of the most promising and inspiring voices of the younger brigade at that time.

'Are you still composing?' asked Joe.

'Yeah, bits here and there. But there's not much funding for the music I like to write. These days they seem to go for music that sounds like it was written two centuries ago. And as you probably know, orchestras are struggling. They have to back pop artists to make it viable.'

'Whatever happened to that guy you were living with, the double-bass player who owned all those old pinball machines?' asked Joe.

'Oh Andy?' replied Johnno, with a smile. 'We're still together.'

'Really! You were never one for long-term relationships.'

'That's true, Joe. But who is, until the right person comes along? How's your love life going?'

'You'd remember Kate, Seb's sister?'

'Yeah! She was a gorgeous girl. Lucky you. Have you two tied the knot?'

Joe laughed. 'Come on, Johnno. Who'd ever marry me?'

They talked about the good old days, how they'd regularly played to audiences of six hundred plus at various school and community dances.

'I must say, I was surprised to see you here. With your achievements,

I thought you'd be playing in New York, London or Berlin. Not here at The Junction.'

'The irony,' said Johnno, 'is that now I've become accomplished as a musician, I'm lucky to have fifty people in the audience some nights. But I'm not complaining. It pays the bills. How are you getting on?'

'Doing well.'

He gave Joe the once over. 'I got to say, Joe, you look a lot better than the last time I saw you over at Manly that night.

Joe could remember the night. 'Must have been ten years ago,' he said, a little embarrassed. He'd snubbed Johnno on that occasion, not because he didn't want to talk with him but because he was embarrassed to be seen in such a drugged-out state.

'Probably longer. Anyway, good to see you looking well. Are you still singing?'

'I haven't done much in public for a while, Johnno, but Sebastian and I are reviving the old duo. I'm staying at his mum's old place at the moment. She passed away a couple of months back.'

'Yeah, I remember his mum. She was a lovely lady. Used to make us lunch when we rehearsed at Seb's place. Say hello and pass on my sympathy to Seb. It'd be good to catch up with him. The last time I saw him was in Newcastle. I was doing a gig up there at the Workers Club. He was working at some youth joint.'

'Yeah, he's still there. You'll have to come along when we play.'

'For sure.'

Joe and Johnno had a laugh about Joe's encounter with the manager at The Bay earlier in the night, and Joe milked him for information on the current scene.

'It's not like the old days when nearly every pub and club had live music. I get enough work, but I still have to hustle for midweek gigs. You two should do ok. You both sing. You'll need to get in with an agent though. They've got the scene sewn up. There was supposed to be someone dropping in tonight to see me about a gig on a cruise.' Johnno looked at his watch. 'I have to play another set, Joe. Are you going to stay for a while?'

'I've got to go into town, but I'll stay for a few songs.'

Johnno made his way back to the keyboard and took a sip of his drink before playing an inspired version of the David Bowie classic, *Under Pressure*.

He then put Joe under pressure by inviting him onto the stage. He who hesitates… thought Joe. He got to his feet, smiled, and made his way onto the stage.

'You'll remember this one,' said Johnno handing Joe the microphone. A moment later a drumbeat started. Johnno sped it up a fraction then began playing.

It took Joe a while to realise it was a song that he and Sebastian had written. He couldn't believe how quickly Johnno had set the tempo. They used to play it using two guitars. Both top and bottom E strings were taken down a tone to D. It had minor chords in the verse and shifted to major chords in the chorus. It used to go down well with a variety of crowds and worked acoustically or with drums and electric guitar. Johnno soon had the hypnotic bass happening with his left hand while his right stayed on the beat, pushing out the chords.

An extensive vocal range was required to do it justice, peaking on C#, a note Joe could hit without having to sing falsetto, while going as low as middle C. The song had just four chords; Johnno was always going to add more.

Joe engaged the audience from the get-go and looked the part. It had been a while since he had performed without holding a guitar. But he knew the moves, and his rugged presence gave the performance credibility.

Waking up, such a beautiful day.

Feel the breeze across your face.

Tracing the steps of a childlike vision,

Hungering for a taste.

Johnno had switched the volume up a notch or two, and once Joe was in full flight, people began filtering through from the public bar to see who was singing. There were only a few words in the chorus and by the time he did it for a third time, a few of the patrons were singing along. When he finished, the crowd applauded and some at the front asked for an encore. Again, Johhno surprised him, remembering another song they had played together years ago. Medium paced, it was a haunting song with a catchy melody.

Is there always a choice?
I wonder.
The sound of the ocean
At my window.
The sometimes perfume
Of the deadly nightshade
Forever fills me
With delights of living dreams.

When they'd finished, even the normally indifferent bar staff applauded. Joe was on a high afterwards. There had been a few hesitations, but nothing that was too obvious.

'Hey Johnno, thanks for that, man. I really enjoyed it. How in the hell did you remember those songs?'

'How could I forget? We played them often enough.'

They spoke together for another minute or so, before Johnno had to continue with the set.

'Ok, Joe. You've got my number. Keep in touch… and by the way, your voice is sounding as good as ever.'

Wow… a compliment from Johnno, thought Joe. That didn't happen too often.

'It's been great to see you, man.'

As Joe walked towards the exit, he was approached by a stylishly dressed gent, probably in his mid-thirties. Joe had noticed him and another man come into the room and stand at the back while he'd been singing.

'Steven Wiseman,' he said, shaking Joe's hand in a firm no-nonsense fashion. 'I enjoyed the song, man. You've got an impressive voice. Are you singing with a band?'

'With a duo actually.'

'My agency is always on the lookout for quality acts.'

Wiseman handed Joe his card.

'That last song one of yours?'

'Yeah... you bet. Co-wrote it with my mate.'

'Give me a call when you're playing next. I'll try to get along and have a listen.'

'Yeah, sure. I definitely will.'

'Might hear from you then,' said the agent, and he shook Joe's hand before heading up to the front of the room.

The moment Wiseman left, the fella who had been standing beside him during the performance caught Joe's attention. Up close the face was familiar.

'Hey, that was impressive. My name's Rob, Rob Martin.' The man had a broad Scottish accent.

As the two shook hands, Joe realised why the face was familiar. Martin had been the drummer in Risky Business, one of the most successful bands to come out of the country in the past decade. The band had broken up just a few months ago amid some dispute over copyright and ownership of material.

'I've been putting together a show band. We're covering a bunch of soul classics. Down the track we intend to record a few originals. I've already got gigs lined up in Sydney and Melbourne as well as a stint in Thailand in a few months, but we've had trouble finding a quality singer who's available.'

For once Joe was lost for words. This was totally out of the blue. 'Sounds interesting, I'll give it some thought.' he replied, wondering whether Martin had heard him mention the duo in his conversation with Wiseman.

'Sure, have a think on it, man,' said Martin, continuing the conversation as he wrote down his contact number on a pub coaster. Joe was surprised he didn't have a card.

'If you're interested, get back to me within the next few days. You'd need to come along to a rehearsal to see if it worked out, but from what I saw tonight I reckon you'll fit the bill. Hope to hear from you, man,' he said, holding Joe's gaze momentarily before walking off.

Joe laughed to himself as he made his way out onto the street. He could talk to the hotel manager another time. Maybe he wouldn't need too. Martin seemed genuine enough. The fickle wind of fate, he thought. You can play for years and nothing happens, then you sing a couple of songs and two opportunities present themselves. He looked at the classy little maroon, gold and white card. There was a mobile number plus an email address for Steven Wiseman, Executive Director Full-On Promotions.

But it was the red and grey coaster he was clutching tightest as he fantasised about performing with one of the best drummers in the country. He had done soul before, not long after the school band had broken up. His mind was racing. What a buzz. He felt like a musician again as he walked down the street towards his car, singing a few bars of the Wilson Pickett classic, *Midnight Hour.*

He thought back to his earlier experience with Saunders and how little the man wanted to pay for musicians. He wondered whether he would ever get decent paying gigs playing with Sebastian.

11

Justice

Sebastian awoke in the early hours after another strange dream. Once again, he had experienced the unnerving sensation of feeling he was a child again, living in his old Napier Street house. Finding it impossible to get back to sleep, he got up and picked up the tv remote to search for something to watch. A pair of piercing yellow-grey eyes seemed to jump from the screen, seeking him out and reaching into his very soul. The all-too-familiar creature stretched its neck to the sky and unleased a bloodcurdling howl, sending a deep chill through Sebastian's spine and rendering him motionless. He grabbed the remote and turned the tv off.

Sebastian sank back into the lounge and tried to make sense of what he'd witnessed. Soon he was berating himself for his spineless behaviour; it was just an image on a screen for godsake. Once he'd regained his composure, he searched and found the channel again. As it turned out, he'd tuned into a documentary about an American woman who nursed injured and sick wolves back to health. The animal that had terrified him was a black-coated wolf.

He was still lying on the sofa four hours later when the time came to get changed and go into town to pick up Deon.

The traffic moved quickly through Charlestown, and Sebastian had time to spare. He decided to take the scenic route, via Mereweather beach. Approaching the turn-off, he was late to move into the right-hand lane and had to push in front of a Ute. This attracted the ire of the driver, who threw him a two-fingered salute. Being a relatively small city, motorists in Newy were familiar with the roads, and could be impatient with those who weren't.

Sebastian slowed down as he approached the water. There was an offshore breeze blowing, creating an excellent wave along the length of the beach. There were numerous board riders out on the water, taking advantage of the conditions. After passing through Bar Beach, Sebastian drove up through The Hill. Making a left turn, he could see down to the harbour, where a coal ship was leaving port. What Sebastian loved about Newcastle was that wherever you lived it was never that far to the beach.

Sebastian found a two-hour parking spot up the hill from the courthouse. If he needed more time, he'd come out and move the car. The courthouse was a grand Victorian edifice with a large arched-tower entrance. Sebastian climbed the sandstone steps and made his way inside.

The courthouse was a hive of activity. There were people seated, others in the queue, a few filling out forms. What was noticeable were the number of hardened, grim faces. Just being in the building made him feel like a criminal. He searched for the appropriate document from the plethora on offer in the wooden cubicles. Unable to find what he was after, he joined the queue. After a short wait he reached the front.

'Hello, my name's Sebastian Darcy. I'm here to pick up Deon Murray.'

Sebastian presented to the woman behind the counter – Sarah, according to her nametag – the documentation Greg Wright had e-mailed.

Her eyes scanned the sheet of paper, and then she raised her head. 'ID?'

Sebastian reached into his trousers, pulled out his wallet and produced his licence. Sarah held it up to the light to check its authenticity, while simultaneously slipping her free hand deftly under the counter. Without even a glance downwards, she pulled out two forms.

'Bring them back to me when they're completed.' She turned, pressed the intercom button, and mumbled something Sebastian couldn't make out.

He hastily answered the questions, after which he re-joined the queue. When he returned the documents to Sarah, a frown appeared on her face

'You have to answer all of the questions, sir.' She tapped her forefinger at the section that dealt with the security bond. 'You need to list assets, to the value of two thousand dollars.'

'Excuse me, madam, but Greg Wright from Juvenile Justice said I wouldn't have to put up a bond.'

Sara's vacant expression made it clear she didn't know Greg Wright from a bar of soap.

'I'm the coordinator of Maitland Youth Services. This is to do with work.'

His declaration carried no favour.

'We have to have security, or we cannot release the prisoner.'

'Can you ring Greg Wright? I have his number.'

Sarah pointed at the queue forming behind Sebastian.

'You're only liable for three hundred dollars anyway, not the full two thousand.' she said, as though letting him in on a secret. 'Most people put down their house if they own one.'

Sebastian's nostrils flared in response.

'My house? You are kidding, lady! I'm not putting up my house as security. What a preposterous idea!'

Sarah didn't respond. She simply turned her attention to the next customer.

Sebastian was left stranded. Checkmate. Back to the booth he went. This time he listed his Holden as security.

He re-joined the queue, even forcing a genial smile as he handed the form back to Sarah. Sarah exhaled slowly. Clearly, she was dealing with an idiot.

'Sorry, Mr. Darcy. Motor vehicles are not acceptable. We get into trouble if we accept motor vehicles as security.'

'What? You are kidding me! The car's worth forty bloody grand, for godsake,'

This was an exaggeration on Sebastian's part but proved to be irrelevant anyway. Sarah had had enough. She turned to her co-worker.

'Loretta, can you deal with this one?' The woman ignored Sebastian. 'Next,' she called.

Sebastian was taken aback. He wanted to walk out but he couldn't just leave Deon. Should he ring Greg Wright?

Loretta left the recalcitrant customer standing in no-man's-land for a few minutes. When she approached Sebastian, she was stone-faced and displeased. It was clear the changing of the baton had not been for his benefit.

'Look, mister. It's that simple. Motor vehicles are not accepted.'

Customers in the queue were glaring at him, and these were not the type of people you wanted to mess with. He was considering asking to see Loretta's boss, when a man in the queue said, in a gentle voice, 'Have you got a TV, mate? Just put down TV and stereo.'

At that moment, Sebastian's attention was diverted to the adjoining room, where a trapdoor was opening. Deon appeared, accompanied by a beefy warden.

When he sighted Sebastian, Deon's downcast demeanour lifted considerably. Sebastian knew he was beaten – he could hardly let them return Deon to the cells. He hastily listed a stereo and a television as security. Unable to remember the brand names, he made them up.

To Sebastian's surprise, the form was readily accepted. Validating the market value of the non-existent assets wasn't an issue. Loretta then produced an Agreement of Surety form which Deon and then Sebastian were instructed to sign. They were both handed a copy of the bail undertaking. Deon was also given a copy of the charge sheet, a copy of the facts relating to his arrest, a tape of his police interview, sheets of paper informing him of his rights, and a NSW Police Service information handout explaining bail and court procedures. He was instructed to report to the police station weekly until his court appearance. His personal items were returned in a plastic bag: wallet, mobile phone, a small notebook, a few coins, and a bunch of crumpled Centrelink papers.

As they were about to leave, Loretta caught Sebastian's eye. 'Sebastian Darcy?' she called.

Sebastian was sheepish, thinking he was in trouble again, but this proved not to be the case. Loretta was holding up a piece of paper that she wanted him to take.

'We do not usually pass on messages, Mr. Darcy,' she said, a sprightly politeness to her tone that said his earlier transgression was now forgiven.

She handed him a folded memo sheet. He had no idea who it could be from. When he read it he got a real surprise.

Please meet me at 1 pm today, Blackbutt Reserve. Frances.

What a strange thing to do. Why didn't she simply phone or text. Was what she had to say really that urgent? And why Blackbutt? Was she now chasing him? Now that was an intriguing thought. The beast had been awoken and carnal feelings stirred within. He sent Frances a message.

'I'll be there.'

Clutching the note, Sebastian checked his watch, as he and Deon walked from the building and out onto the street.

'Thanks Sebastian... for getting me outta there.'

'Oh, that's ok. How you feeling?'

'I wouldn't mind a cold drink, man. Me throat's so dry.'

They walked across to a café on the corner and Sebastian brought Deon a Coke.

'Are you hungry, mate? 'Yep... sure am. I didn't feel much like eating in there.'

'We'll drop in at Maccas if you like.'

Deon nodded enthusiastically. Sebastian drove to King Street and turned into McDonalds. After hoeing into a burger and chips, Deon was soon back to his old self, joking and laughing.

'Hey Deon, why did you leave that group house you were in? I thought it was going ok.'

'Rules, man. Too many rules... can't do this, can't do that.'

'Shit, Deon, you waited ages for that to come up. I thought you would at least give it a bit more time.'

'I couldn't stand it there Seb. You couldn't fart without a worker having a policy on it. Me mates wanted to drop over, and I had to always get permission. Man... it was like you was a little kid.'

Sebastian checked his watch again. There wasn't enough time to drop Deon off at Charlestown if he was to be on time to meet Frances at

Blackbutt Reserve. He'd only been with Deon for ten minutes and already he was cramping his style. He reminded himself that it was only short-term.

'I can't believe you were mucking around with guns and stuff, Deon.'

'We was nowhere near the boys... me and Michaela, we didn't take nothin'. And that kid Jacob had the fake gun... Donny grabbed it off 'em, and then they made up all this fucking shit for the cops.'

'Deon!'

'What?'

'You swear too fucking much.'

'Sorry... sorry, Seb,' he said, apologetic, oblivious to the irony. 'We'll have to get a swearing jar going again, eh Seb?' said Deon, referring to the time a group of them had stayed at Myall Lakes. 'You made a fortune out of that.'

'Yeah, I wish! By lunchtime you were all out of coins.'

Sebastian hadn't known Deon very well before the camping trip to Myall Lakes. But it became apparent during the trip that there was far more to the boy than just the jocular, happy-go-lucky lad he'd appeared to be on the surface.

The group had been walking though the bush between Mungo Brush and Tea Gardens. The guide stopped near a lagoon, at the base of the sandhills. After taking a small shovel from his pack, the guide began digging in the sand. As he dug deeper, he became excited at the prospect of finding water.

Deon had stayed well back from the group. Sebastian noticed he was becoming increasingly agitated. When the guide struck water, cupped his hands and drank, he invited the others to do the same.

At this point Deon stormed over, his mouth curled up in disgust.

'You can't drink that water. There's burial places round 'ere,' he declared, pointing to the surrounding hills.

Everyone was startled. Some of them thought at first that he was joking. Nobody had ever seen him so fierce and irate.

'The water you're drinking... it's passed through the remains of dead people. People are buried in the hills. Ya don't dig for water 'ere.'

He continued to berate the hapless guide. 'No respect, it's fucking wrong... you should know these things. How would you like it if I went to your sacred places, ya churches and cathedrals, and started playing around? Or if I went to the cemetery and dug up the graves? How would you like that, eh?'

The guide was embarrassingly stung, and he stopped drinking the water. Whilst he had obviously just been trying to do his job, the day's outing turned a little sour from that point. The guide, to his credit, tried to patch things up later when he attempted to display his empathy and awareness of Indigenous culture by making a reference to the spiritual significance of crows. But he had lost Deon's respect. Deon caught the man's eye before he spoke.

'They'll eat ya bones when ya die, man.'

Blackbutt Reserve could be seen in the distance as Sebastian and Deon made their way up Carnley Avenue. The tranquil bushland was tucked away beneath a busy bypass road that meandered along the ridge, to the west of the city.

Sebastian had been there often with Astrid and Jenna. Sometimes just the three of them, other times with groups of friends. Jenna had been fascinated by the peacocks and brush turkeys that roamed wild. Astrid loved seeing the koalas and emus. They'd walk up the hill to the koala enclosure where there were also birds, reptiles and a nocturnal display. They'd invariably finish up at the playground.

'What 'ave you got to do round 'ere?' asked Deon.

Sebastian was less than truthful. 'It's to do with work. I've got to pick up something I forgot to get earlier. I'm supposed to meet Frances... you know Frances?'

'Yeah, she came along to watch us rehearse the other week up at the council hall.'

'Did she? Was she impressed?'

'Yeah, I suppose... you should ask Thommo,' he added with a snigger.

'Why Thommo?'

'He and Frances seemed to hit it off pretty good.'

'Does he like her?'

'Thommo? I don't know. But I reckon she likes him by the way she was carrying on.'

Sebastian visualised Frances, ingratiating herself to the teenage boy.

'She's old enough to be his mother,' he snapped, barely containing himself.

They turned into the car park.

'Bloody racist, this place,' said Deon.

Sebastian was still thinking about Frances. At first, he thought Deon was referring to the previous conversation. 'Who's a racist? Frances?'

'Nah, not Frances.'

Deon pointed to the signpost near the entrance to the parking area. 'Blackbutt... the name's racist. Should call the place Whitearse or something. You'll find more white arses than black butts 'ere... eh?'

Deon broke into his infectious chuckle.

'You are bloody crazy, Deon,' said Sebastian, with a laugh. 'I'll drive home through Redhead if it makes you feel better.'

The inviting aroma of steak and onions drifted across from the BBQ area where a family was enjoying a late lunch. It was just after four and there was no sign of Frances's car.

'Can you wait here, Deon? I'll go see if she's up near the picnic area. I won't be too long. Eat your Macca's and chill out.'

Sebastian walked on past the picnic area, and up to the pioneer's cottage. There were a few children standing on the edge of the lake, throwing bread to the ducks. To the left was the winding path up to the koala display and bird aviary. For a moment, Sebastian thought he had spotted Frances coming down the path. He was just about to wave, when he realised it was someone else with similar straight blonde hair. He wondered if he was going crazy. It had happened a few times lately – thinking he had seen Frances in the distance only to find it was someone else. Sebastian was again reminded of just how much Frances had affected him. He grabbed his phone and angrily hit France's phone number. It rang out.

There was another car park up the top end of the reserve. Maybe that was where Frances meant to meet him. He returned to the car park.

'Deon, I'm going for a walk up to the top section.'

'Can I come?'

'It would be better if you wait here. What if she turns up and there's nobody around?'

'Shit, Seb! I bin sittin' round for friggin' days.'

'Don't blame me for that,' replied Sebastian, sharply.

Deon went quiet and Sebastian softened.

'Come on then.'

Deon's mood changed instantly. He hopped out of the car with alacrity. In the shadows of the late afternoon, they walked back along past the BBQ area, then around the pond and up past the emu and wallaby displays.

Sebastian heard a dog howling in the distance. It might have been half a kilometre away, yet it unsettled him, reminding him of the black-coated wolf he'd seen on television. He mused over the wolf's reputation with Native American Indians of being a shapeshifter. Soon he was imagining wolf-like shapes in logs and branches strewn across the forest floor. Wolves don't exist in Australia, he told himself, but his attempt at being rational did not lessen his apprehension.

Deon eyed Sebastian with concern. 'You're lookin' a bit frazzled, Seb. Ya know that?'

Sebastian became defensive.

'Yeah… chasing around after you. You're wearing me out.'

They had to decide whether to continue along the path that passed the cages and up along the ridge, or head straight through the centre of the vale, along Blueberry Ash Walk. They selected the latter, following the track up the hill past the grey gums and ironbarks, and into the thumping heart of the shady forest.

'See those, bro?' said Deon, pointing to the sandpaper figs, 'You can use 'em to polish up ya spears and boomerangs.'

Up ahead they could hear the light rustling of leaves as a large lizard scurried into the bush.

'Lot of goannas round 'ere. Ever eat goanna, Seb?'

'Nup... not that I can remember. Tasted croc and roo at a community open day. Had a roo stew that was tasty another time.'

'I should catch something and cook up a feed, eh Seb? Nah,' he said with a laugh.

Sebastian huffed and puffed as they made their way up the steep incline. The loose gravel and stones made it difficult to get a firm footing on the slippery surface with his flat-soled shoes. Deon did the climb easily. He pointed to a plant that was near the edge of the track.

'Ya can make jam out of them bush raspberries. Sweet as.' Deon's face beamed with contentment as he imagined the taste. 'Plenty of tucker about. You could live in 'ere.'

They passed a part of the forest where the stench of fruitbat droppings was concentrated.

'You'd want to check that the breeze was blowing in the right direction if you camped here,' said Sebastian, holding his nose.

Deon responded with a chuckle. Sebastian might have been making light of the pungent odour, but he could smell wolf in every molecule he inhaled.

Memories from childhood were flooding his thoughts. Lying awake in the early hours, terrified. Feeling like a prisoner on death row, awaiting the inevitable. His mother had brushed it off.

'Everyone has bad dreams, Seb.'

When his dad found out, he made a joke out of it. 'When you were a toddler, Seb, you were scared of your own shadow.' Then in a cutting, severe tone, 'You're a real sook sometimes, Son. You know that? You need to grow up a bit!'

Sebastian could recall turning inward... disguising his fear, keeping it knotted up and well hidden.

They were high on the western slope and, after encountering a sharp turn in the track, the sound of running water was audible. Filtered by a dense canopy of branches and translucent leaves, the afternoon sun penetrated the forest in blotches of sparkling green. Although the main road was not far away, it was eerily quiet with the massive escarpment insulating the valley from noise and giving the illusion of remoteness. They continued to ascend until they came to another signpost that directed them along a path to the left.

Sebastian thoughts turned to Astrid, and he became nostalgic. For a second, he could visualise her striding out in front, pausing to study a shrub or flower that intrigued her, asking him a question about a plant or animal that invariably he couldn't answer.

Soon they could hear the sporadic cries of children frolicking in the playground up ahead. They were approaching civilisation. When they arrived at the car park, there was no sign of Frances or her vehicle.

'We'll wait for a few minutes on the off-chance,' said Sebastian.

Deon tossed pebbles at a post while Sebastian sat on a log, scrutinising the approaching traffic. After fifteen to twenty minutes had passed, Sebastian decided to give up. They headed back along the southern trail, Sebastian cursing Frances for leading them on a wild goose chase and loathing himself for allowing her to have such a hold on him.

When they got back to the car, Deon was the first to notice

'Fucking vandals.'

The right side of the Commodore had been gouged with something sharp, probably a knife or screwdriver. The cut went deep into the metal, damaging four panels. They looked around for possible culprits. There was nobody nearby, just a family in toddler land packing away their picnic gear, oblivious to the world. Sebastian was livid, not only because of the damage to his car, but because it occurred to him that Frances may have set him up.

He rang Frances's phone and got her answering machine.

What sort of message could he leave anyway? He felt like yelling at her. Where were you, Frances? You missed the rendezvous. Was it you who vandalised my car?

A sense of unease came over him. He thought back to the incident on the golf course. Was that connected in some way to the car being damaged? He pondered the idea and decided it was unlikely. That had happened in Sydney. It had to be related to either Joe's or Matt's activities. Besides, his car wasn't vandalised when he was in Sydney.

There was a warning sign in the parking bay telling patrons to lock their vehicles. Maybe it was vandals. Perhaps it was bad karma he thought, briefly entertaining the idea. At that point, he decided he was clutching at straws.

As soon as they arrived back at the house, Charlie spotted Deon and went berserk, greeting him like a long-lost pal. It was Charlie's lucky day. Deon reciprocated, playing games and giving the dog the attention she endlessly craved. Sebastian showed Deon where things were in the house and gave him a key. He asked him to ensure both doors were locked when he went out.

Deon eyed the tobacco on the table. He was surprised Sebastian smoked. He thought about asking for one but decided it might put Sebastian in a difficult predicament. A smoke could wait. He'd survived without cigarettes for the past few days, he thought to himself.

Deon's phone buzzed. It was a message from Michaela. He turned to Sebastian.

'Hey Sebastian, is it ok if Michaela comes over 'ere later? We was gunna listen to some music and watch a movie.'

'Tonight? Jees, you don't waste any time. That should be ok… but no bongs or drinking.'

'No way. She don't do dope and we ain't got any cash anyway. Hey Seb, I've still got to get my clothes and CD player from Donny's.'

'Just don't you go there alone. You'll be breaching bail.'

'Nah… I ain't that stupid.'

'Maybe we'll have time in the morning. Will Michaela be staying for dinner?'

'Umm... not sure, Seb.'

Sebastian made a coffee and went out onto the veranda. He rang

Frances's home number again. This time when she didn't pick up, he waited for the beeps. His voice came out more forceful than he intended. 'Frances... this is Sebastian. Can you contact me? It's urgent.'

He slammed the phone on the table, cursing the woman and the power she had over him. She was like a necrosis eating away at his core, gnawing in, deeper and deeper.

The house was depressingly empty without Astrid and Jenna. He could feel their ghosts everywhere. The thought of not seeing his daughter was painful. He went to his wardrobe and took out an envelope. It contained a copy of an email Jenna had sent when she was on a school ski trip to Jindabyne last year. It was an indulgence, for a minute, to swim in the nostalgia, to feel her presence for a short time.

It was Sunday morning 6 am as we passed over the Hawkesbury River. We drove through Sydney before we had our first stop. The choice, McDonald's or Kentucky Fried Chicken. I had a salad sandwich (not). Fell asleep and when I woke up, I could feel the chill in the air.

It wasn't long before we were off the bus at Lake Jindabyne.

Camp rules clearly stated no mixing in dormitories. Not a problem we thought. Our vodka is pre-mixed (that's a joke, Mum). There are senior boys from a Sydney high school in the next dorm. Hmm we thought... good luck supervisors (that isn't a joke)!

Next morning up early.

Meet Lydia Bionic Woman. Move outside your comfort zone was her motto. We laughed. She was serious.

Organise ski gear... hit the slopes... Friday Flat... The Gunbarrel.

Watch the snowboarders Jeff and Mario fall on their bums.

Laugh at the Eveready Battery Boys as they play pass-the-ball, kick-the-ball, basketball, football in the hall and even in their bedrooms.

Honestly, you can still hear them going at three in the morning. Tomorrow night we all get to dress up for the farewell party.

Having a great time. Give Charlie Wonder Dog a pat for me.

Love you both,

Jenna.

12

On Your Bike

Sebastian checked the pantry and found an unopened packet of basmati rice. He went to the freezer and took out a lamb korma he had cooked the week before. The bottle of Coopers beer sitting at the front of the fridge was tempting, but he felt the need to get out of the house.

When Deon saw Sebastian getting out his bike, his face became animated. 'Seb, 'ave ya got another bike? I'll come with ya.'

'Sorry, mate. There's one in the shed but it needs a bit of work. If you can fix it up, you can have it. It has an alloy frame, not a bad bike.'

'Thanks Seb... I'll have a look at it tomorrow.'

Sebastian unchained his green Mongoose Switchback, checked the tyre pressure, clipped on his purple helmet and pedalled up the driveway. Deon had come out onto the veranda to wave him off. He watched him start the climb up Algona Road and was about to go back inside when a four-wheel-drive that pulled out from a side street caught his eye. The vehicle, with its distinctive reddish roof racks and Queensland plates, was familiar. He knew he had seen it somewhere before, but he just couldn't place it.

Sebastian had to work hard to reach the top of Algona Road. Puffing vigorously, he sat back and cruised along the flat section to catch his breath.

Near the fire station, he crossed to the right and rode along the footpath parallel to the highway. It wasn't long before he was approaching Kahibah and that crazy intersection where nobody seemed to know who had right of way. There was a car behind him, and he slowed to let it pass before turning left towards the shops. A truck stopped up ahead. Sebastian slowed down as a precaution. It was just as well that he did because the driver began to reverse. The driver appeared not to have seen him. Sebastian gave him a blast with his bell.

'Nice one, mate,' he said, as he rode past.

He rode through Kahibah, past the fruit shop and delicatessen where he and Astrid often shopped when they'd first moved to the area. They'd seemed to have had more time back then, or at least they'd spent more time together. Sebastian had been surprised at the ease at which Astrid had settled into life in Australia. It was exotic to her, and she loved the simplest things, like going for walks along the sand at Redhead in her bare feet. She took to bodysurfing with gusto, and by the end of her first summer was attacking the waves like a local.

Astrid had been intransigent about her decision to return to work, soon after Jenna's birth.

'It's a no-brainer, Seb. As a physiotherapist I earn much more money than you. You can stay home with Jenna. It's the logical thing to do. We will have money to travel.'

That had been fine with Sebastian, and they did travel whenever their finances permitted. They went back to Holland a few times, and off on adventures through outback Australia and South-East Asia.

Sebastian turned right after passing through Kahibah. At the bottom of the hill, he turned left onto Fernley Track. The track ran parallel to the old railway line, which had been built in the late 1800s to carry coal and passengers between Redhead and Newcastle.

There were joggers out pounding the pavement, other bike riders, and people walking their dogs. Two policemen on pushbikes rode by. Sebastian entered Fernley Tunnel and lifted his sunglasses. He was soon immersed in an amalgam of rich, musky odours. In the quiet of the tunnel, he could faintly hear what sounded like a train approaching. He wondered whether he was hallucinating as the steely rattle progressively got louder. Gusts of wind funnelled into the tunnel, adding to the illusion.

Out of the blue, two youths on skateboards came racing through. They were followed closely by another boy riding a motorised bike. Sebastian closed his eyes and conjured up a locomotive's presence, its trail of smoky fumes and the acrid smell of spent fuel palpable. He took a swig on his water bottle before turning around and pedalling back along the track and out onto Dudley Road.

It was a steep climb, and the most difficult part of the ride. For safety he mostly rode on the concrete culvert adjoining the tar. It was also a smoother ride. Occasionally he would glance behind to see if a vehicle was coming, before drifting across the road to give his legs a rest. If he made it to the top without having to stop, he felt a sense of achievement. But as at Blackbutt, he found himself puffing before he was halfway up and had to push the bike the rest of the way.

From the top of the hill, it was a relatively easy ride to the bowling club. Across to the east there were fifteen or so ships anchored off the coast, waiting in a queue for their fill of Hunter Valley coal.

As Sebastian rode along, he became aware of the unusual click-clack rhythm being created by the front brake-pad rubbing lightly against the wheel. He could make out three distinct notes. The tempo was crucial in obtaining the effect and he had to pedal at an exact speed. The rhythm suggested a busy soundscape with a darting keyboard and pulsating bass. A slow-moving guitar would provide the voice of reason needed to counter the mayhem. He remembered he had a set of lyrics that should fit the mood.

Helter skelter summer swelter,
Bushfired out for sure.
Close the gates to the city,
The wolves are at the door.

After riding through the intersection at Whitebridge, he decided to take the longer route home down Bullsgarden Road. Later, he wondered whether this decision gave the maniac he was about to encounter the opportunity he had been waiting for.

Sebastian was aware of the hazards of riding a pushbike on a public road. He'd joked about it with Joe and Astrid.

There are drivers that you need to be wary of if you are to survive unscathed. There are drivers who don't see you and run you off the road accidentally. 'Oh, I'm so sorry,' they say apologetically as they watch you climb out of the ditch. There are drivers who get nervous and slow down to a snail's pace as they warily creep past despite the fact that the road is wide enough to fit a jumbo jet or two. Then there are drivers who detest the fact that you are on their road and insist on driving within millimetres of your handlebars just to give you a shake. There are also drivers who decide to use their vehicle as a weapon.

Sebastian was still gathering speed as he passed the pet shop, which was the only building on the left side of the road. He could hear something approaching from behind but was not alarmed as it was a wide road. Sensing that the vehicle was slowing down and getting too close, he stopped pedalling. He had actually thought the driver was pulling over to the side of the road.

As he turned to see just what the driver was up to, the bull bar of the vehicle whacked into his back wheel. Suddenly his bike was careering out of control. It hit the gutter and he went catapulting into a paddock of long grass and weeds.

The four-wheel-drive that had hit him pulled up parallel to where Sebastian had fallen. At that stage he thought it had been an accident. This theory was soon dispelled as half a brick flew through the air, just missing his head. This was followed by an eerie chuckle as the attacker mumbled something that he could not fully decipher.

The engine roared and the vehicle accelerated down the hill in a cloud of smoke. Sebastian lay amongst the grass and weeds inert, in a state of shock. And then, out of the blue a pair of protuberant eyes was gazing at him.

'Are you ok there, mate?'

Wiping the dirt from his face, Sebastian welcomed the warm and friendly voice. The left side of his body had borne the brunt of the fall. Apart from a few painful lacerations and missing skin on his hip and shoulder, there was nothing too severe.

'Nothing seems broken,' he replied gingerly.

'You wait here. I just live up the road. I'll get my car and give you a lift home.'

Sebastian managed a stifled thankyou. With sweat dripping off him and his body shaking uncontrollably, he waited anxiously for the good Samaritan's return. Every vehicle that passed by made him nervous, lest it be the attacker returning to finish him off. What a relief it was when the good Samaritan returned ten minutes later. He picked himself up off the ground and introduced himself. The man's name was Brian. He wrapped an old tarpaulin around the bicycle and manoeuvred it into the back seat. Then he pulled out a cold bottle of water from his sports bag and offered it to Sebastian, who accepted it gratefully.

Brian looked at Sebastian sympathetically and shook his head. 'You're lucky, mate, I tell you.'

'Did you see what happened?'

'I'd just come out of the pet shop when I saw the Toyota heading straight at you. He had it in for you, mate. No doubt about it.'

'You didn't happen to get the plates?'

'Nah... sorry, mate... it all happened too quickly.'

Sebastian put up a brave front, but he was badly shaken. Brian drove him home and helped him unload the bike. Sebastian thanked him for coming to his aid. As the man drove away, Deon came ambling out of the house.

'What the fuck! What happened to you, Seb?'

'Some arsehole just ran me off the road.'

'What do you mean? On purpose?'

'Yeah... it was deliberate alright. He tried to fucking kill me. Some dickhead in a four-wheel-drive. Can you believe it? A fucking four-wheel-drive!'

'I'll smash him and his car up if I find him,' said Deon, angrily.

He probably would, thought Sebastian.

Deon turned his attention to the Mongoose. 'The back wheel's fucked, man... the frame seems ok, though.'

Sebastian nodded but his mind wasn't on the conversation. He was wondering what would have eventuated if Brian hadn't been nearby when the attack occurred.

Deon stopped fiddling with the bike and gazed into the distance. Something had suddenly clicked. 'You know what Sebastian, that four-wheel-drive… I bet it was the same one that turned out of Bulwa Street just after you rode off. And I'm sure I seen the same one up at Blackbutt, when I was waiting for you in the car park.'

'Are you sure?'

'Yeah … could tell from the Queensland plates, and the red roof racks. I know me cars, man. Someone's tailin' ya.'

Sebastian rang Charlestown Police Station and explained the incident as rationally as he could. The constable advised him to drop in and make a written statement. He showered and cleaned himself up before driving up to the police station with Deon.

The desk officer was polite and understanding but, in reality, what could the police do without knowing the rego number?

They returned home, and Sebastian dialled Frances's number. He wasn't even given the opportunity to abuse the answering machine. She was probably having it off with some young lover, he thought with acrimony. He left another terse text message before ringing Napier Street.

Matt answered. Joe was out. The two speculated as to whether Sebastian's assault was connected to the incident at the golf course.

They were discussing the assailant's vehicle when Deon overheard his name being mentioned. 'Who are ya callin' a kid?' he called out.

After talking about the attack with Matt, Sebastian did feel better, but it really didn't change much. Matt said he'd tell Joe when he came in.

After Sebastian had hung up, Deon was curious. 'Who was that? I could hear a beat in the background.'

'Someone I should keep you well away from,' he replied, thinking about the potent mix the two would make if they teamed up.

Deon was starting to get hungry and offered to make dinner using the leftovers in the fridge.

'Go for it… the curry will keep,' said Sebastian, who was in no mood for cooking. He poured a glass of chardonnay from an opened bottle in the fridge and went to his bedroom. Minutes later he glanced out the window to see a four-wheel-drive backing into the driveway. His pulse raced, and he grabbed a piece of four-by-two that he kept on top of his wardrobe for such a moment. He crept cautiously down the hallway towards the front door.

When he got a clear view of what was actually happening, he felt ridiculous. What a frightened fool he was. At least nobody had seen him. Deon was out the front of the house, grinning like a Cheshire cat, as an attractive young woman sprung out of the front passenger seat and gave him a warm hug.

The car drove away and the two came into the house. Deon introduced his girlfriend to Sebastian. Self-assured and well-spoken, Michaela was nothing like the rough-edged girl he had been expecting.

Sebastian turned on the television and drank some more wine while Deon and Michaela cooked dinner.

'Seb... come and get a feed,' called Deon, about thirty minutes later.

The food was impressive. Sebastian was more than a little surprised at Deon's culinary skills. 'Where did you learn to cook a stir-fry like this, Deon?'

Deon winked. 'I've got a few tricks up my sleeve.'

Sebastian poured another wine and put a large bottle of Coke on the table.

'Michaela's nice, eh?' said Deon, while she was in the bathroom. He was obviously pleased with himself.

'Yeah... she seems like a lovely girl. But she won't look good behind bars,' said Sebastian, sounding a bit too didactic for his own liking.

They talked about Deon's legal predicament. He needed to make contact with his mum in Bre and get the address of an aunt and cousin who lived in Mayfield. And he could try to obtain a reference from the Land Council back home, which would be handy. He could also get an excellent reference from Jillian, the Council Community Officer in Maitland. She would be more than happy to help him out.

Sebastian went out on the veranda to have a cigarette. This time Deon couldn't resist. Sebastian wasn't too concerned. If Deon wanted a cigarette, it was better that he was honest about it. Deon rolled his durry and Sebastian started on a fresh bottle of Chardonnay. It occurred to Sebastian that perhaps he wasn't the best role model for a sixteen-year-old Koori boy.

'Deon... how is Michaela getting home?'

'I was goin' to ask, Sebastian... is it ok with you if she stays over?'

Deon hammed it up, putting on a sad face, while Sebastian considered his request.

'What will your parents say, Michaela?'

Deon was the one to respond. 'Michaela's seventeen, Seb. She's had boyfriends stay at her place. Haven't you, Michaela?'

Michaela nodded convincingly.

Jenna and Michaela were almost the same age. 'Do you mind ringing home, Michaela? If your mum says it's ok, then it's fine by me.'

Michaela did as Sebastian asked. He wondered what his answer would be if he were to receive that call.

Sebastian spoke briefly to Michaela's mother. She said it was, all cool.

'There's another mattress under the bed and spare sheets and blankets in the wardrobe if you need them.'

'Thanks heaps, Sebastian. We'll probably stay up and watch a movie.'

You had to hand it to the boy, thought Sebastian. He knew how to make himself at home.

'Sure, that's fine. But we haven't got much of a collection. Jenna has a few there you might like.'

'Nah, that don't matter... Michaela's got stuff on her phone. Thanks again Seb. We won't be noisy.'

After ensuring Charlie had water for the night, Sebastian double-checked the locks before saying goodnight to the young lovers and heading off to his bedroom.

Mentally and physically drained, he wondered whether the lunatic would dare come to his house. The madman obviously knew where he lived. After vandalising the car and running him off the road, what was he capable of next? And why? It had to have something to do with Frances. It was all too coincidental. Was someone trying to make her look bad? Again, he wondered whether the attack was linked to the gunshots fired on the golf course. Perhaps it was related to the Community Centre's AGM? He had certainly made some enemies that night. Still, he couldn't think of anyone who would take it so far.

What were the words the good Samaritan had used? "He had it in for you." Did that mean there was only one person involved?

He should have had the presence of mind to ask for Brian's number. Then he remembered his out-of-control former neighbour. They'd had a falling out when Sebastian complained about his parties with loud music that often went into the early hours. The man and his girlfriend had since moved to Cessnock, but he was the vengeful type. And he and his mates all owned four-wheel-drives.

What if Graham or his wife had heard that broadcast last month? Today FM radio had done a segment on feuding neighbours. Jenna had emailed them a set of Sebastian's lyrics, *Love Thy Neighbour*. The station had mentioned both Sebastian and Jenna's names. Was that so ridiculous to contemplate?

As Sebastian lay in bed, he could not get that cold haunting voice out of his head. What had he said? Was it, "I'll be back" or was it "Watch your back"? What did it matter? They meant the same thing.

He checked to ensure the block of wood under his bed was reachable, gaining some solace from the thought that he wasn't in the house alone.

As he drifted off to sleep, he recalled the lyrics of his not so neighbourly song.

On they blast this neighbourly delight,
The same bloody songs that never get tight.
All through the day and all night long,
The band only stopping to have a bong.
Met the boyfriend out the front,
Came on with that Aussie grunt.

Abused me from across the fence,
The atavistic creep is really dense.
But just so we set the record straight,
No, it wasn't me who unhinged their gate.
When I left home the lights were on,
Was probably a fuse, an appliance gone wrong.
No, officer, I didn't poison their lawn.
No, I don't phone at four in the morn.
No, I didn't order those truckloads of sand,
Probably some poor soul who booked the band.
Despite their antisocial behaviour,
I'm all for love; love thy neighbour.

13

Spiders

Hot winds were gusting from the north-west, as Joe and Matt left Maroubra Junction. Bushfire warnings had been issued for much of the state, with temperatures soaring into the mid forties out west. Father and son had been shopping for groceries and doing various errands which, for Joe, included putting on a few bets at the TAB.

Joe and Matt had an exciting afternoon and night coming up. Yesterday, Joe had been on the verge of ringing Rob Martin to audition for his band. The offer had become too enticing to ignore. He'd decided to simply tell Sebastian it had been impossible to find work, and that the opportunity had come along. Sebastian would understand.

Then he got a phone call that rendered that plan redundant. The call came from Steve Wiseman who said he'd been thinking on it, and had been so impressed by what he'd heard at The Junction that he wanted Joe and his co-writer to record *From Here to There*, and a couple of other originals. At his expense.

Wiseman said he had meetings lined up with radio station executives, to promote his clients. He wanted the recordings done as soon as possible so he could include Joe in the pitch. Wiseman then asked Joe if he could start recording the next day.

Joe jumped at the chance. He rang Sebastian immediately and told him the news. Joe knew Sebastian had to come down to Sydney, so he said he'd try to line up studio time to make it coincide with his visit. Sebastian said he would talk to Deon, and then get back to Joe to finalise times. Joe had been using some of Matt's beats, and they agreed it would be a good starting point for recording their songs seeing as they didn't have a drummer.

Wiseman wanted Joe to record *From Here to There*. Joe selected *Life in the West* and told Sebastian to pick the third song. Sebastian decided on *Amsterdam Lady*, which Joe hadn't played, but Sebastian knew he would pick up quickly.

Joe and Matt pulled up outside the Napier Street house.

'Come on Matt, let's get these bags inside quickly so we can get out of the heat. I need you fresh for this afternoon.'

Matt paused near the gate. There was a parcel poking out of slot at the top of the mailbox. He strolled over to find a small cardboard box wrapped in brown paper. He took it out and saw it was addressed to Mr De'Gabriel.

'Hey... check this out, Dad. Who'd send a parcel to us? It's not even a birthday or anything.' Matt spun the package around in his fingers. 'There's not even a sender's address on it. And the date on the stamp is old, the fourteenth of June.'

'Probably some marketing gimmick,' replied Joe. Matt put the parcel in his pocket while he helped Joe with the shopping bags.

Once they were inside, Matt began fussing over the package. It made him feel a touch sentimental. 'It might be from old Henry. He could have dropped it off.'

Henry was Matt's grandfather on his mother's side.

'Henry high pants? Don't get your hopes up, Matt. You're unlikely to get anything from that miserable old bastard.'

'He's sent me late birthday presents before.'

'Matt, he hasn't done that since you were eight. You have more chance of getting a present from the tooth fairy.'

'The tooth fairy, eh? Well, the tooth fairy sure owes me a present or two by now!'

Matt untied the string and removed the brown paper to reveal a white box with two small holes on either side. In his own fastidious way, he slowly peeled back the tape in two long parings, ensuring it didn't rip. The lid was on a hinge, and he flicked it open, anticipating a bracelet, or even a watch. He withdrew his hands at lightning speed.

'What the fuck!' shrieked Matt, as he watched the box drop to the floor.

'It's a fucking funnel-web… a fucking funnel-web spider!'

Matt looked across at Joe, with an expression of utter horror on his face. He stayed well back from where the package had fallen.

A large dark spider lay motionless on the ground.

'Calm down, Son. It's probably dead,' said Joe, as he came out from the kitchen to check it out.

'It's not dead, Dad. It reared up when I opened the lid. Why do you think I dropped the fucking thing?'

'I'll get a jar and catch it,' said Joe.

Before he had a chance to find a container, Matt called out again.

'It's moving... it's fucking moving!'

Joe hurried over to where Matt was standing. The spider was heading for the sanctuary of Matt's bedroom. Joe ripped his thong from his foot and, in almost the same motion, brought his arm down hard, squashing the spider on the spot. Its innards oozed out over the linoleum floor.

'It's dead now... we'd never have found the bastard if it had gotten into your room,' said Joe, squatting on his haunches to take a closer look at the creature.

Joe studied the box as he spoke. 'The address has been typed and pasted on. The stamp was attached to make it look like authentic mail.'

Matt was fuming. He'd put the box in his pocket. 'What sort of wacko would send a spider in the mail?'

'The same sort of fucking wacko who would shoot at us on a golf course.'

'Probably the same weirdo who ran Seb off the road, I reckon.'

'What? Ran Seb off the road? When did that happen?'

'Yesterday, when he was out riding his bike. He rang this morning. You were having a shower. Sorry, I forgot to tell you.'

'What else did he say?'

'Said he would get here Thursday. Stay two nights, I think.'

'You think?'

'I'm not your secretary. Ring him your bloody self.'

'Come on, Son. You should have told me. I've been waiting on his call.'

Joe put the remnants of the spider back into the box and went out to the front of the house.

The street was unusually quiet, the heat and humidity keeping even the perennial gardeners inside. The curtains were drawn on the house opposite, which was a pity because the woman's curious nature could have been useful for once. Joe went back inside where Matt was studying the spider. He'd downloaded some images from an arthropod site.

'I reckon it was a male funnel-web, Dad.'

'No... I don't think so Matt. It was a trapdoor.'

'What... you're an expert on spiders now, are you? I've got a picture of a funnel-web and it looks just like that thing.'

'Ok... you believe what you want. But I'm telling you, it's a trapdoor not a funnel-web. Guarantee it! People often mistake trapdoors for funnel-webs, but the funnel-web is a bit darker in colour and, as you know, much more venomous. One bite could kill you.'

'But it reared up at me. Trapdoors don't do that shit.'

'Matt... Matt, they do. They'll rear up at you alright. I do know me spiders, Son. When you were little and we lived on the Central Coast, I used to capture funnel-webs and take them into the labs for milking. I know what they look like.'

Matt's eyes sparkled with mischief. 'I remember that... you used to stage fights between them. Put funnel-webs in jars with redbacks and scorpions, to see which one survived. How sick is that?'

'Hey, don't knock it Matt. I made some good money betting on spider fights.'

Joe rang Sebastian and they spoke about the bike and spider incidents. Sebastian put a positive bent on what had happened to him, telling Joe that although the bike was totalled, he only had a few scratches.

If there were any doubts that someone was playing mind games, they were now dispelled. And Joe was certain that their tormenter, or tormenters, were not going to simply disappear. But what was the purpose of attacking Sebastian? Were the incidents linked? The problem for Joe was that with so little to go on, it was difficult to know where to start. He mulled over the situation and decided he'd take a drive over to Bondi and call in on Sophia, Matt's mum. It was something he had been meaning to do since he moved back over to this side of the harbour. As long as he didn't stay for too long, he'd be back in plenty of time for the recording session.

Sophia was a ubiquitous eastern suburbs identity who had lived all her life in and around Bondi. If anybody knew who's who in the zoo of crims and unstable types in the eastern suburbs, it was her. If the arcane prankster was someone from their past with an old score to settle, and there were a couple of names that sprung to mind, there was a chance Sophia would know their whereabouts.

'Hey Matt, I'm going out for a while. Keep the place locked up,' instructed Joe as he picked up his keys from the table.

'Where are you going?'

'There's someone I want to see. An old friend.'

'Not the TAB again?'

Joe shot Matt a guilty look, as though he'd been caught out. 'See you soon, Matt. Just be careful until I get back. I won't be long.'

It had been a few years since Matt had seen his mum. He didn't even ask about her these days. If Matt knew where he was going it would probably just upset him. Better to say nothing. Since her accident, Sophia had been prone to fluctuating mood swings and it was potluck as to what state of mind she would be in.

Joe followed the coastline through Coogee, up the hill past Bronte, then along Bondi Road, turning off before the beach.

He turned into Sophia's street. There was a new blue Honda that had been configured for wheelchair access parked outside. Sophia's house was a converted shop; a large structure with an extension out the back. Joe walked in through the gate to find the door ajar, so he knocked on the screen door. He didn't receive the reception he'd expected.

'Go away, will you! I've already got a religion. Can you just piss off and leave me alone?'

'Soph... it's me, Joe,' he shouted.

'Who?' enquired Sophia, in a tone that suggested she didn't quite believe what she was hearing.

'Joe... Joe, your partner in crime.'

'Oh... sorry, Joe. Give me a sec.'

'I get a lot of religious wackos around these parts,' muttered Sophia, amidst the clicking of locks and the metallic rattle of a chain.

The door finally opened, and Sophia rolled her wheelchair forward, greeting Joe with a hug.

'Come in, Joe. Good to see you. Anything wrong?'

'Nah... nothing too serious.'

Sophia Azar was the daughter of Greek parents who migrated to Australia after World War II. They'd had high hopes of making a go of it in the land of opportunity. Unfortunately for Sophia, this meant long dour hours spent sweating in a fish and chip shop after school and most weekends. That was until the age of sixteen, when the wild child rebelled and, to her parents' disgust, ran away from home with her twenty-five-year-old boyfriend.

The romance didn't last, but Sophia became pregnant and was determined to have the child. Her son Damien was born but, despite having a child, her thirst for the wild life was insatiable. When she met Joe, the chemistry was explosive. They were a lethal combination, spinning off each other, both risk-takers, indestructible, and in love. They were off the gear while Sophia was pregnant, and for a while afterwards, but it wasn't long before they were both sucked back into the black hole of addiction.

Sophia gave Joe a warm hug and Joe followed her down the hallway and through to the kitchen. Incongruent with the messy surrounds, there were stylish paintings and sculptures on display throughout the house. Most were from well-known Australian artists. Sophia had aged considerably since Joe last saw her, but her handsome features were still apparent.

The two sipped tea and reminisced over old times. Joe told her about the upcoming recording session, and she was thrilled for him. Joe found it hard to follow the thread of her conversation, as she spoke in a desultory fashion, switching topics often. Her speech at times verged on incoherent as she raved on about what were, to Joe, a plethora of inane dramas. Suddenly a change came over her face, as though now she was getting down to business.

'So, how's Matt doing, Joe?'

Just give her the good news, thought Joe. 'Not too bad really. He's full-on into his music.'

'Can you tell him that I'd like to see him? I've been thinking about him a lot lately.'

'Yeah, I'll tell him Soph.' He wondered just what she knew about the boy's recent escapades.

'What about Damien? What's he up to these days?' asked Joe

'Damien's doing alright, I suppose. He tells me he's a used-car salesman, but the crew he's in with are a bit shady for my liking. In some ways he's worse than you were Joe, and that's sayin' something.'

She smiled then looked into Joe's eyes. 'Hey Joe, let's get out of here. We'll go down the pub for a while if it's alright with you?'

That was fine with Joe. Sophia grabbed her bag and locked the house. Once they were out on the street, Joe pushed Sophia along the footpath, following a trail she traversed so often you could almost see the wheelchair ruts in the pavement. The two mucked about like insouciant teenagers as they made their way towards the Beach Road Hotel in the muggy afternoon swelter.

When they reached the intersection, Sophia insisted on taking control of her wheelchair. Totally careless in attitude, she careered across the busy intersection as if she had a death wish. After forcing a car to break, she waved to the not-so-amused driver. Joe chided her for being reckless, but she just laughed it off. Joe wondered whether she was putting on a show for his benefit.

They entered the hotel, and it was an effusive Sophia who greeted all and sundry with warm-hearted hellos. The two made their way through the main lounge and out towards the beer garden. Meandering through the narrow spaces, Sophia nudged the tables and chairs of a table of unsuspecting drinkers, who were too slow to get out of her path. Most saw the maelstrom coming and lifted their drinks up off the table.

'Like the old days, eh Joe?' she said, and Joe realised what she was up to.

Back then they'd make a point of being noticed when something big was going down that they were a bit too close to. It would give them an alibi if the police came knocking.

Joe followed from behind, now and then shouting, 'Excuse me,' and apologising for the destruction Sophia left in her wake.

They found a table and Joe was pleased Sophia was stationary.

'What are you drinking, Soph?'

'Double bourbon and Coke for me, thanks. Can't have anything too strong with my medication.'

She winked at Joe, and he got a laugh out of that one. The two shared a few stories, the conversation continuing in a lighthearted vein, until Joe began to fill Sophia in on recent events.

'Who else was with you on the golf course, Joe?'

'Just Matt and Seb... you remember Sebastian Darcy, don't you?'

'Course I do... my memory isn't that fucked. He was a nice bloke. One of my girlfriends was keen on him. Seb's hardly the type to be upsettin' crims, from what I remember. You still dealing Joe?'

'These days I only do a little smoko.'

'A little smoko, eh... I reckon it could have something to do with that.'

'Well, it's the most obvious reason, Soph, but I'm not doing anything over this side of the harbour.'

They discussed the present circumstances of a few hard nuts from the old days. As he had hoped, with Sophia's knowledge he was able to eliminate a couple of suspects.

'Red Mullane lives over in Perth these days, runs a laundry business.'

Joe looked at her with raised eyebrows.

'No, Joe. Not money laundering. He's got a family. Gone straight from what I've heard. I wouldn't worry about McGuiness, he carked it a few years back. Sounds like his style though. Spiders in the mail... pretty quirky. I'm trying to think who'd do something like that. I've got it... why didn't I think of it earlier? Spiderman... you've been upsetting Spiderman, Joe. Now he would be difficult to deal with if you got tangled in his web. Joe verses Spiderman,' she chuckled again.

'Soph,' said Joe, in a reprimanding tone.

'Tell you what I'll do, Joe... I'll have a chat to Uncle Paul. And Damien as well. One of them might know something.'

Paul Souriss was a big player in these parts. Ostensibly, he was a successful, eastern suburbs entrepreneur, but his real money came from sex and gambling. He was astute and well-connected, with tentacles reaching into the police, law and politics. Souriss was an enigma to most. Only a few of his most trusted had direct contact regarding his business affairs, and most of this inner circle were family. The odd magazine article and the occasional smear campaign only seemed to enhance his reputation.

'I thought Souriss would be lying low these days. Didn't the crime squad clean up all that stuff?' Joe added, in a less than serious manner.

'Come on, Joe. You know Uncle Paul. He's managed to keep most of the ethnic gangs in check, so you can imagine how popular he is.'

Sophia had a special spot for Uncle Paul. After the accident he was the one who had stood by her. He made sure she got the best treatment possible, helped her out financially until she received the insurance payout, and then ensured she used it to invest wisely. She had refused the help of her own parents, who had made her feel like a liability and a disgrace.

'A white Toyota van, you reckon. Shouldn't be too many of those around Sydney,' she said with a laugh, 'I'll see what I can do'

When Joe returned home, Matt was in the kitchen. During the drive back out to Malabar, Joe had mulled over what Sophia had said, and decided to tell Matt that he'd seen her. It was pointless to try and hide it. Sophia was a determined woman, and if she said she wanted to see Matt then she would. But he didn't tell Matt the entire truth.

'Hey, Matt, I ran into Sophia when I was out.'

'Oh yeah,' he replied, showing little interest.

'She said she would like to see you.'

'She didn't even want to see me when I was a kid. Why does she want to see me now?'

'Don't be too hard on her, Matt. It wasn't all her fault. She was never the same after the accident. And she had Damien to contend with... your mum's a good woman.'

Sophia and Joe did live together for a few years after Matt was born. It was a real struggle. Damien had a few years on Matt and viewed him as a cuckoo in the nest. As the two grew older, Damien bullied his younger sibling, and it brought out the worst in Joe. Sophia and Joe's arguments grew worse, and eventually the situation became intolerable for both. The fact that Sophia and Joe were using again didn't help matters. In the end, Sophia and Joe faced the inevitable. Joe took Matt and moved into his own place.

Then came Sophia's dreadful accident that left her a paraplegic. Joe did what he could for Sophia after the accident, but he had been struggling to stay above water himself.

14

Surreal

In the crepuscular light, Sebastian is pushing Jenna in a pram out around the headland between Bondi and Tamarama. It is a walk they did often many years ago, but today the scene is ominous. Massive waves are crashing onto the rocks nearby. Unnerving moans emanate from deep within Earth, and the translucent ocean hisses as sparks of bright, flickering red light dance across the water. The wind howls wickedly, like starved wolves searching for prey.

Sebastian's face contorts from the strain, and he looks down at his daughter who is surprisingly undaunted by the situation. Suddenly a more powerful wave crashes onto the rocks and Sebastian must quickly manoeuvre the pram to prevent the spray from drenching them both. Bracing his body, he holds on grimly as the backwash threatens to sweep them away. It occurs to him that he should turn back but, as if in response to the thought, a dense mist rolls in, swallowing the bay and covering the path behind them. He gathers his strength and pushes on.

After advancing a further ten metres or so, he is startled by a tall lanky creature in a shiny silver suit who seems to have materialised out of nowhere. The body is human, but the face is unmistakably that of a wolf. The creature bends its villainous neck towards Sebastian and speaks in a deep resonating voice, 'Bet you'd like to know the way out of this one.'

Sebastian is terrified and as he attempts to escape with Jenna, his body will only move in slow motion. The creature hovers above, seemingly amused by his futile attempts to flee. Then, as suddenly as it appeared, it evaporates into thin air.

Up ahead, Sebastian can hear people talking and shouting. It gives him some hope. His body is free to move normally again, and he continues out along the headland, intent on finding the source of the uproar. They come upon a large cave. Inside there are five men dressed in blue overalls who are sitting on stools around a rectangular wooden table. One of the men turns and greets them with a welcoming smile, so Sebastian wheels Jenna into the cavern, relieved to find some respite from the storm.

The men are drinking a grey liquid from large wooden mugs. What a bizarre sight they are as they fill their mugs from an oak cask, clicking them together and downing their drinks in unison.

In the stygian atmosphere they seem to be enjoying themselves, occasionally breaking out in boisterous laughter as though they have just shared the funniest of jokes. They are conversing in a kind of inane slang, making it is impossible for Sebastian to decipher what they are saying. They don't even flinch when a wave reaches into the enclave and threatens to sweep the table away.

A translucent circle of light appears near the entrance to the cave. About two metres in diameter, it has a shimmering concave inner core. The men continue to party, taking no notice of this peculiar phenomena until one of the drinkers gets to his feet, places his cup on the ground, and turns toward the circle of light. Raising both arms above his head, he performs a stunning acrobatic backflip, landing feet first into the circle of light and vanishing from sight.

While Sebastian is trying to make sense of it all, the half-wolf creature lopes into the cave. It raises its head and starts to sing, displaying astonishing vocal agility as it descends in quarter-note intervals, creating an eerie, hypnotic atmosphere. When the creature starts manoeuvring towards Jenna, Sebastian knows he is in a precarious situation. He takes one last look at the dismal surrounds, clings on tightly to Jenna with one arm and, dragging the pram with the other, steps into the circle of light.

In a split second the landscape is transformed. They are near the entrance to a massive sandstone amphitheatre, the dusty surrounds, stunted vegetation, and rows of similar houses reminiscent of an outback

Australian town. The people in the vicinity are hurrying towards the amphitheatre where, judging from the commotion, a performance is in progress.

Curious to see what the attraction is, Sebastian pushes Jenna through the arched entrance and into the amphitheatre. The three actors on stage are dressed in colourful outfits. As they peg socks and shirts onto a clothesline, the audience laughs wildly. Sebastian has no idea why the audience finds this funny. He thinks back to the men in the cave. Once again he is the odd one out, but at least there is no sign of the stalking wolf-like creature.

There is a commotion near the entrance to the amphitheatre. Two security guards are menacing a middle-aged lady. The lady is protesting, but the people standing nearby take no notice, seemingly oblivious to her plight. Sebastian is terrified. He rocks the pram back and forth, waiting for an opportune moment to flee. The audience is captivated when the actors move to the front of the stage and start chopping wood. Sebastian notices that the security guards are busy dragging the unfortunate woman towards a paddy wagon.

He pushes the pram along to a side entrance and bolts.

Emerging onto a tar road, he pushes on past a series of derelict buildings and reaches the outskirts of the town. Nobody is around and the landscape is bleak, with a few desert shrubs the only semblance of life. Sebastian glances down at Jenna who is wide awake and unmindful of the ordeal. There seems to be no option but to continue, so he follows the road out of town where it meanders between two large sand dunes.

In the distance he sees a mass of purple. As he gets closer, he realises there are two lines of massive jacaranda trees in full bloom leading up to an imposing, dilapidated timber house. The presence of the trees is incongruent, absurdly out of place with the stark setting, the fallen flowers forming an elegant purple carpet. Sebastian follows the trail to the back of the building where there are four train carriages that have been converted into living quarters.

Two ladies appear at the window. They wave in a friendly manner, giving Sebastian the impression that they are expecting them. They point with enthusiasm to a door. Sebastian tries to fit the pram through, but the entrance is too narrow. He eventually gives up, lifting Jenna into his arms and ducking his head so they can get through. Once inside the carriage, a strange calm envelopes him.

The older of the two women is wearing a long white robe with a Mother Hubbard- style bonnet covering her head. The younger woman is attired in a mission brown uniform and has her hands clasped together as though in prayer. Sebastian's peace is short-lived. He becomes edgy when the robed woman gapes at Jenna in an odd way. He feels he is being set up when the same woman insists there is something he must see and asks that he leaves Jenna with the younger woman and follows her through to the adjoining carriage.

Sebastian shakes his head vigorously, cocooning Jenna to make it clear that he has no intention of relinquishing her. This makes both women angry and they berate him, accusing him of not taking proper care of his child.

It's then that Sebastian notices the bushy, silver grey fur protruding from their garments. In the split-second Sebastian is distracted, the younger woman pounces with dazzling speed to rip Jenna from his arms. Sebastian desperately tries to retrieve her but once again his body will only move in slow motion. The more enraged Sebastian feels, the more impossible it is for him to move, and he can do nothing but howl at Jenna's abductors. Displaying a distinct lack of emotion, the younger woman's wolven features intensify as she rocks baby Jenna to and fro, humming a sickeningly sweet lullaby. Both women back away slowly towards the adjoining carriage as Sebastian's wailing intensifies.

The anguish he feels is excruciating, and the more he struggles and calls out, the more intense his pain becomes. As he watches on helplessly, Jenna is being taken further and further away, and the acrid taste of bile fills his mouth as he begins to shake uncontrollably. His protests become fever pitched, and he feels as though his entire being is shutting down.

Sebastian awoke in a confused state but with a profound sense of relief to discover he had been dreaming! He felt sure he had been there in that carriage. It had been gut-wrenching, and it took some time to readjust. It wasn't until he attempted to move from his recumbent position that he realised how stiff and sore he was. The memories of the bike incident came flooding back in frightening waves.

A muffled voice nearby alerted him to the fact that someone else was in the house. The voice was unfamiliar, so he listened intently. There was the distinct sound of a bed squeaking, followed by an occasional lover's whimper.

Of course, Deon was in the house. Michaela had stayed the night.

His thoughts turned to Jenna, and he began fretting about her wellbeing. Sure, what he had experienced was just a dream, but he needed to know she was safe. From the moment he'd held her in his arms when she was born, he knew the love he felt for his daughter was unique. He picked up his phone from the bedside table and sent her a short text.

Hope holiday going well.

Love you,

Dad.

If he called it a holiday, then the assumption was they'd return home after the holiday was over. That was Sebastian's thinking.

Eventually he arose from bed and staggered into the kitchen, hoping that the aroma of fresh beans would lift his spirits. Turning on the jug, he anticipated the jolt to his senses that a strong brew of coffee would provide. His hopes turned to disappointment when he opened the fridge door and realised there was no milk left.

'Typical selfish teenagers,' he muttered to himself, cursing Deon and Michaela for not leaving enough milk for the morning. He'd have to settle for a black coffee, he thought begrudgingly. He could go and get some milk, but the run in with the four-wheel-drive had taken its toll. He was feeling too disorientated and fearful to venture outside.

What if the maniac was still out there waiting for him? As he mulled over that thought, he realised he was being a coward, giving into the fear and letting it grasp a deeper hold on him. Was he so pathetic as to succumb to his tormenter and hide away because of what might happen? He thought of the insidious way school bullies had impacted on the lives of some of the teenagers who turned up at the Youth Centre. 'Face your demons,' he said to himself. He went back into the bedroom and slowly changed into a pair of shorts, T-shirt, and sandals. The cuts and bruises were there for the world to see, but so what? He'd just tell the truth if anyone asked; he'd fallen off his bike.

The shop was only five minutes away, but he was too stiff and sore to walk. Grabbing his wallet and keys, he stepped out of the house. At the top of the driveway, he scanned the area nervously in each direction, on the lookout for that four-wheel-drive with Queensland plates.

On his way back home, Sebastian noticed a scruffy character near the top of the hill, sitting by the side of the road. His hair was cut military style and his limbs were covered in tattoos. While the man's head was turned, Sebastian took a furtive look and reared backwards. Staring directly at him from the man's forearm, a jackal bared its sharp jagged teeth.

Sebastian became suspicious. When he was back inside the house, he peered through the blinds and studied the man, wondering whether he should call the police. He was about to do so, when a van with a McDonald's Homes logo pulled over to the side of the road and the man hopped in.

As Sebastian made a coffee, he chided himself for being so paranoid and judgemental. He should know better than to make assumptions about people based on their appearance. Wasn't that the type of attitude he'd been so critical of? Was he no better than Vanessa Hadley and her ilk? He picked up the phone and dialled a number that he now knew by heart.

Finally, Frances answered her phone. She was curt.

'Hello.'

'Hi Frances. I've been wanting to talk to you.'

'Talk to me? What in hell for? I can only presume it's to do with the meeting tomorrow. And by the way, stop sending me those weird text messages.'

Sebastian was taken aback by the harshness of her tone. His lips were quivering as he tried to remain calm and plough on. He told her about the memo, the Blackbutt rendezvous, and the damage to his car. She didn't even respond. It was only when he told her the memo was supposedly from her that she spoke.

'Listen Sebastian, how many people know both of us around town? Half the bloody population of Maitland. And you've made your fair share of enemies around the place.'

'You mean Hadley,' replied Sebastian, defensive, as he wondered who else she could possibly mean.

'Do you really think I'd organise a secret rendezvous? Do I seem like the rendezvous type? Some of you blokes use incredible logic.'

Her comments made him feel foolish. And he resented being classified as "one of her blokes".

Perhaps it had been a mistake to ring her, but he wasn't going to be deterred. There had to be a connection.

'Yesterday, someone ran me off the road while I was out riding my bicycle. A four- wheel drive.'

'Why are you telling me? Get some lessons on how to control a bicycle.'

'Do you know anyone who drives a four-wheel-drive with Queensland plates and red markings on the roof rack?'

'Queensland plates,' she repeated hesitantly, as though something had just twigged. This was the first chink in her armour, and he took the opportunity to get on the front foot.

'You know the vehicle I'm talking about, don't you?'

'What? A four-wheel-drive with Queensland plates? There'd be about forty thousand of them at least, at a guess.'

'You know something, don't you?' he persisted.

As soon as he had made the accusation, he regretted it. Such tactics were bound to fail with Frances. Not only did she again deny having any knowledge of the vehicle, but she went on the attack.

'How dare you ring up and accuse me like this. You've got a lot of nerve, particularly after that offensive note you left at my house. You need psychiatric help if you ask me. Don't call me again.'

Sebastian was still analysing his encounter with Frances ten minutes later when Deon came bouncing out of his room, full of youthful ebullience.

'Hey, Seb. Watched this unreal movie last night. Michaela brought it with her. *The Tracker*. You seen it?'

'Is that the one with David Gulpilil in it?'

'Yeah, yeah, that's it. Really mad, eh? Got some amazing scenes.'

Oh, to be young and carefree thought Sebastian, a touch envious of Deon's ability to live in the moment. Not even a thought to the police charges and his likely court case.

'I watched it, years ago. It's a great movie.'

It didn't stop Deon from recounting the plot.

Hey, Sebastian... Thanks for letting Michaela stay.'

'That's alright. She seems like a lovely girl. But just be careful who you bring back to the house, ok?'

'Yeah, yeah cool... no way I'd bring back anyone without checking with you first.'

'Particularly that Richo bloke. He's bad news.'

'Oh, he's a dickhead... tries to chat up twelve-year-olds.'

'He lives up near The Square now, doesn't he?'

'Yeah... got a unit up there on Charlestown Road. You're safe anyways, Seb. Ya know Richo said to me that he'd never rip you off because you helped him out when he was in the shit.'

'Well, isn't that honourable of him. I was wondering why I never got burgled. I'll have to send him a Christmas card. What are you up to today, Deon? Much happening?'

'I've got a rehearsal with the boys for The Opera House gig. Can't wait to get down to Sydney and do the show. You still coming to watch?'

'Of course. Wouldn't miss it for quids.'

'Fella at the Land Council reckons I should check out that dance academy in Redfern. Reckon we'll have time?'

'Yeah... we'll make time for it.'

'Walshie was down there for a while.'

'Oh... I didn't know Walshie went there.'

'Not for long. He only stayed for a few weeks. Said he didn't like living in the big smoke.'

'Don't be put off. You'll adjust. You make friends easily.'

'Nah... I reckon it will be great, meeting people from all over the place.'

About an hour later, Sebastian, Deon and Michaela left the house. Sebastian locked up then called out to Deon, who was walking down the driveway with Michaela.

'You got your key, mate?'

A look of panic came over Deon's face as he checked his pockets. 'Yep,' he replied, as though it was never in doubt.

They took a closer look at the damage to the panels of the Commodore and according to Deon it had been done with a screwdriver. It was going to be a costly repair job. The cuts went deep into the metal.

On the drive up to Charlestown Square, Deon rode shotgun, amusing Sebastian and Michaela, giving them the lowdown on every four-wheel-drive vehicle they encountered.

Sebastian feigned composure, but his mind was racing, unlike the impression his countenance portrayed. 'Hey Deon. It's only Queensland plates we're looking for.'

'With red markings on the roof rack, I know. But you can change the plates and paint the roof rack easily enough,' he replied.

Michaela nudged his shoulder. 'Could change cars easily enough, too.'

Deon laughed at her comment, his infectious giggle amusing Michaela.

'Michaela has a point,' said Sebastian. 'This bloke could have two vehicles for all we know.'

After dropping off Deon and Michaela near Charlestown Square, Sebastian took the backroads though Newcastle, coming out on the New England Highway. He checked the rear-vision mirror constantly. Anxiety was his norm when alone.

He'd just passed through Beresfield when an incoming text message caught his attention. It was from Jenna, and he pulled over to the side of the road at the first opportunity.

Hi Dad,

Miss you heaps. All well here.

I've told Mum she should talk to you, but she won't. Not at the moment anyway.

I'll call you soon. Take care.

Love you, Jenna.

15

Fantasy's End

When Sebastian got to work, he made a recording and emailed it to Astrid. It was an attempt to be truthful and, hopefully, to salvage their relationship. Lorraine arrived a short time later and noticed the bandages and scratches on his face.

'You've been in the wars. Whatever happened to you?'

Sebastian told her about the events of the past few days: shots fired at the golf course; the Blackbutt rendezvous and damage to his car; the bike incident; and his heated exchange with Frances.

When he'd finished, there was a short silence before Lorraine spoke. 'Did you know that Frances worked for an employment agency when she lived in Sydney?'

'She told me that she'd worked as a photographer. Still... she could've done both. Why are you so interested in Frances? It's not like you to be so nosey.'

'Callan got himself mixed up with her.'

'Callan, your nephew?'

Sebastian visualised Frances in seduction mode, cajoling the young strapping farm labourer. He tried to play down the jealousy he felt. 'Well, that's not illegal.'

'Well, no Seb, it's not illegal. But as you know, Callan's not the sharpest tool in the shed, and he does have a wife and three kids to support. Anyway, I did a bit of digging. Here's the thing, Seb. A workmate of Frances's from the employment agency got bashed. Apparently, it was quite vicious. The fella was hit from behind. Did a stint in hospital.

Frances's colleagues suspected it was a friend of Frances who did the bashing. It was reported to the police, but there wasn't enough evidence. Frances left the job not long after the bashing. Quite a few people were more than happy to see her go.'

'How did you find out all this?'

'Frances put on her membership application that she'd worked for an employment agency in Kent Street, Sydney. I found them online and rang the manager, Claudia Napa. I told a fib, said Frances had applied for a job in Maitland, and had listed her as a referee. Anyway, according to Claudia, Frances's work was fine. When I mentioned that Frances would be interacting with teenagers and asked about her character, she told me about the bashing. Frances's mate called himself David Stephens, but Claudia reckons it wasn't his real name.'

Sebastian thought back to the awkward phone conversation with Frances. At least he was vindicated for accusing her. He'd suspected she'd held something back.

'Just make sure you're ready for Frances at the meeting,' said Lorraine.

'She won't come. Not after our argument this morning.'

'Oh, she'll be here. She rang me this morning, just before I left for work. Wanted to know about your duties and responsibilities.'

'Really? It's pretty easy to find out. What did you say?'

'I told her if she wanted that sort of information, then she should speak to you.'

'I don't get it. She knows you'd tell me about it. Is she just trying to piss me off?'

'Maybe she wants your job.'

'Ha. Is that a joke? Well at least the meeting will be interesting.'

'Oh, it will be interesting alright,' said Lorraine, a glint in her eye.

'Something else, Seb. Do you know who Frances's father is?'

'Should I?'

'Have you heard of Andrew Vanderburg?'

'The artist? Wasn't he on charges for having sex with an underage girl?'

'And his daughter, according to some.'

'Surely not. The authorities would have stepped in.'

'Morten was charged with neglect after Frances was picked up in the Cross. She was thirteen. But Morten has money and connections. He shunted Frances off to boarding school.'

'She did say something about going to boarding school. Where did you get all this? You should be working for ASIO, Lorraine.'

'It was easy to get hold of. The story about Frances was big news in the papers years ago. And it's all over Facebook and Twitter. Have a look at this,' said Lorraine, passing Sebastian a clipping.

It had been published in *The Telegraph*. The caption read: *Artist and daughter*.

'He actually used Frances as a model when she was a kid. You can see her in some of his early work at the National Gallery.'

'Sebastian, you need to ring Maitland Police Station. Ask for Sergeant Fleming. Explain to him what's been going on.'

Sebastian's phone rang. It was Greg Wright from Juvenile Justice with some good news. The police had re-interviewed Jacob, and he had admitted to being the one with the weapon. The good news was uplifting.

'I knew Deon was telling the truth,' said Sebastian, with pride. 'Maybe the police will drop the charges.'

'Does Deon know?' asked Lorraine.

'No... not yet. Wright's going to call him.'

Sebastian rang Maitland Police Station as Lorraine had advised. He was still taking to Sergeant Fleming when people began to arrive for the monthly meeting.

Frances rocked up. Dressed in a grey suit, with shoulder pads and heels, she may well have been auditioning for a role on *The Bold and the Beautiful*. Sebastian got the surprise of his life. Frances was so unexpectedly pleasant, it was disarming. Then he had to endure the painful sight of watching her endear herself to the other four committee members. Boy, did she turn it on! A harbinger of what was to come, Frances bragged about being on the school debating team, naming the prestigious Double

Bay establishment where she had honed her skills. She even had the audacity to make a joke about being expelled for taking a joy ride with a friend in the PE teacher's Maserati.

What was worrying about the spectacle to Sebastian was that people actually warmed to her meretricious manner. But what were her motives, Sebastian wondered. Did she really want his job?

After the completion of pleasantries, cups of tea, coffee and biscuits, as well as gloating over the success of the Vanessa Hadley fiasco, the meeting began. All things considered, Sebastian was feeling relatively composed. Unexpectedly so. He no longer felt haunted by his attraction to Frances. The compelling urge to please her had well and truly dissipated.

Then he remembered something important he'd forgotten to do. With all that had been happening, he hadn't done his usual ring around to remind all the committee members that the meeting was on. How stupid!

When Shirley Strudwick delivered the Treasurer's report in her somnolent, community-group style, one had the feeling that a stray cow could just as well wander up from the river and make a contribution. The tranquil ambience altered abruptly once the meeting was declared open for general business and Frances raised her hand.

'I'm sure some of you will already be aware of some of the issues I'm about to bring to your attention. I've been talking with the neighbours on both sides of us. They've asked me to raise a few matters with the committee. Apparently, there has been excessive noise around the hall of late. It is a quiet neighbourhood so I must ask Sebastian to address that. But the main issue is to do with the groups of teenagers that have been hanging around out the front. You'll remember that Sebastian recently had a run-in with Vanessa Hadley over this. One lady said some of them were smoking marijuana.'

'How do you spell marijuana?' enquired Lorraine, poking her head out from behind her computer. 'It's not coming up on spell check,' she added.

Shirley and Annie quickly accepted the challenge and the meeting stalled as they attempted to spell the word. Lorraine noticed that the interruption annoyed Frances, so she milked it for all it was worth, encouraging the women to continue guessing. It had been clever of Frances to use Vanessa Hadley's name. Since her axing, some in the community thought her treatment had been rather harsh. After all, Hadley and her volunteers did run activities for the oldies.

'I've just re-checked my mail, and I can say I've not received one single complaint on any of those matters raised by Frances,' said Sebastian.

He was relieved when Annie Heatherington, a down-to-earth woman who worked as a mental health nurse, came to his aid.

'Frances... these things are always a problem with our clientele. We know they are not all angels. Some of them have been abused, others kicked out of home. A lot of them have mental health issues. It's good they have somewhere to come where they feel safe.'

'That might be the case, Annie. But don't forget, we as committee members are the ones liable for what happens here. There is a case for working with those we *can* help. The young ones who are capable of doing a proper TAFE course and who want to get a job. Not the desperados whose behaviour, unfortunately, will never change. If we could raise the standard, we'd have better stats.'

'But Seb does get them into work experience and courses, Frances. Next, you'll be suggesting an entrance exam,' said Annie.

In full flight now, and with a cruel curling of her bottom lip, Frances looked directly at Sebastian when she spoke. 'Sebastian. Is it true that you told some of the teenagers that experimenting with drugs was normal behaviour for inquisitive teenagers?'

What a nerve! To use information that he had revealed to her, if not in intimate, then at least in private, conversation and to put her spin on it to make him look bad. He glanced in Lorraine's direction. As Secretary, her role at the meeting was to record the minutes. It was unfortunate because her guile would have been useful. Still, she could have indicated some anger at France's ridiculous claims. Again, he lamented the fact that he hadn't done his usual ring around to ensure there were committee members in attendance who understood the realities of his job. Sebastian knew he was in danger of losing it, so he changed tack.

'Yeah, that's what I told them, Frances. It's all part of the Drug Education Program. You see, we all have a joint or two together in the afternoon. It's just a nice way to finish the day. I'm thinking of doing some fundraising by selling ecstasy tabs on Friday afternoons so we can buy a new drum kit.'

He might have amused Lorraine, but his comments were met with a disapproving frown from Nick Bolt. Frances jerked her head from side to side, like an irate dictator.

'I'd like to remind you, Sebastian, that these are serious matters. I wouldn't be so flippant if I were you. There are legal implications, you know.'

'Legal implications? What are you saying? Have you been seeking legal advice?'

'We can't be condoning law-breaking activities. It becomes a matter for the police.'

'Now, now, I'm sure it's not that bad, Frances,' placated Annie.

Sebastian shot the inexorable Frances death stares. What a deplorable attempt at retribution!

The problem for Sebastian was that she was convincing. If there was any doubt as to the efficacy of Frances's comments, he only had to read the faces around him. Only one committee member had come to his defence. The other two didn't seem to have a problem with Frances hurling invectives at him. He had a strong feeling Frances would put forward a motion. But he had no idea what it would it be.

'Frances, nobody is breaking the law around here. You should check your facts before spruiking otherwise. I provide factual information on a variety of health matters. That's part of the job, so let's put things into fucking context.'

'Language, Seb,' chastised Nick Bolt.

Sebastian wanted to punch the bloke. 'Oh... so sorry, Nick.'

Nick wasn't sure whether it was a genuine apology or sarcasm. He eyeballed Sebastian before he spoke. 'Now, I know that Sebastian's job can be difficult. I'm not disputing that, but we can't have the young ones breaking the law. As Frances has alluded to, it puts us all in a tricky position legally.'

'Thanks for that. Nick,' said Frances. 'I have a suggestion that might help matters. How about we invite the police along to the pool competition. It would be great for community relations, and it will help keep our clientele on the right track.'

Frances knew full well that Sebastian was vehemently opposed to the idea.

'Come on now. We've already discussed this before. I've asked the regulars and they said no. Once a year as a challenge, sure, but that's it,' countered Sebastian.

'But the police do want to come and play in the pool comps, don't they, Sebastian?'

'We made a decision on this earlier in the year.'

'Well, Sebastian, I don't think it's your call. It should be put to a vote. The committee has a right to determine policy matters. I would like to propose a motion that we invite the police along to the Friday pool competition. Nick will second it, won't you Nick?'

Nick nodded in agreement. He was on a promise, thought Sabastian angrily, as Frances braced herself to deliver another blow.

'And if you can't abide by the committee's decision, Sebastian, you should resign.'

Sebastian could hardly believe what he was hearing. The last thing in the world that he wanted to deal with right now after the Community Centre fiasco was more powermongering. He didn't have the energy to fight it. It occurred to him that maybe after six years in the same job, it could be time for a change anyway.

And with Joe so keen, the music option was becoming increasingly appealing.

What happened next was quite peculiar. Attention was diverted from the meeting to the doorway where a man and a woman in police uniform materialised at the top of the stairway. The group gaped at the two police officers as though all the police talk had conjured them up. Due to the heated exchange, nobody had noticed them ascend the stairs.

At first Sebastian thought Frances had invited them to the meeting to ram home her point. But when the booming voice of the moustached sergeant broke through the silence, it became clear they were definitely not on a social visit.

'Is Frances Morten here?'

'Yes... I'm Frances Morten,' she answered, in a tone that made it clear she didn't appreciate being disturbed.

'We would like you to accompany us to the station to answer a few questions.'

'You must be joking. Can't you see we are in the middle of an important meeting? Surely this can wait,' she replied, her tone scolding.

The sergeant's response was stern. 'Frances! It would be in your best interests to comply with our request.'

There were stunned faces and muffled mutterings. The female officer pulled her aside, but Frances continued to protest. It wasn't until they threatened to charge her with resisting arrest, that she became more compliant. Even then, she expressed outrage at being escorted away.

Sebastian turned to Lorraine to gauge her reaction and saw Sergeant Fleming place an envelope on her desk. The meeting dissolved soon afterwards, with the certainty that the incident would be all over town come morning. Sebastian had been more than happy to see Frances stopped in her tracks. But having been made aware of her abusive background, seeing Frances being hauled away by the police gave him little satisfaction.

At that stage, Sebastian thought the police response had been triggered by his call to Sergeant Fleming. That the police had found a link between Frances and his assailant. But, as he was to find out, that was not the case.

Half an hour later, when he and Lorraine were the only two left in the building, Lorraine opened the envelope Sergeant Fleming had placed on her desk.

'What's that about, Lorraine? I saw Fleming put it there. Why are you looking at me like that?'

'Did Frances ever mention an organisation called Fantasies Incorporated?'

'No. Sounds like a group of clowns organising kids' birthday parties,' he scoffed.

'That's not a bad guess. They do parties and costume extravaganzas for wealthy clients. You name it and they'll organise it. They are actually a legitimate business operating out of Darlinghurst, in Sydney, but they also provide another service for the top end of town. The rich at play, one might say. It's called Bohemians Behaving Badly, and it's run by Frances. They create scenarios based on the clients' wishes. The fantasies might involve voyeurism or bondage, that type of thing. On most occasions, classy prostitutes are hired. Sometimes out-of-work actors are used to interact with the clients in public places to add realism. As the advertisement says, the possibilities are limited only by customers' imaginations.

Here's one scenario they use for promotional purposes. It's advertised as a birthday gift, but probably not from the man's wife. First, four or five women are selected from a catalogue by the client. They are then then set up at various indoor and outdoor locations. The client has to decipher clues to seek them out. Each of the women has a script to follow to ensure there is plenty of variety in the activities on offer, so to speak.'

'Why are you telling me this?'

'Because some of these events have taken place at Frances's house.'

'What! Here in Maitland?'

Lorraine nodded.

'You are kidding me,' said Sebastian, his face a gaping rictus of incredulity.

'Frances has a racket going where she makes extra money by using males she picks up as well as injecting herself into proceedings. Oh... and Sebastian, Frances records these sessions.'

Sebastian turned pale.

'As I said, I did a bit of investigating when I found out Callan was involved with Frances.'

He looked on nervously as Lorraine took a USB from the envelope on her desk. Sebastian followed her into the adjoining room where there was a computer and screen. She placed the device into the slot and two files appeared on the screen.

After a few seconds, the camera focused in on a tall buxom, mature-aged woman straddling a much younger woman who was spread-eagled over a leather couch. Then the focus moved to another couple, and Sebastian recognised Frances and Callan.

At first Sebastian was mesmerised, not quite believing what he was seeing. This quickly turned to shame when he realised that he was being drawn back into her vortex; there was no denying that watching a corybantic Frances was a turn-on.

'I'll leave you to watch the main feature,' said Lorraine, and she clicked on the second file, pressed play, and left the room.

Frances was soon in focus again, her slender naked body arched provocatively across the bed. When the camera zoomed in on Sebastian, he knew there could be no denying the identity of the man stimulating the woman and responding to her erotic moans and groans.

He was about to press stop when he saw two eyes poking out from the closet. Frances had cleverly managed to control the situation so that Sebastian had been facing the other way.

He stopped the machine, gathered his equanimity, and went back out. He tried to be as logical about it all as he could to conceal his embarrassment.

'You know what's on that?'

Lorraine nodded. Part of her was enjoying Sebastian discomfort.

'Why me? I'm hardly Mr Universe?'

'Maybe because you were available at the right time and price,' she said, lightheartedly. 'Seriously, Sebastian, I'm sorry to disappoint you but it probably wasn't you that the client wanted to watch.'

'You know who's in the closet watching?'

Lorraine nodded.

Sebastian went into panic mode. 'Has it been downloaded?'

'Frances's site has been taken down. There've only been a few downloads. Thankfully there's plenty of competition for this sort of thing.'

'I know it gives Frances the opportunity to meet people but, really, why bother with all this committee stuff? She must find it bloody boring knowing her background.'

'Remember there were rumours that Frances had to do community hours? Well, they were true. Apparently, she got busted with cocaine. And like you said, the Youth Centre provided her with rich pickings.'

'Are you having a go at me?'

'Have a look at yourself, Seb! You have an incredible wife, a lovely daughter, and you get involved with the likes of Frances. Why in the hell would you do it?'

'I don't know. I fucked up. What will happen to Frances now? Will she be charged?'

'The police were able to get a warrant for her arrest and to close down her site because of the age of one of the participants she'd employed. But Frances isn't stupid. She's bound to get some fancy Sydney lawyer. Apparently, a couple of the young blokes and one of the girls she hired are former clients from the part-time job she had in Sydney. She was supposed to find work for them.'

'Well, she did that, didn't she?'

'You and Callan could sue Frances for breach of privacy, and probably win. But it would get ugly with all the publicity. The press would have a field day.'

'Lorraine, I really appreciate what you've done. I feel completely stupid. I can't believe you pulled that off. I owe you big time.'

The two workmates locked up the building for the night and said their goodbyes. As Sebastian walked to his car, the realisation of how gullible he'd been began to sink in. Frances had reeled him in hook, line, and sinker.

He thought back to the email he'd sent to Astrid earlier in the day. He began having second thoughts about the sense and likely success of such a move.

Today's events hadn't infused him with confidence regarding his understanding of the female mind.

16

Close Call

Deon was feeling fantastic as he nonchalantly ambled down Algona Road towards Sebastian's house. The call from Greg Wright, his Juvenile Justice caseworker, had been encouraging. He was no longer suspected of having been in possession of the firearm. Although he'd put on a brave front, it had been worrying him. He'd had enough experience with the law to know the truth didn't always come out, and he felt fortunate. The rehearsal with the boys had been terrific. In his mind he could see himself at The Opera House, the lights dimming as he and his mates were about to step out onto the stage. He was shaken from his daydream when he became aware of a vehicle slowing down as it came down the hill behind him. Perhaps it was turning into a driveway, he thought, as he turned his head to see a police car alongside him. It didn't stop, but the policeman in the passenger seat looked at him just long enough to catch his gaze, and to let him know his presence in the area had been noted.

That was the second time today and it was starting to really annoy him. Earlier, he'd been waiting for a mate near Hamilton Railway Station, soaking up a bit of sun, when a policewoman approached him. She spoke to him nicely enough, and even smiled when he told her he was on his way to Maitland for a rehearsal, but he noticed that she didn't have a friendly chat with any of the other teenagers in the vicinity.

He thought about the eyes that followed him when he entered certain shops. With some it didn't matter if you paid the last time you were there or not. And it wasn't as though he dressed untidily, with his Levis and Nike pumps. That was interesting in itself. From the way some people scrutinised his clothes, the assumption was they were stolen. What a joke! He laughed to himself at the irony. If you dressed shabbily, you were treated as though you were some deadbeat blackfella.

His nan used to say you can never win with the whitefella. She'd been shifted from pillar to post due to changes in government policy. It was no wonder that in the end she flatly refused the offer of a new house in town, preferring to live in a tin shack by the river.

His pop had told him there were good and bad gubba, just like there are good and bad blackfellas. Pop was a legend around the shearing sheds where he'd spent his entire working life. Deon had seen the respectful manner in which his pop was treated by his fellow shearers and even the bosses.

Thinking of Bre was making him feel homesick. For a moment in his mind, he was back home, lying on the sand by the river, having a yarn with his cousin. But he did like living down this way. He had made some good friends and there were opportunities he'd never get back home. And how lucky was he, to have a girlfriend like Michaela? Apart from her looks, when he was with her, he felt confident and content.

He thought about what Sebastian had done for him and decided he would make something – maybe a woodcarving – to show his appreciation. It occurred to Deon that he never thought of Seb as a gubba. He didn't know many whitefellas like that, maybe a few teachers in his younger days.

The boy from Bre was carrying a blue-and-white sports bag that contained ochre, boomerangs, clapsticks, a headpiece, his lap-lap, and a water bottle. There was a reserve on his right and he decided to take the opportunity to gather some branches for The Opera House performance. Crossing the road, he trod carefully to avoid the thistle and broken glass, and was soon amongst the eucalypts, sorting through the fallen branches. From where he was, it was possible to see through the gaps in the trees and up to the cul-de-sac above.

It was the red roof racks that he noticed first.

He gathered his belongings and quickly meandered through the bush, stopping near the edge of the reserve. The Queensland plates confirmed what he already knew. He pulled out his phone and called Sebastian's number. There was no answer, just Sebastian's voice on the answering machine.

Sebastian had left work forty minutes earlier and was approaching Charlestown. Just a few minutes from home, he was still in a state of bewilderment over Lorraine's revelations. He squirmed as he wondered what Astrid would make of it, if she ever found out. Probably wouldn't give two hoots in her present frame of mind. What would Jenna think? How could he possibly explain? And there had been a few downloads. He tried to reassure himself, recalling what Lorraine had said about there being so many free pornography sites to choose from that Frances's contribution was a mere drop in the ocean. Before he'd left work, he and Lorraine had checked to make sure Frances's site had been taken down. Bohemians Behaving Badly was nowhere to be found.

His mind was instantly jolted back into gear when a four-wheel-drive with Queensland plates pulled up at the lights behind him. The adrenalin started to pump. He then realised it had black roof racks and there was a female driver behind the wheel. Sebastian caught a glimpse of himself in the rear-vision mirror. He could see how being on edge constantly was taking its toll – sunken cheeks, sullen eyes, deepening facial lines. At least the police were now looking for his attacker. There was some comfort in that.

Deon approached the vehicle and saw it was locked. A striped towel was draped across the passenger seat. Faded green curtains partitioned the back from the driver's compartment, making it impossible to see anything but an old mattress and a few tools. But where was the driver? Probably breaking into Sebastian's house, he decided. Why else would he hide the car up here? With one hand on his hunting stick, Deon headed towards

Sebastian's house. Hearing the rustle of leaves up ahead, he stopped in his tracks.

Peering out through the fishbone ferns, Deon saw a thin man with long blonde hair. He was wearing a khaki top, black jeans, and an Akubra hat. The hat made it difficult to see his face. The bloke was assiduously putting together some sort of apparatus. Deon could see it glisten in the sun, but it didn't appear to be a rifle.

He was unsure just what to do. Should he retreat to the house and be ready to warn Sebastian, or find out what this guy was up to? In the end he decided on the latter, backtracking and approaching from the other side of the reserve where there was more cover, and he could get a closer look.

It took him a few minutes to reach the new vantage point. From his new position he could make out the man's features. The long blonde hair didn't look natural, and the moustache seemed fake. The apparatus the man had assembled looked peculiar. It was a pistol attached to a wooden handgrip that fully enveloped his hand. The barrel was much longer than that of a normal handgun.

In the back of his mind, Deon could recall watching a pistol-shooting competition on YouTube, where a similar weapon was used. And if he remembered correctly, they were surprisingly accurate. Some of the competitors were able to hit close to the bullseye repeatedly. But how far were they from the targets? He tried to visualise the distance and decided they were close to half a footy field away. How far away was Sebastian's driveway from the man with the pistol? About the same, or a little less, at a guess. Could this guy be that good? He wasn't stupid, having cleverly positioned himself in a small hollowed-out section of bush from where he could see everything that happened within the vicinity of Sebastian's house.

Deon figured that if Sebastian wasn't at work, there was a good chance he was on his way home. The problem with trying to warn Sebastian, was that he wasn't sure as to which direction he'd come from – down the hill via Dudley Road, or up the hill from Gateshead.

Although he was reticent to do it, he knew he should contact the police.

Getting to his feet, he was about to move to a safe distance to make the phone call, when he saw Sebastian's car coming down Algona Road. If Sebastian got out of his car in the driveway, he would be a sitting duck. Deon watched as the gunman's head turned. He'd also seen Sebastian's car.

With alert eyes protruding from the undergrowth, Deon went on the attack. He moved quickly through the bush towards his foe. When he reached the clearing, he was still about fifteen metres from the man. Treading ever so lightly, avoiding the clusters of twigs and dry leaves, he'd only taken only four or five steps out into the open when the man turned.

Deon, with his hunting stick in hand, was a fearsome sight. The startled man hesitated, and in that split second Deon shaped and hurled his weapon through the air.

The throw was accurate, but the man had seen it coming so was able to twist his torso and avoid a full body blow. The hunting stick whacked into his shoulder, and he let out a muffled cry, losing his balance and falling to his knees. With one elbow on the ground, and clearly in pain, he glowered back at Deon. The pistol was still firmly in his grasp.

The boy from Bre knew what it was like to be the hunted. As the man raised his weapon, Deon began zigzagging, staying low to the ground. He'd soon vanished from sight. Although he'd been near impossible to hit, Deon was surprised the man hadn't fired. Perhaps he was saving his bullets for Sebastian, he thought.

Racing out onto the street, Deon began screaming out to all and sundry, 'There's a man in the bush with a gun. Ring the police!' He ducked in behind parked cars and crabbed his way towards the house, passing an elderly couple who just gazed back at him as though he was part of a performance.

Deon came to an open space near the house, and he could see Sebastian was in the driveway. He could picture the assailant taking aim, so he kept running, yelling and gesticulating in the direction of the reserve.

Sebastian was slow to react because he had his headphones on and was listening to a Van Morrison song.

But when he saw the normally cool Deon in such a state, he knew something was seriously wrong. He took the headphones off and opened the car door, just as a bullet ricocheted off the concrete driveway, missing him by millimetres. It gave him such a fright that he stumbled, banging his knee on the car door. He then threw himself on the ground and crawled behind the back of the car. Deon was soon by his side, just as another bullet whizzed by, splintering the wooden fence behind them.

If the assailant came directly at them, they really didn't have a chance in high heaven. After a short discussion, they decided to make a run for the back of the house. With Charlie the cocker spaniel barking wildly in the background, they raced down the driveway, keeping directly behind the car for as long as possible before cutting across to the side gate and up the stairs.

Sebastian fumbled with his keys as he scrambled to unlock the back door. He was still shaking when he got inside. Grasping hold of his phone with one hand and using his other hand to keep it steady, he phoned 000.

Deon quickly assembled a small arsenal of weapons – two knives from the kitchen drawer, the iron from the laundry, and a couple of Sebastian's golf clubs. He stood near the window at the front, peeping his head out from behind the curtains every few seconds, trying to find out what the attacker was going to do next.

When the police arrived ten minutes later, the man was gone. Deon gave them a description of the shooter, saying he thought the hair and moustache were fake. The police managed to retrieve one of the bullets from the fence. As Deon had suspected, they were .22 calibre. A check on the numberplates of the four-wheel-drive revealed they were bogus. They belonged to a vehicle garaged in Brisbane that was the same model and make.

After the police left, Deon went back into the bush and retrieved his hunting stick. Sebastian was on edge for the short time he was gone. He now knew that his assailant wasn't just trying to scare him. The madman was trying to kill him. He thought to himself that it was fortunate Astrid and Jenna were away in Cairns.

He was thankful to have Deon in the house that night. Drifting off to sleep, he realised his sense of helplessness and dread was not new to him. He could visualise himself as a boy, in his bedroom at the back of the house all those years ago. Although he no longer had such fanciful notions of being hunted by a wolf, back then he'd also thought his days were numbered.

Treading ever so lightly in the darkness,
Dragging the desk across the lino floor,
Jamming it up against the door,
Lying in bed, sweating in fear,
Drifting off to sleep and dreaming.
Oh no... the wolf is on the move.
Panic... it has crossed Sydney Harbour Bridge.
Cold sweat and abject misery,
The wolf is running through the city,
Soon it will be at the door.

17

Cairns

The esplanade was alive with a mix of workers, families and young suntanned backpackers as Astrid made her way past the waterfront lagoon. In the heavy tropical air, the pulsating force of Earth's lungs was palpable. It was cyclone season, and a thin line of dark grey cloud was visible on the horizon. 'A severe low system in the north-west,' the weatherman had said, but it wasn't expected to stretch as far south as Cairns. In fact, there was barely a breeze blowing along the renowned coastal strip, with the thermometer already registering in the thirties.

It wasn't just the biosphere that was sizzling on that particular morning. Astrid's mood fluctuated between anger and despondency, as she thought back to the fiery exchange with Sebastian prior to her departure from Newcastle. The nerve of him to stand there and prevaricate, implying he was the one maligned. Dwelling on the matter made her more incensed. Of course, they had been going through a bad patch, but that was no excuse. And that woman. So damn blatant. It was one thing to ring the house, but to tell her how lucky she was to have a man like Sebastian. Who in the hell did this Frances think she was? It was about work, Sebastian had said. What a load of apocryphal rubbish! Did he really believe she was that gullible? Did he care so little? Frances could have him as far as she was concerned.

Astrid saw her cousin Laura in the distance. Laura worked in the tourism industry, organising holidays for European vacationers. Like Astrid, she spoke five or so languages. Laura's office was nearby, and the two were meeting for morning tea. Jenna was off fishing with her cousins.

The two greeted each other with a warm hug and went into a coffee shop just off the esplanade. Laura had hoped that the tropical vibe would be a panacea for Astrid's connubial woes, but so far neither the splendid magenta sunsets nor the magical mountain views could put a dent in her cousin's brooding mood.

Both women spoke with a slight European accent. Laura at times would slip into a cute Aussie drawl, a result of her laidback lifestyle under the north Queensland sun. They spoke mostly English, occasionally lapsing into Dutch when they talked about home. Laura had spent a lot of time with her younger cousin when they were teenagers back in Holland and loved her dearly. She couldn't remember ever seeing her in such a tormented state.

'Since I've been up here in Cairns, I've been thinking a lot about Holland,' said Astrid.

'You can always go back for a holiday.'

'Yeah, that's true. But I don't have a reason to stay here anymore.'

'You've always told me you liked it here in Australia.'

'It was a great place to bring up Jenna, but it's more than that. It's changed since I first came here. The country seems to be going backwards.'

'I know there are issues. But the weather is great up here in Cairns. And don't forget how cold the winters are back home.' Laura let out an animated shudder to prove her point. 'Stay up here. You'll easily get a job.'

'It's beautiful, for sure. Tell me this Laura, how many jobs do you think there will be up here once the Reef is gone?'

'The Reef's not all that bad. Not yet anyway.'

'That's the thing, Laura, everyone pretends. I see up here they are pushing for another coalmine. That disturbs me.'

'Astrid, no place is perfect.'

'Laura, I want more out of life than good weather. You have Jimmy, who adores you, and your children. What are my options without Seb? Buy a house and spend my life working to pay it off, just in time to be put into a substandard aged-care home? No thanks.'

You should come out with me and my friends tonight, Astrid... life's too short to mope about. Come out and enjoy yourself.'

'Thanks Laura... but I'm not very good company at the moment.'

'Not good company? Look at you... still so young and beautiful. Men still notice you, Astrid.'

Astrid mused over the "men still notice you" comment. She thought about one of Laura's attractive workmates, and the attention he'd bestowed on her during a previous visit.

'I'm really okay Laura... you go out and have a good time. I need time to think.'

'Oh... Astrid,' said her cousin with concern. 'Sometimes you can think too much. You know what? I don't think that bastard deserves you. Dump him and get on with your life.'

The comment drew a smile from Astrid; the first one for a long time. 'Thanks for your support, Laura. I do really appreciate it.' It was comforting being around her cousin again.

It was soon time for Laura to return to work. The two exchanged hugs.

'I'll see you at home. Tot Ziens, said Laura.

Once alone, Astrid again felt annoyed. Her sense of purpose seemed to have deserted her. She'd been putting off opening the attachment Sebastian had sent, and at one stage nearly erased it without finding out what it contained. But her curious nature got the better of her. Now or never, she decided, plugging in her headphones and turning on her phone. There was a song, but it was Sebastian's spoken voice that she heard first, and it startled her.

Dearest Astrid,

Ever since I first laid eyes on you in Ireland all those years ago, I knew you were the one I wanted to share my life with. I will always love you. There are so many amazing things about you: your humour, depths of perception, sense of fairness, love of adventure, empathy, intelligence... I could keep on going.

Please forgive my deplorable behaviour. For that I truly apologise.

Astrid, you are the love of my life. Please come back. Or let me come to you.

Love you always.

What followed was Sebastian singing unaccompanied the song that had won her heart in Amsterdam, all those years ago. *Amsterdam Lady* he'd called it.

Astrid noticed a young musician setting up his gear in a café across the road. He was about the same age she and Sebastian had been when they first met. Something about the young man's swagger reminded her of Sebastian all those years ago. She found an empty seat nearby and watched the young musician go about his business.

When she'd told her mother she was moving to Australia to live with Sebastian, her mother had been horrified. 'Not Australia… it's the end of the world. And you can never trust a musician.' Her mother had been right, thought Astrid, with bitterness.

The night Sebastian had sung *Amsterdam Lady* was the moment Astrid had fallen in love with the carefree Australian traveller. It had been just after Sebastian returned from Spain. She'd borrowed a bicycle from a friend, and they'd decided to ride into town and see some of the city's attractions. Astrid could remember that day as though it was yesterday.

They'd followed a route along the canals to Anne Frank's famous wartime refuge. From there they'd ridden to Nieuwmarkt. Sebastian had been fascinated by the circular dome rooftops of the haunting De Wang building. They'd visited the Zeedijk Temple and wandered through the boutique shops nearby. After cruising through the red-light district, they'd stopped for lunch at a small café. Sebastian had had to duck his head to get inside the low doorway. The building was over four hundred years old.

After lunch they'd cycled over to Vondelpark, checking out the rose gardens, sculptures and bronze statues. A theatre troupe had been rehearsing near the edge of a pond. The performance was in Dutch, so Astrid had translated the dialogue into English for Sebastian's benefit. An hour later they were still sitting on the grass, intrigued by the story. It was about a Dutch girl who had been shanghaied and taken to sea by a notorious Dutch sailor.

That night they'd gone out for dinner to a popular student eatery close to Astrid's flat, where it was possible to get a decent meal at a reasonable price while listening to live music.

On that particular night, musicians in the audience had been invited to perform. A female vocal duo had done a hot rendition of the Eagles classic, *Hotel California*. This was followed by an inebriated man who'd fumbled his way through Dylan's *A Hard Rain*.

When Sebastian had gotten on stage, Astrid had been taken by surprise. Using the house guitar, he'd quickly adjusted a couple of strings before strumming a catchy, hypnotic rhythm. The tune had been uplifting.

I read your letter over and over,
Talked about it with Sam.
Sam's a man who understands (he say),
Get a ticket to Amsterdam.

As Sebastian had explained later, he hadn't played one song, he'd put together two unfinished songs. It had been a gamble, but luckily it had worked. As he'd repeated the phrase "Get a ticket to Amsterdam", he'd begun playing a riff. Singing in a high haunting voice, Sebastian had made it clear he meant every word. Astrid would never forget the frisson of sheer joy she'd felt when she'd realised he was singing about her.

Glad to see your face my friend,
Glad you've come my way again.
You know there's something
So incredible about you, Astrid.
Just can't live without you.

It wasn't just the song. It had been his display of unexpected and unrestrained emotion. The audience had lapped it up, and after the applause Sebastian had put his guitar back on the rack and spoken into the microphone.

'Astrid, you are truly so beautiful, in body and spirit. Thanks for inviting me into your world.'

On social occasions for many years later, Astrid would lightheartedly refer to it as the night the cunning Aussie bastard sang that beautiful song. Thinking about it today made her bitter.

'The bastard had probably inserted the name of the city and whatever woman he was trying to impress,' she cursed out aloud.

18

Back to the Big Smoke

Sebastian awoke with a headache, feeling the strain of the previous day's attack. He went through to the lounge room to find that Deon was already dressed and ready to go. Sebastian walked to the front of the house and stared out through the curtains. Deon alleviated his fears by telling him he'd already scouted around outside and there was no sign of the assailant or his vehicle. Sebastian was also glad to hear that the police had driven by the house an hour earlier. He dashed to the back of the house to check on Charlie. The cocker spaniel became energised on seeing him, scampering to the door in anticipation of a morning walk, hanging her head in disappointment when she had to settle for a pat and a fresh bowl of water.

'Today we're off to the big smoke,' said Sebastian.

Back inside the house, Sebastian showered, dressed, tossed some clothes into a bag, and brewed a strong coffee for the road. With Charlie on the lead, he and Deon made their way to the garage at the bottom of the long driveway. With Deon riding shotgun and Charlie nestled up on the back seat, they drove out onto Algona Road.

Sebastian hadn't really wanted to take Charlie all the way to Sydney, but there hadn't been a choice. There wasn't anyone he could impose on at short notice, and he didn't want to leave the dog at a kennel. He'd have hell to pay if Jenna found out he'd done that, he thought. At least Napier Street had a large backyard. And considering recent events, having an alert dog like Charlie patrolling the boundaries might be useful.

They wound their way through the mountains, and Sebastian's mood lifted as the tranquil blue waters of the Hawkesbury River came into view. The ancient sandstone hills and the dense forests of bloodwood, scribbly gum and stringybark conjured up images of a less frantic time. Affected by Deon's presence, Sebastian imagined the original inhabitants, the Guringai people, watching from the clifftops as the English rowed up the Hawkesbury River over two hundred years ago. He wondered what they would make of the country now. He thought about some of the First Nations boys who frequented the Youth Centre, their fractured, disconnected lives, the ripple effect of dispossession and disempowerment that still damaged them.

Up ahead there was a cross by the side of the road. Flowers had been left in memory of a loved one; the victim of a road accident, no doubt. Seeing the flowers reminded Sebastian of his mother's funeral. He considered himself to be the type of person who could handle most things life threw at him, but his mother's death had really affected him.

Further along was a message painted in verdant green along a guardrail. *All things must pass.*

Sebastian looked at it twice. Were the flowers and the message related? Perhaps the universe was mocking him, laughing in his face over the state of his relationship with Astrid. Immediately he chided himself for being negative and superstitious. He mulled over the words again. The message was likely to have been left by a friend. It didn't sound like something a lover, or a family member, would say.

They pulled off the expressway near the Hawkesbury River to give Charlie a run. It felt odd to Sebastian, being there without Astrid and Jenna. After being delayed on the Cahill Expressway due to a minor accident, they eventually made it to Anzac Parade. When they reached the Austral Street turn-off, Deon, who had been quiet for most of the trip, pointed to the high brick walls crowned with barbed wire.

'That's Long Bay Gaol, eh Seb?'

'Where did you think you were going?'

Deon let out a restrained chuckle. The comment was a bit close to the bone. 'Got a few rels in lock-up... make sure I don't follow them, eh Seb?'

'Don't be too hard on yourself. Everyone has a slip-up now and then, Deon. You've just got to be more careful who you hang out with.'

'Ya get to Lapa if you keep goin' along that road, eh?'

'That's right... Little Bay, La Perouse. Then there's Botany Bay. Have you been out there?'

'Yeah... been out that way once.'

'Joe and I used to walk around the rocks from Malabar when we were kids. Years ago, there used to be a ferry that went across to Kurnell.'

'Kurnell... was over there that Captain Cook landed, eh Seb?'

'I'll take you for a drive over there if we get the chance. What do you reckon?'

'Yeah... we'll see, eh,' replied Deon, not overly enthusiastic about the idea.

When they arrived at Napier Street, Kate's Toyota was parked out front. Sebastian had been expecting to see Joe's Falcon. Charlie went berserk once she was let out of the car, pulling hard on the lead with her nose to the ground, sniffing out her new environment.

On approach to the house, the throbbing sound of a synthesiser bass could be heard.

'That music reminds me of an old Doctor Dre song,' said Deon.

'Doctor Who?'

'Not Doctor Who, Doctor Dre,' said Deon, laughing when he realised Sebastian had been making a joke.

The side entrance was locked, secured from the inside with a chain and a padlock. Welded on top of the gate was a rectangular metal bracket, making it near impossible to scale. Joe must have done that, thought Sebastian. The screen door was locked, so Sebastian banged his fist on the aluminium frame.

'Kate... open up.'

The curtain moved and Matt's face appeared at the side window. There was the sound of keys being shuffled and then the door opened.

'Hey, Seb,' said Matt, fumbling for the key to unlock the screen door.

'It used to be a safe neighbourhood once,' said Sebastian.

'We thought you might need extra security while you're here, Seb,' said Matt with a wry grin.

Deon thought that was really funny.

'Joe just rang. He said to tell you he'll be back shortly.'

'Oh yeah... I know all about Joe's "shortly".'

Matt nodded. 'Tell me about it.'

When they got inside the house, Kate was busily moving around the kitchen. She had a cookbook open and a pot on the hotplate. It confirmed what Sebastian had suspected; there was definitely something going on between Kate and Joe. After they exchanged pleasantries, Sebastian pulled Matt aside, asking him not to offer Deon drugs. He had enough on his plate without having something go astray while Deon was in his care. Sebastian wasn't sure whether he was just telling him what he wanted to hear, but Matt assured him he would do as he'd requested.

Charlie was wriggling and rolling, vying for attention. Deon roughed her up with playful vigour.

'Don't get her too excited or she'll be dropping her barker's eggs on the carpet,' warned Matt.

Deon looked at him funny.

'Barker's eggs. Dog shit,' said Matt.

Deon laughed. 'Never heard that one before,' he said.

'They make a great watchdog, the cocker spaniel,' said Kate, affectionately.

'Umm... yeah, that's true,' said Sebastian. 'The trouble with Charlie is that she reacts to everything within four blocks.'

'You need to listen to her different barks, Seb. Each one is telling you something.'

'Well as far as I'm concerned, Kate, what Charlie's bark is telling me is that she needs a good kick up the arse. Anyway, with all that's been happening, I'm thinking of trading Charlie in on a pit bull.'

'Nah, you're much better off with a wussy dog,' said Matt. 'When we lived in Manly, our neighbour had this fluffy white thing. I used to look after it sometimes. When I'd take it for a walk, all these babes would want to have a pat. A cute dog is a pickup accessory, like a fancy car,' he asserted.

'Yeah, but they're interested in the dog, not you,' teased Kate.

'Yeah, but they trust you because you have a cute dog. It's a wonder that terrorists don't use them. They should put it in the manual. Be seen with cute dog in public and you become a loveable, trustworthy citizen by association.'

Sebastian took Charlie out into the backyard and surveyed the fence line. He stuck bricks up against the fence in a few places to plug the gaps. When he went back inside, he wasn't at all surprised to see that Matt and Deon had hit it off. Music was the common thread. They chatted about the latest releases and expressed their views on the current state of rap and hip-hop. It wasn't long before the two disappeared into Matt's room.

Sebastian told Kate about the bike incident and the shooting in his driveway. He put on a brave front, giving a blow-by-blow account of how he and Deon had handled the situation. Kate was horrified to hear what had occurred, but relieved to know the police had a suspect. She insisted Sebastian keep in contact with the police.

When Sebastian told her about his strange dreams, Kate stopped what she was doing and opened her iPad.

'I'll google it and see what comes up.'

'Kate... are you serious?'

'Here we go, Seb. This is interesting. It says here that dreams about wolves appear as reminders of loving, powerful and loyal people in our lives, and our relationships with them. Here's another one... wolf dreams can be positive or negative. They can mean you have people to rely on, like me, or they can refer to the sly, the insatiable and the evil. That seems a bit much but consider what's been going on!

'Thanks for that, Kate. I think the dreams are related to me being in the house again, and that it's my subconscious bringing back memories from when I was a kid.'

'I reckon that's possible. Here's another take on it. The wolf can be seen as a trickster. Like in Red Riding Hood. The Grimm's fairytale version. Who's afraid of the big bad wolf, eh?'

'Are you trying to scare me?'

'Here's an interpretation you'll like. Wolf dreams offer the gift of strength, freedom, and the ability to fiercely protect what's dear to us. They invite us to reclaim our power, to run freely, and to live as authentic lives as possible.'

Sebastian wondered how much Kate was making up. In any case, that last bit made him think about Astrid. Was that what she was doing? Reclaiming her power? He asked Kate whether she had spoken to Astrid lately, letting her know Astrid still wouldn't talk to him.

Kate surprised him by saying she'd spoken with Astrid the day before. Sebastian was all ears.

'She didn't say much. Seemed a bit down.'

'Down?' repeated Sebastian. Angry he expected, but not down.

Sebastian gave Kate a brief account of the stormy encounter that had occurred before Astrid left for Cairns with Jenna. He wondered how much Kate already knew.

'She told me she was homesick,'said Kate.

Sebastian's pulse raced. Perhaps his email had done the trick.

'Did she say she intended coming home?' he asked, with anticipation.

From the puzzled expression on Kate's face, it was clear he'd misunderstood. His high hopes were brought crashing down to earth with a thud.

'Homesick, Seb,' she said, giving her brother a gape that questioned his sanity. 'Not for Newcastle. For Amsterdam.'

Afterwards he felt completely stupid. For a moment he'd deluded himself into thinking she might have wanted to come back to him. He didn't doubt that Astrid would be feeling betrayed. But would she really do something that drastic?

Sebastian's attention was drawn to the song Matt and Deon were working on. He knew that Joe had written the lyrics years ago. It had a catchy chorus, and Deon was singing a harmony a fifth above Matt.

Didn't get a proper look, that's what I told the cop with the book.

Kate noticed his attention had shifted. 'The music sounds classy. Deon can really sing.'

'You should have seen him with his mates at Maitland Mall last week. Talk about talent! But it wasn't just the dancing or the music. It was their confidence and attitude, the way they are so proud of their culture. Deon even had the audacity to berate the Mayor for being late for their performance. And he did it in a way that had the audience and even the Mayor himself laughing. Reckon he'll blow them away at The Opera House.'

'Does he play the didge?'

'Yeah, really well. But for the show he does with his mates, he just uses clapping sticks and his voice. The chanting sounds so intense and powerful.'

Kate nodded towards the room. 'Be interesting to see what they come up with. Matt's gotten really good with the production side.'

Sebastian found it peculiar hearing Kate talk about Matt. Kate and Matt came from separate compartments of his life. Usually, when he saw Kate she had her two children with her.

'So, where are Jake and Darren?'

'Staying with their dad.'

Kate took the lid off the pan and stirred the sauce, the mixed aromas of tomato, garlic and spices filling the air.

'Yum... smells good, Sis. You the resident cook now?' asked Sebastian.

'Been staying over some nights,' replied Kate, as she moved about the kitchen, knowing where the conversation was heading.

'Oh, so you're moving in with Joe,' said Sebastian, in a half-joking manner that annoyed Kate.

'Give it a break, Seb. Don't play the protective older brother with me. I'm a big girl now. I can look after myself.'

Sebastian's tone hardened. 'You could have at least told me what's going on.'

'That's what I'm doing. I'm telling you what's going on. Sorry I didn't get your approval, but I knew how you would react.'

The sound of a car could be heard coming to a halt out the front of the house.

'Speak of the devil. That'll be Joe,' said Kate, sounding like a wife heralding her husband's return. 'He's really serious about playing music again you know. He's been working on songs and playing heaps.'

'His voice is sounding great. But you never know about commitment with Joe,' countered Sebastian.

Kate shot him a sharp, hostile look. She knew he was referring to more than the music.

'Sebastian, I'm not stupid. I know what Joe's like. I didn't just come floating down the river on a gumleaf. But you've got to trust people at some stage. It's not like I'm expecting him to move in with me and the kids. Anyway, why are you so critical of him? I thought you and Joe were good mates.'

'We are, but you are my sister and I know the effect Joe can have on people.'

When Joe came in, he was full of beans. He was happy to see Sebastian again. For a while they sounded like soldiers exchanging war stories, with Sebastian filling Joe in on the latest incident in his driveway.

'It was the same bastard who ran me off the road on my bike,' he said.

Joe showed Sebastian the remains of the spider that had come in the mail.

They drew up a timeline of everything that had happened. They were fairly certain two people were involved in the shooting incident at the golf course but couldn't decide whether one member of that duo was the person who had attacked Sebastian. In Joe's opinion, unless the guy spent his time racing between Sydney and Newcastle, it was unlikely to have been the same person who had dropped the spider into the letterbox.

They did know there were two vehicles involved. The four-wheel-drive with the fake plates, and the van the woman with the two children had seen in the parking lot above Malabar pool. In the end, they agreed it was useless to speculate further because they didn't have enough to go on.

Before long Joe was raving on to Sebastian about his chance encounter with Johnno at the Junction Hotel. He poured praise on Johnno's interpretations of their songs and told Sebastian about meeting Rob Martin, the drummer from Risky Business, saying nothing about the offer the drummer had made, or how close he had come to auditioning for the band.

'We have the studio booked for this afternoon and into the night, Seb. I can't wait to get back in there.'

Sebastian should have been excited but, after recent events, the last thing he wanted was to be put under pressure to perform in a recording studio. Right now, he felt like he didn't have a creative bone in his body.

'Joe, I feel totally fucked. I really don't think I'm up for it.'

'Seb, all you have to do is record the vocal tracks, a bit of harmony and keyboard. You already know the parts. You'll probably do it in one take. I'll get you some coke if you need a lift. It'll get you in the mood.'

Sebastian said he wouldn't be taking any cocaine. He then gave Joe the same spiel he'd given Matt about not offering Deon drugs. And he tried to get his head around the idea of going into a studio.

Joe picked up the guitar that was up sitting against the wall and began strumming.

'I reckon we will do this one pretty quickly. I love that guitar riff you worked out. Really conjures up the outback feel.'

Sebastian was soon drawn in.

Dry, dusty, hotter than I ever expected,
It never rains much except in February.
Then the rivers flood.
Life in the West,
Life in the West.

'That three-four part you've added works really well,' said Sebastian.

'Wait til you hear it in the studio. I did the vocals to *From Here to There* in one take. *Life in the West* took longer but wait til you hear it. Wiseman said he'll release the best one or two songs as independent releases, if the sessions work out. You'll really like Billy, the producer, and his lady, Catalina. Really cool dudes. Billy plays drums and bass and was going to put down parts after I left. Tonight, there's someone coming along to take footage for a music video.'

'Joe, you still look cool, but I feel like I'm over the hill.'

'They can always photoshop you or something,' said Joe with a laugh. He then smiled and pointed to Matt's room. 'Seb, neither of us are spring chickens, so I've lined up Matt and his mate Jessie to come along and dance for the video. Billy liked the idea of using Matt's beats. He's mixing it with drums. Said it would make our stuff sound more modern. Matt's done some backup vocals already. From what I'm hearing in Matt's room, it would be great to get Deon singing tonight as well. When you told me Deon played didge, I got excited. Can you imagine how cool it would be to have a didge on *Life in the West*?'

Deon emerged from Matt's room in a musical daze.

'That's mad, man. Should hear some of the beats,' he said to Sebastian.

Joe introduced himself, shaking Deon's hand. 'Love your voice, man. Where are you from, Deon?'

'I'm a Ngemba man. From Brewarrina.'

'The famous fish traps. I played at Lightning Ridge years ago on a country tour and we dropped into Brewarrina to pick up a drummer. Probably before you were born.'

Deon was impressed that Joe knew about his hometown. His face lit up, and momentarily he was lazing by the river again, fishing and yarning, catching yabbies.

'Do you go back to Brewarrina much?' asked Joe.

'Yeah, whenever I can. But not to stay. Not many opportunities for me back there.'

Matt came out a few minutes later to get Deon. 'Come in and see what I've done with your voice, man,' he said, ushering Deon back into the studio.

'Seems like a sensible enough kid,' said Joe, as the two youngsters disappeared into the room.

'In some ways he's really mature. But like Matt, he's got to stay out of trouble,' replied Sebastian.

Kate moved about the kitchen with purpose. Sebastian and Joe continued to yap as they placed the cutlery and various condiments on the table.

'This looks great, Sis,' said Sebastian.

'Was going to have it tonight, but who knows what time you lot will get back. At least it will keep you going.'

Before long the five of them were enjoying the meal. They chatted for the next twenty minutes or so and, as they were finishing up, Joe reached over his shoulder, picked up the remote control and clicked on the television. The voices of the Channel Nine commentary team filled the room.

'Joe, do we really need it?' asked Kate with chagrin.

'Just want to check the score, Kate. It won't stop our conversation.'

Matt sided with Kate. 'Dad, not the bloody cricket.'

When Joe didn't turn it off, Matt decided he wouldn't suffer in silence.

'I can't believe you watch that crap. It's the most boring game on Earth... besides golf,' he added cheekily.

'Do you like the cricket, Deon?' asked Joe, trying to drum up some support.

'Can't get into the test matches. They drag on and on. Don't mind the twenty-over games.'

'The Aussies are two for one sixty-two,' said Joe as he turned the television off. 'Deon, did you know the first cricket team to tour England was Aboriginal?'

'Heard somethin' about it.'

'They probably forced 'em to play,' quipped Matt.

'Matt's into basketball. Drums banging, screeching on bugles, whistling... you can't watch a game without some idiot getting in your ear with something. It's a friggin' circus.'

'When have you ever gone to a basketball game? You're talking shit, Dad.'

'That's why I don't go. Because it's so bloody noisy. You would have played a bit of basketball, Deon, being a country boy?'

'Yeah... we played a lot at school and down the PCYC.'

'Matt was selected for the Sydney Kings junior squad when he was fifteen,' said Joe proudly.

'True? That's cool,' said Deon.

'You must have had talent, Matt,' said Kate. 'Why didn't you stay at it?'

'Because Dad was too lazy to take me to training.'

Joe knew Matt was pressing his buttons, but he still couldn't let the comment go unchallenged.

'That's not true, Matt, and you know it. You didn't want to train four times a week. You weren't willing to put in the time, that's what really happened.'

'Ok Dad. Whatever you reckon.'

Deon found the father and son jousting amusing. Kate didn't. Her eyes moved from one to the other.

'Hey, come on fellas, please.'

'Deon was a really good footie player,' said Sebastian. 'Made the state schoolboys team when he was at school.'

Deon turned to Sebastian. 'Remember little Stevie Campbell? He came up to the pool comp with me one time?'

'Yep. The fella with the long curly hair.'

'Seen 'im in Newy the other week. The Knights signed him on a two-year contract.'

'Really? Good on him. I would've thought he was too small.'

'He's bulked up heaps. And he's fast as lightning.'

Joe leant forward. 'Maybe you should have stayed with the footie, Deon. Great money if you make it.'

'Hmm... don't know if I was good enough to play for the Knights.'

'Nah, not the bloody Knights, Deon... the Rabbitohs. They were Seb's team once, before he sold out,' said Joe, with a wink in Deon's direction.

'Come on, Joe. As if you can talk. How can you be a true Rabbitoh's supporter when you lived in the heart of enemy territory for so long? Manly, of all places... the despicable Sea Eagles!'

'It's loyalty Sebastian. Once a Rabbitoh, always a Rabbitoh. It doesn't matter where you live. It's where your heart is.'

'Who's having dessert?' asked Kate, who was up and moving about the kitchen again.

'Thanks again for the dinner, Sis. You're still a great cook. You didn't happen to bake up a batch of those famous rock cakes of yours, did you?' asked Sebastian, with a cheeky smile.

Kate feigned outrage as she picked up a tea towel and hurled it across the room at him. 'You are such a bastard, Sebastian. I'd forgotten about that. Hey Joe, you know what my nasty brother did to me when I was ten and I'd made my first ever batch of cakes? He tried to bounce them on the kitchen floor. Can you believe it?'

'They made great cricket balls... could even spin 'em.'

A short time later, Joe was on his feet and pacing the room like a caged lion.

'Joe... you alright?' asked Kate. She walked over to him and started massaging his neck and shoulders. Kate knew what the problem was. He was craving an after-dinner smoke. She knew what she'd do if the others weren't there. It turned her on just thinking about it. A medicinal massage, she called it. It certainly did the trick. Joe would lie prostrate on the bed, and she would sit astride him. She would start at his neck and remove his garments one by one as she worked her way down his body. By the time she turned him over, Joe invariably had an erection.

He was a good lover, thought Kate. His curious nature ensured the sex was not repetitive. Initially what had surprised Kate was his stamina; Joe was not a person who you would think of as being fit.

When Kate had finished, Joe thanked her and looked across at Sebastian.

'Since I started cutting down on the smoking, I've got all this energy.'

'What do you want Joe? A bloody medal?' Sebastian replied.

Though unintended, the words came out harsh. Kate threw him a dirty look. She knew her brother was jealous of the propinquity evident between her and Joe. But there was more to it than that. What irked Sebastian was that despite the overt display of affection, there was still not a word to him from Joe about his relationship with Kate. Sebastian did acknowledge one point though. It was probably the least he'd seen Joe smoke since he was sixteen. Still, Sebastian had no intention of joining the poor Joe fan club.

After lunch, the four men thanked Kate and helped clean up before leaving for the recording session. The studio was in King Street, Newtown and, according to Joe, it would take them about twenty minutes to get there.

They joked around in the car, trying to come up with a name for their outfit. Matt got a laugh with his suggestion, Moving Targets, but the more they thought about it, the more they liked it. Sebastian decided on the final arrangement for *Amsterdam Lady* on the way to the studio.

As Joe had said, the producer, Billy, was a likeable character and was easy to work with. He was a Jamaican man with Bob Marley-style dreadlocks and his wife, Catalina, was of Spanish descent. She had moved to Sydney as a teenager and knew her way around the dials, taking over when Billy played drums or bass.

The session went really well, with the producer complementing them on their arrangements and harmonies. Matt's friend didn't turn up, which gave Deon more to do. They tried at first to record the didge with a click track, but Deon found it off-putting. When they replaced it with Billy's drumming, they had it down in a couple of takes.

Billy was an excellent musician and revealed that he'd worked for years as a session musician in London. When Billy told them he would have a master of the songs ready in a couple of days, Sebastian questioned his optimism. His answer was that he worked day and night until a project was finished. He said Wiseman, like himself, didn't believe in getting too fancy with production techniques, preferring a natural sound with strong rhythms and limited effects.

Lucy, the woman who came to shoot the footage, stayed for almost three hours. After a while they became oblivious to her presence. She thought *Life in the West* would be the best for visuals. It featured Deon on didge, and Deon and Matt dancing, and had a wild guitar solo, courtesy of

Joe.

The four didn't get home from the studio until the early hours. Kate was fast asleep; Charlie was in the laundry and had to be settled again before Sebastian could go to sleep. He'd hoped to have heard from Astrid or Jenna and was disappointed that neither had attempted to contact him. Before he went to sleep, he sent a text to Jenna.

Dearest Jenna,

You are an amazing daughter. All that a father could ever wish for. I am so proud of you. At the moment I probably don't seem like the greatest father in the world and for that I am truly sorry.

Miss you, Jenna.

Love,

Dad.

19

The White Van

Sebastian emerges from a fog and finds himself outside an old house. The front door is partially open and he sticks his head inside. Hundreds of multicoloured candles flicker from sconces mounted in small enclaves, forming an archway that reaches down the hallway and out to the back of the house.

In a distant room he hears the faint sound of music. It dawns on him that it is *From Here to There*, but it sounds nothing like the version they'd put down. It has a luscious orchestral backing. And a lighter beat. The arrangement is one that he has never heard.

I cannot forget,
I don't choose to remember.
My sea loving soul
Longs for the living.

Sebastian realises there is another voice singing along softly in the background. It is Astrid's voice, and he stands there mesmerised.

Sebastian follows the avenue of candles though the house and into a rumpus room situated out the back. The scent of burning incense is strong, the heady mixture of spicy fragrances redolent of an oriental market. Walking into the room, he sees Astrid lying on a dark-green leather sofa. Attired in an embroidered cotton top and colourful sarong, her eyes come alive when she sees him. He is overcome with a feeling of tranquility and wellbeing. Astrid rises to her feet and starts swaying to the tempo of the music. She holds out her arm, insisting that Sebastian joins her. As they dance, Astrid sings.

Morning awakens me
To a thousand sunrises
That you once thought
To eternalise.

When the song ends a sombre expression comes over Astrid's face. Sebastian feels guilty and begins to apologise, but she cuts him off.

She takes Sebastian's hand and leads him through to the hallway where there is a ladder set up below the light fitting. Placing a lightbulb into his hand, she points to the ceiling.

Sebastian looks up. The ceiling is extremely high. Ridiculously so. It is out of proportion with the rest of the house and seems to have gotten even higher. He becomes agitated, knowing he has little chance of reaching the light fitting.

Astrid picks up on his hesitation and her buoyant countenance turns gloomy. Her sense of melancholy flows through his whole being and he knows he cannot let her down.

He walks over to the ladder, which is also growing in length. He glances across at Astrid, who now seems hopeful, and he knows he must at least attempt the task. Stepping onto the first rung, he begins to climb. Higher and higher he goes, until he has reached the second-last rung. To have any chance of reaching the light globe, he must stand on the very top of the ladder.

After hesitating for a split second, he warily steps up. Fighting to retain his balance, he raises his arm above his head and reaches out for the globe. As he touches it with the tip of his fingers, the ladder starts to wobble. He loses his balance and falls. Tumbling thought the air, he braces his body in preparation for the inevitable impact. But seconds pass and he doesn't hit the ground.

He just keeps on falling and falling

The falling sensation had been too real, and frightening. Afterwards, Sebastian lay on the bed recounting his dream. It had left a powerful after-effect, the experience somehow galvanising his attachment to Astrid and leaving him with a deep yearning to be with her.

Sebastian became aware of Joe's voice, and the click-clacking of Kate's leather shoes on the kitchen floor. He heard the jangle of keys and the slight squeak of the front door opening. There was a brief silence (Sebastian imagined Joe and Kate quietly kissing) before the door closed and Kate left for work.

An hour later, Sebastian and Joe were sipping coffee at the back of the house while entertaining Charlie by throwing balls for her to retrieve.

Joe checked the weather forecast and found out that there was the possibility of a thunderstorm later in the day. The two decided to play nine holes at Bondi while conditions were favourable.

Deon and Matt were in Matt's room, working on another song. The success of the previous night had given them both more drive and determination. When Sebastian and Joe walked into the room, Matt and Deon were so involved in what they were doing, it took a few seconds for them to realise they were no longer alone.

'We're going over to Bondi to play nine. Be back in a couple of hours,' said Joe.

Sebastian turned to Deon 'Come and have a hit with us, mate.'

Deon hesitated, glancing across at Matt.

'Don't play golf, man. Stay here and we'll keep working on this song.'

'Is that ok, Sebastian?' asked Deon.

'Yeah, yeah, that's fine. We won't be long.'

Matt turned to his father. 'Hey Dad, will you leave the car please? I'll need to go down the shops.'

A smile came over Joe's face. 'See how nice and polite he can be when he wants something.'

Matt tapped his fingers lightly on the table. 'We've started putting together a really cool song.'

'Yeah, I know, Son. I reckon the whole neighbourhood knows the beat.' Joe did an impressive ad lib of the beat with his voice and hands before continuing. 'Plenty of food in the fridge, Deon. Make yourself at home. And Matt,' he said, pausing to get his full attention. 'Make sure you lock up properly when you go out.'

Sebastian rang Maitland Police Station. He'd hoped they might have found his assailant by now, but that turned out to be wishful thinking. They didn't have any further information. Since he'd been in Sydney, Sebastian had managed to forget about the precarious nature of the situation he was in but, once he'd left the house, he began to feel apprehensive again.

'Hey, you seem a bit uptight, Seb.'

'Yeah, well… this maniac with the pistol. The police still have no idea where he is. How can I relax while he's still on the loose? I thought they might have at least found that four-wheel-drive by now.'

After they'd put their golf clubs in the boot, Joe decided he would have to reassure his friend. He had a quick look up and down the street before tugging on Sebastian's sleeve. He then lifted his shirt for a split second. A triumphant expression appeared on his face.

'I've got your back, Seb.'

Sebastian gazed back at him, dumbfounded.

'Is it real?' Sebastian asked, still not quite believing what he'd seen.

Joe patted the spot where the weapon sat snugly in its holster. 'Of course it's fucking real. It's a 22 Baretta semiautomatic.'

'You are bloody kidding! So, what's going on, Joe? Are we fucking gangsters now?'

Joe was taken aback. He had thought Sebastian would appreciate the fact they were now less vulnerable.

'You've had some fuckwit nearly shoot you. Next time, mate, you mightn't be so lucky. Have you forgotten what happened the last time we were on a golf course? What is it with you? Don't you get it?'

'I do get it Joe. It's simple. It's called the law. If this nut case appears, we call the cops and let them deal with it. That's what people do.'

'What… after or before he puts a bullet in ya?'

'For fuck's sake, Joe, you can't take a gun out onto a golf course.'

'I'm not stupid. Nobody will see it. We've got to do something to protect ourselves.'

'You had it with you last night, didn't you? In that bag you wouldn't let out of your sight.'

'Fuck, man. I wish I hadn't shown you.'

So, what are you going to do, eh? Have a shoot-out on Bondi golf course?'

'What if there are people around?'

'What if... what if... fuck, man! What if Deon hadn't been around when this bloke went after you? From what I understand, you'd have been killed or seriously injured. So, get real, Seb. The cops can't find him. We'd be idiots if we didn't take precautions. It's just insurance. And it's only a short-range pistol anyway,' he added, in an attempt to mollify him.

'Now, that's a relief,' replied Sebastian, sarcastically.

Joe pointed to the back seat of Sebastian's car. 'What's that cricket bat and the piece of four-by-two? They're weapons.'

'Oh, come on, Joe. It's hardly the same.'

'It's for the same thing – self-defence. Even if they are useless. You fight guns with a gun, not a piece of wood. What are you going to do? Bat the bullet away? Hit it for six?'

It's not a joke, Joe. I hope you know what you're doing.'

'You bet I do. I had a practice in the bush at Lapa yesterday. I'm still a good shot. This fucker appears, I won't hesitate.'

They didn't speak for a while. Sebastian wouldn't admit it to Joe, but knowing his mate had a weapon did alleviate his angst somewhat. And it was true what Joe had said, a cricket bat would be useless against the madman.

Bondi Beach was alive with joggers, surfers, and the morning latte crowd. They stopped at a fruit shop off the main drag and bought a bag of bananas. The high-energy food was standard fare for the two when playing golf, almost as important as golf balls.

'Good thing we decided to play early,' said Joe, pointing to the south-east where clouds were gathering. 'I reckon we'll get an almighty storm this arvo.'

Joe began to tell Sebastian about a documentary he had seen recently. It was about a paraglider who had been sucked up into the clouds while practising for a competition out west.

'This German lady was swept up over nine thousand feet and amazingly survived. Totally fucking awesome, eh? Imagine if you were up there in a plane and you looked out and saw her. You'd think you were trippin' or losin' it.'

'Joe... nobody could possibly live through something like that. Sounds like you got the facts mixed up. Had you just smoked some weed?'

Joe was affronted by Sebastian's skepticism. 'Fair dinkum, Seb! She went up higher than fucking Everest. I thought you would have heard about it. It was all over the news at the time. What did they say? The odds of surviving were similar to winning the lottery five fucking times in a row!'

Sebastian rolled his eyes.

'You're so gullible, Joe. Someone's stringing you along. The air is too thin once you get up that high. How could she breathe for starters? And besides, you would freeze to death. It drops to something like minus thirty.'

'Yeah, well here's the thing that saved her. She went unconscious. Some doctor who was talking about it reckons that's the reason she survived. Her body functions slowed down, and she was fucking hibernating, man.'

'Humans don't hibernate. You sure she wasn't a bear, Joe? Did she growl?

'Fuck you, Seb. Do you think I would make something like that up?

'Well, what about her gear? It couldn't possibly survive. Some glider she must have had! Made of some secret material.' Sebastian sniggered.

'I'll show you the story when we get back. You'll see, you smart-arse.'

'Perhaps she was an alien? That would explain it.'

Joe couldn't stop himself. He had to convince Sebastian.

'Odds of a billion to one. I'm telling ya, Sebastian, the lady couldn't believe it herself when she came out of the storm alive with the glider still in one piece. The officials on the ground wouldn't believe it, but she had a tracking device on the craft.'

'Yeah, sure Joe… it's easy to fake a tracking device. Next you'll tell me she thanked the angels for saving her life.'

Joe looked at Sebastian who was smiling to himself. A "got you" moment.

Joe kicked the side of Sebastian's shoe. 'You bastard… you've heard the story. Smart-arse. Can't help yourself, can you?'

Sebastian got some satisfaction out of leading Joe along.

They unloaded their clubs from the car and paid their green fees. It was a quiet morning, and they didn't have to wait. But once they started to play, it was clear from their lethargic manner that the Bondi game was lacking its usual zest. Bondi might have been a short golf course, but it still required effort. Last night had been fun, but it had also been draining. Also weighing on both their minds, particularly Sebastian's, was the fact that last time they had attempted to play golf they had been shot at.

Even though they'd agreed to break their usual rule and bring phones due to the alarming events of the past week, Sebastian became irritated after Joe's Lone Ranger ringtone sounded as he was about to hit a shot. The irrepressible Joe tried hard to create some fun by prodding Sebastian with his seven-iron as he was lining up a shot.

'Need to bend your arse more, mate.'

Another time Sebastian might have laughed, but he flicked the club away. 'Fuck off, Joe. Grow up, for fuck's sake.'

Both Sebastian and Joe kept to themselves as they played the hole. Even though neither, in particular Sebastian, were in the best of moods, the thrill of recording their songs together the previous day had had an unusual side effect; neither of them seemed to care too much about beating the other. Of course, knowing someone out there had it in for you did put the importance of winning a golf game into perspective, but it was more than that. Bragging about beating the other at golf seemed incongruous with the unity and camaraderie they'd experienced during the recording session. When they talked about music, the antagonism between the two dissipated.

'I can't believe how well it went,' said Sebastian. 'Even *Amsterdam Lady* went down without a hitch. That Billy is a really topnotch producer. And Catalina too. The delay she put on Deon's didge was brilliant.'

'How good was Billy's drumming?' said Joe.

'I was really buggered before we started, but once we got into it, I seemed to get more energy.'

'I get a real buzz out of knowing our songs have been professionally recorded. I wish we'd stayed to see what Billy did with the mixing.'

'Got a big night ahead of him.'

'Sure, but with all that gear, it's not like the old days when you had to splice tapes and over-dub vocals to get a convincing sound. Did you know Paul McCartney used to record his own voice over and over to get a thick vocal sound? Queen used to do the same with their backup parts. Now you can digitally enhance with the flick of a switch.'

'I remember a story from the sixties, about Johnny O'Keefe. He recorded the lead vocals to one of his hits something like a hundred and twenty times. They ended up using the first take.'

'Anyway, Joe. Let's hope Wiseman's happy with the result.'

Joe thought about how close he had been to auditioning for Rob Martin's band. He hoped he'd made the right decision. Again, he thought about the routine and regular money he'd forgone. Still, after the success of the session, he did feel that his decision was validated. Of course, whether their sound would stand out and give them the edge over the hundreds of other classy outfits vying for attention in the behemoth that was the music industry was a matter for the gods.

Perched on the headland to the north of Bondi beach, the views from the golf course were spectacular. Some of the holes followed the coastline and a poor shot to the right on some holes meant a ball lost over the cliff. Unless you had abseiling gear or a death wish, it was impossible to retrieve a ball.

They were on the fourth hole when Joe hit his ball over the cliff. His eyes almost popped out of his head as he looked over the ledge and saw the booty lying in a crevice below. There were four large boulders that had broken away from the main formation and seemed to be clinging to the top of the cliff by the skin of their teeth. Nestled amongst the tufts of grass that had somehow managed to get a footing were about twelve golf balls. Joe lowered his wiry body down onto the rocks.

Sebastian had walked over to his ball which was about thirty metres away on the other side of the fairway. When he turned around, he could only see Joe's golf clubs. It seemed as though Joe had vanished into thin air. Then, from out of nowhere, he heard Joe's voice.

'Hey, Seb… you up there?'

'Joe… where the hell are you?'

Sebastian walked over to the edge of the fairway and looked down. 'Joe… come back up. Are you fucking kidding? It's too dangerous!'

There was a lull, and nothing happened for a moment, then golf ball after golf ball came whizzing through the air up onto the fairway from the crevice below.

'Manna from heaven,' yelled Joe, as he continued on his merry way, moving amongst the stones and rocks, seemingly oblivious to the fifty metre drop onto the jagged boulders and turbulent waters below.

Joe was about to come back up when he noticed another half a dozen balls precariously placed in a gap between two of the boulders. He eyed them purposefully to see if they were worth the effort. Some of the balls looked brand new. It was too tempting a challenge.

From up above he looked like a giant spider closing in on its prey as he crawled along on all fours. Fragments of loose rock slid over the edge, crashing onto the rocks and into the water below.

Sebastian watched on with awe and consternation.

'Joe, that's enough. You'll kill yourself you stupid fucker. Come back up.'

'Just a few more,' said Joe, stretching his long limbs to gather in the last of the bootie.

A minute or so later and Joe was back up on the fairway, grinning from ear to ear, like the proverbial fisherman who had just landed a boatload.

'Check 'em out, Sebastian.' Methodically, he assessed his catch. 'Some brand newies ... Callaway... Titlist...' He tossed Sebastian all the quality Callaway balls, knowing they were the ones he preferred.

'Joe... you are one crazy bastard,' exclaimed Sebastian, shaking his head and laughing in relief as he gratefully accepted the gift.

Joe's act of madness seemed to give them both a boost and they were in high spirits as they played out the hole.

They'd just putted out when Joe received a text from Sophia. *Contact me ASAP*. Joe didn't like to say too much on the phone. When he showed Sebastian the message and told him he'd asked Sophia for help after receiving the spider in the mail, they decided to give golf a miss. Sophia's place was only five minutes away.

Back at Napier Street, Matt and Deon were working on a set of lyrics when Matt encountered a serious problem. He was out of cigarettes. Grabbing the key to the Falcon, a few minutes later he pulled off the road and stopped outside the newsagency in a no-parking zone. Deon stayed in the car while Matt crossed the road and went inside the shop to buy a packet of Winfield Blues.

Further down the street, a white van parked about twenty metres away on the opposite side of the road caught Deon's attention. He leant across to the passenger seat in an attempt to get a better view. There was a fella sitting in the driver's seat, smoking a cigarette. When he realised the van was a Toyota his heart raced. A few seconds later, a woman with short, cropped blonde hair came strolling along the footpath with a bag of groceries and hopped into the van.

Were these the same two he had heard Joe and Matt talking about? Had he accidentally stumbled upon who had shot at them on the golf course?

The driver flicked his cigarette onto the road and started the engine, lurching out into the traffic without indicating. He then threw a U-turn, turned onto Anzac Parade and accelerated away. Deon didn't want to lose the van. He was contemplating jumping across to the driver's seat and driving off after the van alone, when Matt came out of the shop. He blew the horn of the Falcon to get Matt's attention, then got out of the car and pointed to the white van.

When Matt saw it, he ran across the road, hopped into the driver's seat and quickly pulled out onto the road.

Meanwhile, the lights ahead had turned red, and they found themselves stuck behind a delivery truck. Matt grew increasingly impatient. He waited for an opportune moment before pulling out around the truck and running the red light. As he sped off in pursuit, Deon gave Matt a description of the two people he had seen.

They drove past Matraville High School. When they reached Austral Street, they still hadn't sighted the van. With Long Bay Gaol on the left and clear vision on the right, Matt put his foot down. They reached the crest of the hill and saw the white van in the distance.

'Don't wanna get too close,' said Deon.' They might recognise Joe's car.'

Matt heeded his advice. They probably did know that Joe drove an old Falcon. He was fairly sure they hadn't noticed the car at the shops. The pair had been acting too casually for that.

The van continued along Anzac Parade until the Port Botany intersection where it turned right down Little Bay Road. It then made a left turn at the bottom of the hill into Nurla Avenue. Matt and Deon arrived at the corner of the street to see the vehicle disappear into a driveway. Matt pulled off the road. Before he'd turned the engine off, Deon had opened his door and sprung from the car.

'What are you doin'?' shrieked Matt.

'Nobody will notice a blackfella round these parts. You stay 'ere. They know you.'

Deon was enjoying himself, getting off on the adventure. He knew the drill and it wasn't long before he returned.

'It's a white weatherboard place, number sixteen. There's a side gate and the van is parked in the driveway. The blinds were closed, so I couldn't see what was happening inside.'

He told Matt where he thought the lounge room and bedrooms would be.

'Are you going to ring ya dad? I should tell Seb.'

'They'll still be playing golf. They'll have their phones turned off. We don't even know for sure that it's them yet. I'll call him later.' Matt considered his next move. 'I'm going to drop by home and pick up a few things.

They drove back to Napier Street. Matt searched through his drawers and found what he was looking for.

Deon smiled when he realised what Matt was doing. Matt quickly changed into a pair of blue overalls with a Goddard's Plumbing logo on the front.

'I got the overalls when I did work experience there. These steel boots will come in handy too. It's an old trick I saw in a movie.'

'Did he get away with it?'

'Who?'

'The guy in the movie.'

'I'm not sure. Suppose I should check,' said Matt with a chuckle.

When Matt was changed, he went out the back of the house. While Deon played with Charlie, he got a toolbox out of the shed.

'How do I look?' he asked.

'Mad,' said Deon.'

'Look, Deon. I'm not going into that house until the van is gone and I'm sure no-one is around. Mightn't even get the chance today. Maybe you should stay here. I don't need you to come back with me.'

Deon was affronted by the proposition. 'Fuck no... I'm with ya, Matt,' he said, as though Matt's suggestion was the silliest idea he'd ever heard. 'It's too risky to do by yaself.'

When the two arrived back at Little Bay, they cruised along Nurla Avenue, slowing as they passed the house. The van was gone. The curtains were drawn, and the house seemed to be empty.

Matt parked across from the house in behind a Ford Ute. Apart from a middle-aged lady checking her mailbox, there was nobody else out on the street. He told Deon to stay in the car so he could warn him if the van returned, or anyone approached the house. With toolbox in hand, Matt strolled up to the front gate. He was the epitome of a suburban plumber. If someone was home and came to the door, he'd claim to be at the wrong address.

He knocked on the front door and waited for half a minute. When nobody came to the door, he went around to the side of the house.

'Hello! Anybody home?' he called, doing his best impersonation of a laidback tradesman on a job. Reaching over the side gate, he slipped open the latch and strolled into the backyard. He climbed the back steps and pushed hard against the back door. It wouldn't budge. He banged on the laundry window which gave a little. He glanced around at the neighbouring properties as he slipped on a pair of thin leather gloves. Taking a screwdriver from his toolbox, he had little trouble forcing the window open. It was a small space but large enough for him to squeeze through.

Once inside, he noticed a key hanging on a hook above the washing machine. As he had hoped, it was the key to the back door. Matt laughed at the lackadaisicalness of the occupants of the house as he went back outside and retrieved his toolbox. After having a peep in each room, he sent Deon a text message to let him know he was inside.

There were a few Kodak photographs on an empty display cabinet in the lounge room. They had been taken in the backyard, and the sour-faced female he had seen jump into the van at Malabar was in one of the shots. The scruffy bloke grinning beside her appeared to be her boyfriend, and he was definitely the one driving the white van.

Matt pulled out his phone and took a few photos. Someone he or Joe knew would surely know at least one of them.

The kitchen was sparsely stocked. It contained just the bare essentials. After quickly checking the drawers and cupboards, he went into the first bedroom off the hallway.

There was a queen-size bed and an old wardrobe. On the walls was an eclectic mix of posters - the Roosters league team, a Madonna and a Nirvana pin-up. What caught his attention were the Ruger and Mossberg advertisements with life-size pictures of weapons. The occupant of the room sure liked guns, and he felt he was on the right track.

There was a pair of jeans draped across the bed, and black leather shoes on the floor. Matt had assumed the room was occupied by a male, but when he opened the wardrobe and began searching through the drawers, he realised he was mistaken. There were bras, tampons and female cosmetics. Stuffed at the bottom of the wardrobe, was a fishing rod and carry bag. It seemed odd, considering nothing else he had seen in the house suggested the occupiers had any interest in fishing. And the carry bag was certainly large enough to conceal a rifle.

Matt pushed ahead; more confident than ever he was on the right track. After eliminating the obvious hiding places, he began searching more obscure locations. Five minutes later, he came across something unusual. Tied to the underside of the bed was an object tightly wrapped in opaque plastic. That got him excited. Quickly undoing the bundle, he was soon gazing at a Winchester 1000 SB with a shockproof hunting scope.

Matt continued to search, thinking the ammunition might be nearby. If he found a bullet, he could compare it to the one he'd found on the golf course. There was little doubt in his mind they would match. After a fruitless few minutes, he took a photo of the rifle and carefully re-wrapped it, placing it back under the bed as he'd found it. He decided to try the other bedroom.

When he entered the room, he was met by a sickly stench. The bed was unmade and the sheets needed washing. It seemed like the window hadn't been opened for weeks, if not months. He screwed up his face as he noticed the mould on the ceiling. It was disgusting to Matt, who was fastidious about hygiene.

The walls were littered with truck posters and porn. There was an old television sitting on a small table in the corner. He noticed a black sports bag stuck behind the wardrobe and was optimistic. A smile came over his face when he undid the zip to discover wads of fifty-dollar notes.

Still staring at the money in disbelief, he was startled by the sound of the back door opening. He grabbed the screwdriver from his pocket and stood motionless, listening to the floorboards creak. Somebody else was in the house. They were stepping quietly, as though they were aware there was an intruder in the house. Preparing for the worst, he braced his body and slowly stuck his head out around the door. He caught a glimpse of a figure moving down the hallway and was about to pounce when he was met by Deon's beaming face. He breathed a loud sigh of relief.

'What the fuck, man? You scared the shit out of me. You were supposed to stay in the car.'

'Thought someone might have caught you. Couldn't just sit there waiting forever. Ya reckon it's them?'

'Yep. For sure, I'd say.'

Matt told Deon about the weapon. Deon scrutinised the photos of the two suspects and shook his head.

'It definitely ain't the same dude who was after Seb.' The cold eyes of the man he saw in the clearing with the pistol were indelible imprints on his memory.

'Let's split,' said Matt, 'I've found all I need in here.'

The two cautiously made their way out of the house and back to the car.

When they were driving up Little Bay Road, Matt nudged Deon and pointed to his toolbox.

'Open it up.'

Deon did as Matt said. He was gobsmacked. 'Fuck, man.'

'Found it stashed away in the fella's bedroom,' said Matt, proud of his achievement.

Deon did a quick count as they drove along. 'At least four grand, probably more.'

'Half each,' said Matt.

Deon was blown away by the generosity of the offer. He eyed the bundles of cash voraciously, before shaking his head. 'Nah, you keep it all… I can't risk it.'

'Don't say anything to Joe about us breaking into the place. He'll go nuts. We'll just say we followed the van back to the house.'

'No worries… you better say something about the rifle, though.'

'We'll say we saw them take it out of the car.'

Although they had only met the day before, watching them together, one would have thought they'd been close friends for years. They were kindred spirits on the adventure of a lifetime.

20

The Penny Drops

'Miracles do happen,' said Joe, as Sebastian found a parking spot directly opposite Sophia's place.

Sebastian and Joe strolled up to the front door. Joe knocked a couple of times, put his ear to the door and heard movement inside.

'Sophia... it's Joe!'

A minute later the door opened, and Sophia appeared.

Talk about a quick response... you blokes are quicker than the ambos.'

'We've been playing golf just up the road, Soph. You remember Sebastian?'

'Gidday Sebastian. It's been a while,' said Sophia with a smile as she welcomed them both inside.

They went through the hallway and into the kitchen. There was a bong sitting on the table, already packed. In an arc surrounding it was a bowl of mixed weed, a packet of cigarettes, a lighter and an ashtray. Sophia picked up the lighter and lit the bong. After sucking in the full contents, she wheeled herself over to the back door and opened it to allow the smoke to disperse. She pointed towards the bong and accoutrements.

'Have one if you like.'

Neither of them took up the offer. As Sophia put on the kettle, Sebastian's mind was elsewhere. He was thinking about a picture he had seen as they passed through the hallway.

'Sit down fellas. I'll make us a pot of tea,' said Sophia, refusing Joe's offer of assistance.

She wheeled her way around the kitchen with purpose, placing the milk, sugar and a plate of Tim Tam biscuits on the table. 'Been doing some detective work, Joe,' she said, in a tone that suggested her efforts had not been in vain. 'That white Toyota van you mentioned... I'm pretty sure it belongs to Sandra McDonald and William Bates. Sweet Sandra and Wild Bill move quite a bit of gear around the eastern suburbs. Mostly marijuana and ice.

'Now, Sandra is an interesting character. You might remember a case from about eight years back. A girl on her way home from work was abducted near Lewisham Station. There were four blokes involved. They raped and then murdered the girl.'

'Shit yeah... it was all over the news,' said Joe.

'Well, anyway, Sandra McDonald is the little sister of two of those charmers. When sweet Sandra was a teenager, she was put in juvie for knocking off cars. Her method was interesting. She'd wait until the driver was opening the vehicle then whack the victim over the head with an iron bar and take the keys. She's applied a number of times to join the Australian Army but keeps being rejected. She has a reputation around the traps for knowing a bit about weapons.'

'Probably needs to be able to defend herself, when you consider who her relations are. Well done, Soph,' said Joe.

'What about this Bates bloke?'

'Hang on, Joe... I'm getting to him,' she replied in a forceful manner, letting Joe know who was running the show. 'Bates used to work up the Cross, running errands for the gangs. He's a bit of a show-off, a big mouth. The thing is... Bates has been bragging lately about how he is having a bit of fun getting even with someone who has been operating on his turf.'

Joe got to his feet and began pacing the kitchen. 'Working his turf? Do you know where they live, Bates and McDonald?'

'I'm working on it. That van is registered at some phoney address. Something else I found out. Bates has done some work for Uncle George.'

'George Souriss? They work for George Souriss?'

'Calm down, Joe. Nearly everybody around here in the game either works for George or operates with his tacit approval. It's just that some of them don't always know it. But I can tell you, Joe, it's not his style. He wouldn't muck around with warning shots and spiders in the mail. Tends to be a bit more direct.'

There was a break in conversation.

'Do you mind if I use the bathroom, Sophia?' asked Sebastian.

'No, of course not. Down the hallway to the left.'

Sebastian made his way down the hallway, pausing in front of the artwork that had caught his eye on the way through. He glared at the face of the girl on the swing, who was the subject of the painting. If the solemn face wasn't Frances, then it was her double. The scrawl in the bottom right-hand corner said AM. He realised that the painting had been done by Frances's father, Andrew Morten. As expensive as it would be to buy, having a painting by Andrew Morten probably just meant Sophia was a shrewd investor, he thought. Maybe it was just a coincidence and had nothing to do with the strange events of the past week. Should he just ask Sophia? he wondered. He decided to wait and talk to Joe about it. After pretending to use the bathroom, Sebastian returned to the kitchen.

Joe was on his feet. Since hearing about Bates and McDonald, he had become restless. 'We better be going,' he said to Sophia, 'I need to get back home and have a chat with Matt.'

Sophia followed them through the hallway to the door.

'Thanks, Soph. I appreciate your help,' said Joe.

'I'll keep my ear to the ground. Good to see you again, Seb.'

Joe, and then Sebastian, leaned forward to give Sophia a departing hug.

'Take care, Joe, and don't forget to tell Matt I want to see him. I need to try and make it up to him before I cark it.'

'Cark it?'

Sophia smiled.

'No, no, I'm not dying yet… not that I know of. But I do need to fix a few things up.'

Once Sebastian and Joe were alone, Sebastian told him about the painting hanging in Sophia's hallway. Joe said that Sophia had received a generous payout after her accident and had purchased a few artworks as investments. He thought it was unlikely that Sophia had meet Morten and couldn't see how it was connected to their problems.

Sebastian had already told Joe about what Lorraine had discovered in regard to the shooting, but this time he told Joe about his one-night fling with Frances and her organisation, Bohemians Behaving Badly.

Joe thought it was hilarious, saying it sounded like something he would have become mixed up in, not Sebastian. In Joe's opinion, it might explain why Sebastian had been targeted, and if the police were on to the guy then with their resources they'd probably find him. But in his opinion, Bates and McDonald were the likely culprits regarding the shootings on the golf course. He reiterated what Sophia had told them. The more he thought about it, the more likely he thought the golf course attack, and the spider in the mail incident were linked to the actions of his contumacious son.

By the time they got to Napier Street, Joe was in an agitated state. Would Matt ever learn? He'd had twenty minutes to stew on what Sophia had told him. Sebastian tried but couldn't placate him.

Matt had just come out of the bathroom as Joe entered the house. Joe was blunt.

'Matt, we need to talk,' he growled.

Matt was wary. 'What about?'

'These people fucking us around. Nobody would fire shots at somebody on a golf course without a reason. Come on, Matt. Think about it. Have you done anything that might've stirred things up?'

Matt shrugged his shoulders.

'Have you been dealing around here? Done anything in the eastern suburbs?'

Despite Joe's bellicose state, Matt was relieved. He'd thought Deon had told Joe they'd broken into the house. There was a stand-off for a few seconds.

'I moved a few eckies. So what?' he exclaimed with attitude.

Joe was in his face. 'You are friggin' joking!' he bellowed, raging with anger. 'Why in the fuck didn't you tell me about this before?'

Matt threw his arms in the air. 'You're impossible to talk too. Look at the way you carry on.'

Joe reigned in his temper. 'So, what's a few, Matt?'

'I got a couple of hundred from that Telford fella.'

'Where did you off-load them?'

'Matraville and Maroubra. Just in a couple of pubs.'

'So, it didn't occur to you that it might be the reason behind all this shit that's been going on?'

There was no reply. Just a glare that said, don't push it.

'Jees you're a fucking idiot, Matt! That's why these arseholes are hassling us. Blind Freddy could have worked that one out.'

'Listen, Dad. I don't need a life coach.'

'No. You need a fucking babysitter.'

'I needed the money for some music gear. Anyway, I'm not scared of these dickheads.'

'No, you're too fucking stupid to be scared. You know how it all works, Matt. Why didn't you ask me for some money?'

'Ask you? You're always such a tight-arse. I'm sick of living off your frigging change.'

'For godsake Matt, I'm trying to stash some money away for the future. Your future. I'd be stupid if I spent every cent I made. Are you a complete idiot?'

'Oh yeah, don't give me the how much you care bullshit. You were so fucking out of it most of the time. Didn't give jack shit about me when I was little. Couldn't even look after me properly. Now all I hear is, don't do this, don't do that, do it this way.'

'Don't try the guilt trip on me, Matt. It won't work this time. Think about it. You've got to admit it, Matt. I mean, by any definition you've acted like an absolute fucking idiot.'

'I couldn't give fifty thousand flying fucks about what you think.' Matt was surly. 'I'm pissing off for a while. I'm not putting up with your rubbish.' He moved with speed, grabbing his jacket from the chair on his way out the door.

As Matt walked along Napier Street, it occurred to him that he hadn't told Joe that he and Deon had followed the white van out to Little Bay. Deon was sure to tell them, he thought. He would text Joe later after he'd calmed down, just to make sure.

Joe poured a glass of water and went out into the backyard where Sebastian was playing a ball game with Charlie. Deon was still in Matt's room, singing along to some music with Matt's headphones on, seemingly oblivious to the spat that had occurred in the next room. He had heard Joe and Matt arguing and had assumed it was because Matt had told Joe they'd followed the white van, and that Joe was annoyed because Matt had done so without informing him. He now felt guilty for not at least texting Sebastian about it. Best to stay in Matt's room, he'd decided. Keep out of the firing line.

'Sorry to put that on you, Sebastian. At least I now know what's been going on.' Joe was quiet for a few seconds 'It's true what he was saying though. I can't really blame him for being like he is. Couldn't even get him to go to school half the time. You know they wanted to put him in foster care at one stage. I had to fight them like you wouldn't believe. You know what? I think Matt might have been better off if I had lost custody.'

'Come on Joe, most people have problems of some sort bringing up kids. And it's even harder being a sole parent.'

'I still feel bad when I think about all my fuck-ups. What I've put him through.'

'Well, there's no point beating up on yourself over the past. At least you're getting your act together now.'

'Getting my act together. That's me, Seb. That's all I ever seem to be trying to do. Getting my fucking act together.'

Joe sat there in silence, his fingers across his face. When he spoke, his voice was gentle and loaded with emotion.

'How do you do it, Seb? You're so together. You don't have a major drama every second day. What's your secret?'

'Me, together? You must be kidding. I've been shot at on a golf course, run off the road while riding my bike by some maniac who is trying to shoot me, and my wife has pissed off to Cairns with my daughter and won't even talk to me. Yeah… I've got it all together, really together,' said Sebastian, with an uncomfortable, self-deprecating laugh laced with despair.

'Astrid has pissed off? You didn't tell me! I thought she was just away on a holiday.'

'I thought Kate would have told you about it.'

Joe grimaced. 'Ah... Kate… I've been meaning to tell you about that.'

Joe's phone sounded and he moved away from Sebastian to take the call. Sebastian went back inside. He still hadn't heard a word from Astrid and right now he missed her more than ever.

After three attempts, he realised she wasn't going to answer his call. He felt the urge to take the bull by the horns, no longer content to just let things drift along. The worst thing that could happen was that she'd hang up. He made a call to Laura's house phone in Cairns. His heart skipped a beat when Jenna picked up.

'Hi sweetie. It's Dad here.'

'Dad… how are you going? Miss you heaps.'

'I miss you too, Jenna. Things ok?'

'Yeah, fine. It's really cool up here. I'm having a fantastic time. Going diving tomorrow out on the Reef. Aunt Laura knows these people with a boat.'

'You be careful won't you,' replied Sebastian, glad for his daughter, but more than a little despondent that he wasn't there with her.

'Dad, there's a band up here that wants me to play violin with them,' she said, enthusiastically.

'But you play viola.'

'Yeah, but I still remember how to play violin. They got hold of an electric violin for me. I played along with their CD, and they loved it. I used some of those things you showed me… flattened notes, ninths and sixths and all that.'

'That's great, Jen. Is Mum there?'

'Yep… do you want me to get her?'

'Yeah, thanks Jen. I'll be in touch again soon.'

'Ok, love you Dad.'

Sebastian was left with, if not a sense of redundancy, then a glimpse of its impending certainty. Dad was no longer required, at least not in the way he had been. It wasn't just a matter of geography. Dad's little girl was growing up and spreading her wings.

'Hello, Astrid. How's the holiday going?'

'Holiday... who said anything about a holiday?'

'We need to talk, Astrid.'

'About what?'

'Us.'

'Us? There is no us, Seb.'

'Oh, come on, Astrid!'

'Let's talk about you. And what a dishonest man you've proven to be. And the total disrespect you've shown me.'

'I'm really sorry about that. Did you get the parcel I posted?'

'Words, Sebastian, just words. You can say anything with words.'

'Will you please come home, Astrid?'

'Why?'

'You have your job, and Jenna has school. And I need you.'

'I can get work anywhere. There's plenty of work for physios all around the world. And guess what? There are schools everywhere as well.' Astrid's tone changed. 'You've not needed me for a long time now, Seb.'

'I'll change, Astrid. It was one indiscretion. I am sorry.'

'You call it one indiscretion. But it's more than that.'

'What do you mean?'

'This has been coming for a while.'

'Astrid, please... come home. I've been doing a lot of soul-searching.'

'And so have I. The truth is, Sebastian, we have been distant from each other for a long time.'

'I've been in a rut. It's because of work.'

'Ha... that's a laugh, Sebastian. Have you ever wondered how long we would have stayed together if Jenna hadn't come along?'

'It wouldn't have made a difference. We were in love.'

'What if I had insisted on staying in Holland?'

'I would have stayed as well. It would have been an adventure. Still would be.'

'In love, an adventure. What do these words mean to you? I'm sorry to disappoint you, Sebastian, but you are not the free-spirited man I fell in love with all those years ago.'

'But you admit it, then… about being in love.'

'Sebastian, I'm not having you twist what I say. You seem to think this is a debate to be won.'

'I'm trying to get you to open up your heart. There must be some way I can make it up to you.'

'You want to make it up to me?'

'Yes!'

'I'll tell you how you can make it up to me, Sebastian. What is the name of the place you took me to in Sydney last year? The place where we had fish and chips and people jump off the cliff?'

'Oh, Watson's Bay, The Gap.'

'That's the place. This is how you can make it up to me. You can go to Watson's Bay and jump off The Gap.'

'Astrid, Astrid,' he pleaded, but she'd hung up.

Jenna had stayed by the phone, eavesdropping.

'Mum... why don't you at least try to reconcile things with him?'

Astrid shook her head violently. 'No, Jenna. I'm not a fool.'

'You say that I'm stubborn,' retorted Jenna with filial arrogance.'

'Jenna… you don't understand. Your father has lied and cheated on me.'

'I've seen enough to know that all relationships go through difficult times. You always told me that people make mistakes and that it was important to forgive,' said Jenna, sounding like an expert on the matter of conjugal betrayals.

'It is not always that simple, Jenna.'

'I thought that Dutch people were supposed to be liberal.'

'Jenna... we had an understanding. I gave up a lot to come out and live here in Australia.'

'Come on, Mum. You told me once you were happy to escape the clutches of your family. And besides, it's not as if Dad doesn't want to be with you.'

Astrid sounded uncharacteristically bitter.

'It's about self-preservation Jenna. You can't let people walk all over you. He rejected me.'

Jenna continued to throw light into the shadows, to shake her mother's cerebral bulwarks. She was the best advocate that Sebastian could have hoped for, and Astrid listened to her daughter, her eyes welling.

Jenna's sagacity had caught her by surprise.

It was late when Sebastian got to bed. He'd been in tears after talking with Astrid, and wished he'd not made the phone call. That night he felt as lost and lonely as he'd ever been. Sleeping on a mattress in the room where he'd slept as a kid, in his half-awake state he began to dream.

The boy is frightened and alone, and the wolf is closing in. He screams out, losing control and wetting his bed. The boy gets up and goes inside to tell his mum. She brings out new sheets and they change the bed. She is still out there when his father gets home.

'Please don't tell Dad,' he pleads.

She doesn't. His father comes out.

'Can I sleep inside, Dad? Please, just tonight.

His mother looks at his father. 'No... he's far too old for that.'

They have no inkling of his terror. His father calls him a sook. They both leave.

He's all alone, sobbing. Soon it's a muffled pathetic whimper, vacillating between fear and humiliation.

21

The Unit

Deon was eating breakfast and Kate had already left the house by the time Sebastian got up. Joe still hadn't heard from Matt.

'I'm not overly worried, Seb. Matt's probably crashed at a mate's. It's not the first time he's pissed off after a disagreement. I reckon he'll come to his senses and show up today or tomorrow.'

Sebastian checked his emails and there was a message from Lorraine in his inbox. She'd sent him an attachment from *The Maitland Mercury*. One of the policemen, or someone at the meeting, must have leaked the story to the paper.

Ostensibly, the article was about moral issues in the community but, in reality, it attempted to cash in on the sex angle. Frances Morten was described as a youth worker (untrue) and daughter of the famous artist, Andrew Morten. She was a person of interest, in a "bizarre sex tangle". Not many details were provided. A house in Maitland was mentioned but no address was given. A woman, who purported to be a neighbour of Frances, reported seeing naked men and women making out in the backyard.

That was a real possibility, knowing Frances, thought Sebastian.

Sebastian was thankful there was no mention of the Youth Centre, or himself for that matter. The picture of Frances as a child, painted by her twisted father, had him wondering what she would have been like with a more normal upbringing. He soon found himself reminiscing and feeling sympathy for Frances, but then quickly reminded himself of her contribution to his estranged relationship with Astrid. Whatever she might have had the potential to be, here and now she was nasty and dangerous.

He switched his attention to another story on the same page, reading it out aloud to distract his own mind from Frances and to entertain Deon who was sitting nearby.

'Hey Deon… listen to this. It's from *The Maitland Mercury*. Lorraine sent it to me. The story is titled, The Who Dun It That Mesmerised a City. It happened at Blackbutt Reserve. Remember Blackbutt?'

'Yeah, Whitearse. Course I remember.'

'A diamond python named Fluffy was stolen from one of the displays. The situation worsened when Fluffy's male partner, Jaws, couldn't assist the police. Get this – the only other witnesses were night owls who, according to the reporter, couldn't give a hoot.'

Deon's raucous laughter filled the room. Throughout the morning, Deon hadn't shown the slightest sign of nerves. This had surprised Sebastian. He'd expected Deon to be nervous in the hours leading up to a performance at The Sydney Opera House. He knew he would be.

Sebastian checked *The Newcastle Herald* and saw there was a short story on a shooting at Charlestown that police were investigating. No address was given.

Joe wasn't his usual chirpy self. With Bates and McDonald on the loose, and despite his upbeat analysis of the situation, Joe was concerned about Matt's welfare. When Sebastian saw Joe coming in from the yard after taking a phone call, and grinning from ear to ear, he thought that Joe had been talking with Matt.

'You won't fucking believe this, Seb! Get this – Steve Wiseman listened to the recording session we did with Billy, and he's stoked. Says he wants to release two of them as singles. Has offered us a fifty-fifty deal.'

'What's that mean?'

'We split the profits, after he recoups his recording costs.'

'Really?'

'He likes the name Moving Targets that Matt came up with. You happy with that?'

'I'm hopeless on names. Just go with it, Joe. Wiseman seems to know what he is doing. Which two songs does he want to release?'

'He didn't say, but there's something else, Seb. He's asked if we have enough material to do a three-hour gig. Wiseman said he was desperate for a duo.'

'Are you serious?'

'Serious, Seb.'

'What did you say?'

'I said I'd talk to you and get back to him.'

'It's a four-week residency. With the possibility of fucking well extending it! But here's the funny part. Guess where?'

'Come on, Joe. Just tell me.'

'In some ritzy resort in Cairns.'

'You are kidding me! That's where Astrid and Jenna are.'

'I know. It's fate, Sebastian. Fucking fate. I can't believe it. But here's the problem. He wants us to start next week. The duo he had booked has apparently been involved in a serious car accident and has had to cancel. Wiseman wants an answer on both matters as soon as possible.'

Sebastian really wanted to do the gig. It was obvious that Joe did, too. The recording deal was a foregone conclusion.

'What the heck!' said Sebastian. 'I'll take leave from work. Say yes Joe, on both counts.'

And so, Joe did. The more they thought about the Cairns gig, the more they realised it was a great opportunity, and it set their minds racing. Could they get their act together in time? Neither was prepared to say no. Deon took Charlie for a walk while Sebastian and Joe got stuck into a long and intense practice session. There was a lot to do, but an excellent reason to do it. They became more efficient now, agreeing on arrangements quickly. There was little time to waste. Both were in buoyant spirits as they discussed the logistics of getting up to Cairns in a week. Was it even possible?

Sebastian and Joe kept working on material until it was time for Sebastian to drive Deon to The Opera House.

Twenty minutes later, Sebastian and Deon were travelling along Elizabeth Street towards Circular Quay. Deon's eyes darted around the city. He'd only been in town once before, catching the ferry across to Taronga Zoo as part of a school excursion. Moments later, they turned into Macquarie Street and found the parking station that Sebastian had booked online.

Walking down to The Opera House, Deon was taken aback by the high-rise apartments.

'Why would anybody want to live in 'em?'

Deon was grinning from ear to ear as Sebastian wished him luck before the two parted company at the backstage entrance. With over an hour to kill before the show started, Sebastian decided to go for a wander. In the distance, the cars and trucks looked like mice scurrying across a mantelpiece, as they made their way along the Cahill Expressway. This part of the city was a tourist hotspot and there were people by the water's edge, taking snapshots of the iconic grey arch of steel spanning the harbour. A Dixieland jazz band was welcoming patrons aboard a brightly lit showboat for an afternoon cruise. Up ahead, the sandstone steps leading down from the Botanical Gardens jutted out like an apparition, an anachronism, absurdly out of place amongst the nondescript cafés and tourist shops.

Sebastian paused to read the words of Robert Louis Stephenson engraved on a plaque attached to the walkway – *There is material for a dozen buccaneering stories to be picked up in the hotels around Circular Quay.* He decided to heed the advice. A large group had formed around one of the buskers strutting his stuff along the waterfront. After tossing a few coins to a duo playing banjo and mouth harp, he continued on past the wharves and into the heart of The Rocks area.

After browsing through a few tourist shops, he turned down Kendall Lane and made his way to the Orient Hotel. He'd played at the hotel with Joe a few times years ago, and the place held pleasant memories.

While waiting for his drink, Sebastian watched a quality singer-guitarist perform in a corner of the bar. He applauded at the end of the song – the only person to do so. The other patrons seemed indifferent to the music. Sebastian speculated as to whether audiences were harder to please these days. It gave him a thrill to think that he and Joe would be playing together again. And that Wiseman was pleased with the recordings. Just when he'd almost given up on music, two great opportunities had come along, thanks to Joe. He wondered how Astrid would react to him lobbing in Cairns. If he could see her in person, maybe he would be able to convince her to give him another chance.

He went out into the beer garden and found a table. A tour group was soaking up the atmosphere, studying the large sandstone blocks that had been used to construct The Coach House and Unwin's Store. When the guide turned and pointed, the group swarmed with her, moving close to where Sebastian was sitting. He listened to the commentary.

'Just up the road is Essex Street. It used to be called Gallows Hill. Back in the early days of the colony, crowds of people would gather there to watch public hangings.'

'Did they hang women as well?' asked a woman with an American accent, who appeared to be advocating equal execution rights for females.

The guide was not sure about that one, however she did have another interesting fact to offer. 'For many years, males in the colony outnumbered the females four to one.'

'That's why Australians drink a lot of beer… yes?' joked a man with a strong European accent.

Sebastian downed his beer and got another. Just sip it, he told himself. Forty minutes later he left the hotel and strolled back towards The Opera House. There were more people on the move and the ferry terminals were busy.

He reached The Opera House steps and followed the groups of mostly First Nations people into the concert hall. It was an awesome sight. He'd only been inside once before, and that was when Johnno had given him a ticket to a concert featuring one of his compositions. The use of brush box and birch timbers had given the space a rich organic feel. Enhanced by overhead lights, the high, arched ceilings created a regal ambience, along with the massive pipes of a grand Baroque pipe organ that stood in the shadows like an esteemed observer. As Deon had promised, his seat was in a perfect position, right in the centre of the hall.

The auditorium was filling quickly as more and more people streamed through the entrances. If the place names embroiled on the jackets were any indication, some in the audience had travelled from the far reaches of the state. Directly in front of Sebastian was a group from Wilcannia. An announcement made from the stage microphone was met with displeasure. The group from Brewarrina had pulled out due to a bus breakdown. That would be disappointing for Deon, who had been looking forward to catching up with some of his relatives.

After the traditional welcome and a bit of fiddling with the sound, the concert got underway. Some performances combined Indigenous themes with modern dance. The younger ones came on first with a group of girls from Narrabri pulling off some amazing acrobatic feats. A group of primary students from out west danced as an array of animals with backing from a didgeridoo player.

When the big moment came and Deon swaggered up to the microphone to introduce his troupe, Sebastian felt goosebumps up and down his spine. The lights dimmed and Deon smiled at the audience for the briefest of moments before his demeanour changed to warrior mode. His voice burst through the speakers and a powerful hypnotic chant filled the space. The stage sprung to life with a wash of red and yellow light. One spot remained fixed on Deon while another followed the dancers as they entered from the side. Lights flashed, and photographers who had been lurking in the shadows scurried to the front anticipating something special.

Their traditional song and dance had the audience mesmerised. Two elders sitting across from Sebastian were overwhelmed by the moment, tears welling in their eyes.

They finished their set with an original rap number, and from the admiration bestowed on the group by the younger members of the audience, one would have thought that a famous rock group had just been on stage. At the completion of the song, Deon and his mates received a standing ovation.

For Sebastian, the occasion was pure magic. He had been more than impressed watching the boys perform at Maitland Town Hall. Here, at The Opera House, the quality and size of the sound system, combined with the professional lighting display, lifted their act to another level. Sebastian was perplexed. How was it that this group of five boys, all of whom had been unsuccessful academically at school, could put on such an outstanding performance and become so artistically accomplished in such a short period of time?

After the show, Sebastian waited on The Opera House steps for Deon to come out. When he did, he was still painted up and wearing shorts and a T-Shirt. High on adrenalin after the performance, and with sweat dripping off his body, he was a surreal sight. The white ochre handprints imprinted on his body seemed to take on a spirit of their own dancing in the afternoon light. Eyes darting ahead, Deon became the inquisitive wallaby he had conjured up earlier as he searched the crowd for Sebastian. As he descended the steps, tourists along the harbour foreshore looked on in anticipation, thinking they were about to witness a historical re-enactment. Deon was grinning from ear to ear, pleased with himself, enjoying the afterglow of success.

'That was fantastic, Deon!' exclaimed Sebastian, giving Deon a congratulatory slap across the shoulders.

'Be on TV tomorrow. They were all there… eh… the papers, too. SBS said they want to do a program on us.'

'Good on you, mate. You slayed them. It was brilliant.'

'Hey… was funny before we started. The other groups and some of the officials backstage were lookin' for a didge. Couldn't believe we didn't use one. We had to explain to them that the traditional dances we did never used one.'

They walked back to the parking station and got into the car

'You're still sweating, mate. Put something on or you'll catch a cold. There's a jumper in the back there.'

'Nah… I'll be right.'

Deon felt good, just the way he was.

Back at Napier Street, Joe was playing music and enjoying the solitude, when there was a knock at the door. Matt hadn't taken his key, and Joe had thought it was his son returning home. He opened the door to see Matt's friend, Gavin, standing there. His agitated countenance gave Joe reason for concern.

'Joe... I think Matt's in trouble.'

'What sort of trouble?'

'I left him at the Malabar shops, and he was walking back to Napier Street when this van pulled up behind him.'

'Was it white?'

'Yes... how did you know?'

'It doesn't matter, go on.'

'Well, at first I thought they were mates of his, but then this bloke pushed him into the back of the van and slammed the door shut. He had a look about then hopped into the passenger seat and the van zoomed off. I've been trying to phone Matt but he's not picking up.'

Joe was on his feet. After three unsuccessful attempts at contacting Matt, he rang Sophia. As he switched off his amp and PA, he told Sophia what Gavin had just told him. He left the house minutes later, dropping Gavin off at Maroubra Junction before hightailing it over to Sophia's place. He kept trying to contact Matt along the way but was unsuccessful.

Joe arrived at Bondi to find Sophia on the front veranda in the middle of a phone conversation that didn't seem to be going too well. The longer the conversation went on, the more anguished and frustrated she became. Sophia was sweating profusely when the call ended abruptly.

'Fucking Damien. I can't believe he's my son sometimes!'

'What did he say?'

'Nothing that was helpful... just his usual abruptness and rudeness... thinks he's the bloody ant's pants because he works for Uncle Paul. I'm sure Paul only puts up with him as a favour to me. Damien doesn't tell me anything anymore.'

It wasn't all bad news, though. Sophia had managed to contact Stan, an old family friend of hers. She told him about Matt's abduction and the likely abductors. He'd gotten back to her half an hour later. There was a unit up the Cross that was leased to William Bates. Stan didn't know the address, but he'd try to find out. Word around town was that it was used by Bates for parties. According to Stan, and Sophia assured Joe he was credible, it was the most likely place that Bates and McDonald would have taken Matt.

'Souriss must know about this unit at the Cross.'

'Uncle George… what would he know?'

'You did talk to him.'

'Yes, I spoke to him earlier… but he didn't say much.'

'He does know that Matt's a relative?'

'Yes, of course he does.'

'Can I have his number?'

She gazed back at Joe. 'He won't talk to you, Joe.'

'Soph!' Joe barked.

'Ok, I'll try him again. But sometimes he's impossible to get through to.'

Sophia entered a number manually and put the phone up to her ear. 'See,' she said, handing the phone to Joe.

The recorded voice said that the number was temporarily unavailable. Joe looked at Sophia with scepticism.

'Come on Soph!'

'I don't want Souriss involved. People will get hurt.'

He knew she genuinely cared for Matt's wellbeing, but he also had the feeling Sophia had her own agenda.

'Give me some time, Joe. I'll try a few other avenues.'

Joe was snarly. 'Time? For fuck's sake, there is no time! We've got to do something, now.'

'Joe, we'll find him… he's my son too, you know.'

Joe rang Deon's number on the off-chance that Matt had made contact. He also wanted to fill Sebastian in on what he'd found out.

Deon turned on his speaker so Sebastian could listen to the conversation. When Joe told them Matt was in trouble, Deon was really concerned and confused. Then he realised that Joe didn't know he and Matt had followed the white van out to Little Bay.

At that moment he felt like he'd let everyone down. He knew, for Matt's benefit, he had to spill the beans. He told them everything that had happened, from seeing the van by chance at the Malabar shops, to Matt breaking into the house, finding the gun under McDonald's bed and stealing the dosh.

Joe was surprisingly calm. He was grateful that Deon remembered the address of the Little Bay house and could verify the registration plates of the white van. After a short discussion, they decided to meet back at Napier Street.

Sebastian had listened on in astonishment as Deon revealed his and Matt's escapade. After the call ended, he was speechless and could only shake his head. He cast a scathing look in Deon's direction.

'You are fucking kidding me! You are unbelievable, Deon. I really don't know whether to laugh or cry. You've only just got out of lock-up for chrissake and you go breaking into a house. You still have to go to court, you know. How do you think it will look if you are charged with break and enter?'

'Sorry, Seb... but Matt was gunna go into the place anyway. I couldn't just let him do it alone.'

'So, if Matt jumped off a cliff, you would too? I thought you were a leader.'

Sebastian drove back to Napier Street angry and anxious, trying to make sense of it all. He wondered whether Bates and McDonald were linked to his woes. Was he involved because he had been seen with Joe and Matt? Or did his problems stem from knowing Frances, as Lorraine and he had assumed. And who was the third person? His thoughts were confused, and it occurred to him that Bates might have been the one who had run him off the road in the four-wheel-drive and who had shot at him outside his house in Newcastle. He brought it up with Deon, who assured him that was not the case.

Kate was in the yard playing with Charlie when they arrived back at the house. Charlie performed what was now her standard airborne greeting on seeing Sebastian and Deon.

'I thought you'd be at work,' said Sebastian

'Joe told me what had happened to Matt, so I left early.'

It wasn't long until Joe pulled up outside. He was in a real state. The earlier calm he had displayed talking to Deon had vanished. He'd already been out to the Little Bay house and there was nobody there. Deon told them Matt had taken photos of the two from ones they'd found in the house. They ransacked Matt's room on the off-chance he'd downloaded them, but to no avail. Deon was able, however, to give them a description of Bates and McDonald.

Joe was abrupt. 'Goin' out to Little Bay, again. I wanna check out that house properly. Go inside and see what's there.'

'I'll come too if you like,' said Deon. 'I know how to get in.'

'You are kidding, Deon. No way,' said Sebastian.

'I'll be right,' said Joe. 'Be best if you two go up to the Cross. See if you can spot that white van. We can meet at the fountain later. I'll ring you if I find out anything we don't know.'

Deon told Joe about the back window Matt had prized open to gain entry into the house. Sebastian wanted Kate to wait at Napier Street, in case Matt came back. His real motive was to keep his sister out of harm's way. Kate wouldn't obey. She got annoyed with Sebastian for even suggesting it. Old tensions resurfaced.

'The same sort of thing Mum used to try and do. Wrap me up in cottonwool. Why don't *you* stay behind, Sebastian?'

When they attempted to lock the dog in the backyard, Charlie, as if inspired by Kate's defiance, just wouldn't cop it. According to the neighbour, Charlie had been barking relentlessly all day. Kate wanted to take the dog. Sebastian wanted it left behind. Joe's temper flared as brother and sister bickered.

'For fuck's sake! Does it really matter?'

Sebastian capitulated, and Charlie grasped the opportunity, scurrying towards the side gate as though she'd understood what they'd been discussing.

Joe and Kate drove out to Little Bay with Charlie nestled snugly at Kate's feet. Kate brought up a matter that had been playing on her mind since Joe told her the news.

'So, Joe… you took that Cairns gig?'

'It's a great opportunity.' Joe glanced across at Kate. 'Did you expect me to knock it back?'

'No… of course I didn't expect you to knock it back. It's just the way you've been speaking, it sounds as though you'd like to stay up there long-term.'

'Shit, Kate… the offer just came out of the blue. With Matt missing and all, I've got no idea what will happen. I don't even know what Seb will do, really.'

'What Seb will do? You're actually more concerned about Sebastian. Don't worry about me… about what I think.'

'Jees, Kate… is this the time for this? Who knows how it will turn out?'

Kate spoke softly, with melancholy in her voice. 'Yeah Joe, who knows?'

Joe did try to smooth things over, but Kate had been hurt. She felt a sense of abandonment. She had become more attached to Joe than she realised. And with Sebastian leaving as well…

When they arrived at the house there was no sign of the white van. After parking the car, the two stepped out onto the street with the energetic Charlie pulling on the lead. Joe was innocuously dressed in T-shirt and jeans, while Kate still had on her grey work blouse and white top. It was dog-walking time in suburbia, and they melted into the surrounds perfectly. The smell of coriander and peanut sauce drifted into the street from a nearby house, whetting the appetites of both Joe and Kate. Neither had eaten much since Matt had been abducted.

Approaching the house, they came upon an elderly gentleman in shorts, digging bindies out of his lawn. Like many of his generation, his sun-blotched face bore the effects of too many days spent outdoors in the Aussie sun. Charlie behaved like a trained circus performer, gushing up to the man. Kate told him they were looking for an old friend who used to live in the house two doors down. While Kate stood cockatoo and engaged the man in friendly chitchat, Joe continued on to the house, opening the side gate and walking through to the yard. He checked to ensure he wasn't being watched by anyone from the adjoining dwellings before prising open the laundry window with a screwdriver, as Deon had suggested, and sliding his body through the narrow opening.

After quickly scanning the place to ensure nobody was hiding or asleep in one of the rooms, Joe went back to what he deemed to be McDonald's bedroom. When he looked under the bed, the rifle that Deon had told him Matt had found was gone. This caused him further distress. He went back to the kitchen and ripped open the mail that was on the kitchen table, desperately hoping to find some reference to the Darlinghurst unit. It was wishful thinking really, but at least he came across a letter from a real-estate agent confirming that William Bates and Sandra McDonald actually lived at the Little Bay address. That was some consolation. He went back into the lounge room and soon found the photos Deon had spoken of. He quickly took a few shots with his phone.

In a flat up at Kings Cross, William Bates and Sandra McDonald were laying low. Matt was lying prostrate on a dirty mattress in the corner of the room. His hands and feet were tightly bound, and black gaffer tape covered his mouth. His attempts to wiggle loose proved futile. Wild Bill might not have been a great intellect, but he knew how to tie a knot. Bates cowardly kicked out at Matt as he passed him on his way to the bathroom.

'Leave the kid alone,' yelled Sandra.

It wasn't that she cared about the prisoner. If the decision was made to bury him in the bush, she wouldn't lose too much sleep over it. But she had spent a lot of time with Bates lately, and he was getting on her nerves. It had reached the point where practically everything he said and did antagonised her.

After initially feeling pleased with themselves for successfully pulling off the abduction, they now had a problem. They still didn't know where their money was, and they needed to find out before the boss arrived. The boss wasn't the type of man one wanted to disappoint. The two had given up interrogating Matt for the time being. The problem was that when they removed the gaffer tape, he screamed at the top of his lungs. Normally they would have bashed the information out of the prisoner, but they were under strict orders from the boss to just guard him until he arrived. Sandra had her own ideas on what was required to get Matt to talk, but she needed to get rid of Bill for a while.

'Hey Bill, will you go to the shop and get me some durries. I've run out.'

'But there's still half a packet left, love.'

It made her blood curdle when he called her love. She knew he did it deliberately to annoy her. She felt like kicking him, but she needed him to comply with her wishes.

'I need something to eat as well, Bill. Get me a burger and chips while you're at it.'

'But Sandra, we were told to get everything before coming in. We can't be seen all over the fucking Cross.'

'You're paranoid. Do you know that? Go by the backstreets. Nobody will notice you.' She ushered him towards the door.

Bill rarely got much action from Sandra these days. Not like when they first met, when she'd given him head jobs and they'd fucked nearly every night. What he particularly liked about this type of assignment was the effect it had on her. The violence and danger were an aphrodisiac for her, so there was a good chance she'd be up for it tonight.

Sandra knew her sexuality was currency. She also knew she would dump Bill tomorrow if a better offer came along. Hopefully it soon would. Although the boss was a few years younger than her, she had noticed his lascivious eyes undressing her of late. And she would be more than happy to accommodate him. It was sexy, the way he oozed confidence and power. And how had he described her only last week? The kind of girl a bloke could easily fall for. She wouldn't think twice about jumping ship and hooking up with him if the opportunity came her way. Still, she wasn't stupid. In this business, a bloke was necessary. Even a bloke like Bill. For the time being.

After checking the mailbox on his way out, Bill legged it up towards Darlinghurst Road for food and fags. He fitted in perfectly around the Cross, just one of many sleazy denizens most people tried to avoid. With his head slightly downcast and his eyes peering myopically ahead, Bill was hardly noticeable. Although it was not evident from his morose exterior, he was feeling happy with himself. He was thinking about how his luck had recently changed for the better. Fancy having access to a unit at the Cross that he could use for parties without having to pay one cent of the rent. It wasn't as though he didn't deserve it. He had paid his dues, and now he was being treated with respect. They wouldn't ask you to be the lessee of a unit at the Cross unless you were trusted by the big wigs of the organisation. All the years of hard work were beginning to pay off. That was how Bill saw it.

Back at the unit, Sandra had waited until Bill was safely out of the way. Then she propped Matt up in the corner and braced her body provocatively, giving Matt a clear view of her breasts. Resting one hand on Matt's thigh, she proceeded to traduce Bill in an attempt to win Matt's trust. The groundwork complete, she motioned for him to remain quiet as she removed the gaffer tape fastened to his mouth. This time Matt did as she asked. His eyes darted around the room. He'd heard the door close, but needed to know for certain that Bill was gone. He knew this might be the only opportunity to escape he was going to get.

Sandra started on her version of sweet talk, praising his pale skin and taut body while lifting his T shirt and running her fingers along his stomach.

'We could have some fun together, you and me. But first you need to tell me where the money is.'

Occasionally, with the hint of a smile on her face, her hand would wander lower, her eyes following in anticipation of a tumescent response.

Matt's thoughts were in overdrive. He played along, but at the same time was under no illusion of what wild Bill's reaction would be, and who he would take it out on, if he came back unexpectedly and saw what was going on.

'You are the quiet one, Mattie. And you seem to have lost your tongue. Is the money you stole in the house out at Malabar?'

When Matt still didn't reply, Sandra acted as though his silence was confirmation of her hunch.

'Ha… it is, isn't it?'

Matt knew his reaction gave nothing away. But alarm bells were ringing. He didn't want McDonald or Bates going anywhere near the Malabar house. He had to think of something quickly.

'So, if I tell you… will you let me go?'

'Yeah… sure… of course. Why else would we be keeping you? So, where is the money?'

Matt didn't believe her for a second. He could only imagine what she and Bill were likely to do to him once they got their money back. If he could get his hands free, he would overpower Sandra and be out of the place in seconds. 'It's buried in a park, near Maroubra beach.'

'Which park is that, Mattie?' asked Sandra, putting her face so close to his their lips were almost touching.

'I don't know the name of the park, but the money's buried next to a tree near the road. If you untie my hands, I'll draw you a map.'

Sandra feigned delight. 'You'll draw me a map, will you? If I untie your hands, is that what you'll do?'

Sandra had spoken in such a meretriciously sweet fashion, that when she drew back onto her haunches, Matt actually thought she was going to oblige by getting him a pen and paper. But the fury in her wild green eyes told a different story. She raised her hand and slapped him solidly across the face. The power of the strike sent his body reeling and his head whacked into the wall.

'Don't fuck with me. This is your last chance.'

Her emollient tone was unnerving. After he'd recovered from the sudden blow, he gazed straight back at Sandra, tying to stay strong, daring her to hit him again. Sandra would have probably obliged but her ears pricked up and her attention was diverted elsewhere.

Someone was unlocking the door. Sandra moved with efficiency, replacing the gaffer tape and pushing her prisoner flat to the ground. She quickly adjusted her clothes and tidied herself up.

At first Sandra thought it was Bill. He was always forgetting his wallet. But when she glanced down the hallway, she was shocked to see it was The Boss. He had come early.

The Boss cast an angry gaze around the room as Sandra ambled down the hall to greet him. Wearing designer jeans, a navy shirt and a brown leather jacket, his dilated pupils were a giveaway. He was on something strong and, from his bellicose mannerisms, appeared to be on a very short fuse. The Boss's aggressive vibe didn't seem to bother Sandra. She was more concerned with her own raddled complexion.

'Where is the bastard?'

'He's in the lounge room, tied up. He still hasn't told us what he did with the money.'

The Boss couldn't have cared less about the five grand. That was their problem. But he had a good idea where he might find it. He thought back to the false floorboards and Joe's strange habit of digging holes in the backyard at night. Joe would have quite a stash of cash and valuables by now.

'I thought Bill would be here. Where the fuck is he?'

'He went out to get some food and a packet of durries.'

The Boss growled. He wasn't happy.

'I told Bill not to go,' said Sandra, enjoying distorting the truth, and relishing the chance to cast Bill in a bad light.

The Boss stepped up close to Sandra and pressed his mouth firmly against her lips. Sandra responded with vigour, but just as she was getting into her stride, he pulled away.

'Not now,' he whispered. 'I really need to talk to little Mattie.'

Sandra wasn't disheartened. She knew what men were like. Now he'd had a taste, he'd be back for more.

The Boss turned and strode into the lounge room with a smug grin on his face. His plan had worked perfectly. The Boss was no musician, but he had played Sandra and Bill like a maestro, plucking the chords that resonated within their feckless natures.

When Matt got a glimpse of the man Bates and McDonald called The Boss, he could hardly believe his eyes.

Damien stood glowering at his half-brother with contempt.

'I knew when my stupid mother had been to see that solicitor something was going on. And then I heard her talking about her will and poor little Mattie.' He clenched his fist and banged it down hard on the table. 'How dare that bitch fuck with me! Nobody fucks with me. And as for you, ya little cunt... you don't deserve a fucking cent. Half the inheritance? That's outrageous. It's my fucking money.'

He reeled in his temper momentarily. 'So, Mattie, I couldn't believe my luck when you turned out to be the rogue dealer. You stupid idiot. Think you can walk in on someone else's territory and do as you please? But I should thank you for it, really. Do you believe in providence? I think it was meant to be. And who'd let a chance like that go by... eh? Be doing Uncle Paul proud. Protecting his turf. I could even be Big George's successor, if I play my cards right. I could sit on my fat arse and be the fucking big shot. And as for my mother, she won't be alive all that much longer. But she'll outlive you.'

Damien seemed to remember something that infuriated him. He kicked Matt before continuing. 'What has she ever done for me anyway? Couldn't even bring people home she was so off her face and such an embarrassment. According to the fucking quacks she should have died years ago. What has she got to fucking live for, anyway? Be doing her a favour, really.'

He had thought about knocking off his mother before. Now he was wishing he had followed through with the idea.

22

The Big Shot

In an exclusive businessman's club not far from the unfolding saga at the Cross, Paul Souriss was chatting to one of his lieutenants. He was conservatively attired and to an observer might be mistaken for an accountant or a bank manager. Not that the affable and respected South Maroubra Surf Club stalwart didn't have the common touch. Though it was also fair to say that few of his club buddies ever ventured into this establishment or onto his luxury cruiser docked at Darling Harbour.

Souriss was a perspicacious man, having displayed the rat cunning and ruthlessness to survive the vicissitudes of the underworld through turbulent years. These days he prospered on the power and respect that his wealth provided. Though not a student of classical business theory, his business model had a proven track record, and it included a few basic concepts: he didn't involve himself in grubby operations, he didn't suffer fools, and he demanded results.

Despite his vigorous workout schedule, Souriss still looked overweight. But he was strong, with a powerful upper body, and when he spoke his torso moved with the aggressive swagger of a rhino about to charge. And today, the more he heard, the more charged up he became. He'd planned to spend the day at home with a lady friend by the pool, not attending a crisis meeting.

'I pay people like you good money to avoid these situations. This fantasy crap, sex frolics and videos, tell me, Roberto, what are we running? A frigging circus? Ain't just having a good fuck enough anymore? What's happening to the world?'

His lieutenant interjected. 'There's good money in it, Paul. We do get excellent returns from our online assets.'

'Returns... for how long, eh... for how bloody long? Have you gone crazy too?' He threw his hands up in the air in frustration. 'Have I got a bunch of deviants working for me? Fold up this fuck-up incorporated. And these abductions, kidnappings. Now I hear it's a relative of mine that's been abducted by another. What the hell's happening? Cain and fucking Abel?'

'Damien runs his own race, George. You do him a favour, give him a good job. What does he do? He uses some phoney identity. He skims from the honey pot. And he has a voracious appetite for the drugs, that boy. I don't trust him, George. He's a loose cannon.'

Souriss turned towards his lieutenant, eyeballing him with his piercing, no-nonsense gaze. 'Well, for fuck's sake, Roberto... do something about it. Soon, real soon. You should have reeled him in long ago. And talk to Sophia. As for those two idiots taking pot shots on a golf course,' A touch of menace appeared in Souriss's voice. 'Drop 'em in Perth or fucking Bagdad. Somewhere far away from me. Can you do that for me?'

Roberto didn't like being dressed down by Souriss. He had a reputation for being reliable and effective. Dealing with Souriss's relatives, that was the problem from where he stood. Souriss had two sets of rules operating, one for the family and another for the rest.

Frances sat on the balcony of her father's Coogee beach apartment, gazing out over the pines adorning the picnic area and across to the gentle blue waters beyond. She was sipping on a vodka and orange. Frances didn't usually drink during the day, but events of the past few months were taking their toll.

Her father was in Greece, sweet-talking one of his rich benefactors who saw more worth in his licentious artworks that she did. Stupid fucking Andrew and his art. He was largely to blame for her present predicament. She hated every brushstroke of his with venom. What type of father uses his teenage daughter as a muse? If he hadn't put her on canvas, Damien wouldn't have seen the paintings and become obsessed with her.

When Damien told her she needed loving, she'd almost laughed in his face. What sort of idiot sleeps with a woman a couple of times then declares his everlasting love; a nut case like Damien. And clearly, that's what Damien was. She told herself she should have known better. It had been a big mistake to get involved with him in the first place. It wasn't as though she was unacquainted with narcissistic, rapacious men. That was standard fare for her from an early age. Protection meant controlling. Loving meant possessing, like she was a fancy watch or a luxury car.

Well, once she might have needed love, but no-one gave a flying fuck about her back then. Maybe her life would have been different if her mother hadn't died when she was a child. But the world was full of what ifs. She'd decided long ago that wondering what might be was a waste of energy. It had taken her years to understand how her father's neglect and abuse had affected her. At least it had taught her to be resilient and to stand strong.

There was no doubt that Damien was getting worse. He'd bashed a number of men she had been associated with and had graduated to stalking and shooting at them. Worse still, he was the reason she'd lost her fledging business that'd had the potential to make a small fortune. Now she was being investigated by the police. She had no intention of going down with him.

When he'd turned up at her door she'd given him a clear message, and the message was "not tonight". Did that stop him? He'd raped her, that's what he'd done. Sure, in the end she decided it was useless to resist, but while he was thrusting inside her she made a decision. He would get his just desserts. She'd been a victim before, and she swore back then it would never happen again.

The fool seemed to have no idea there was a tracking device on his car. It had made it easy to avoid him. He'd actually given her the idea, bragging about how he'd used one to check up on his mother.

And what sort of idiot rapes a woman, then afterwards brags about his get-rich-quick schemes? At the time she wondered whether he was suffering from drug induced psychosis. Not that it would get him off the hook. She doubted there was any truth in his assertion that there were hundreds of thousands of dollars buried in a backyard at Malabar.

Frances walked from the balcony through to her father's room, unlatched his wardrobe and pulled out the top drawer. Her father wasn't a total loss. His way of showing that he cared was to teach his daughter how to handle a handgun. He'd even taken her for a few practice sessions out in the bush near Katoomba. She searched and found the pistol in a holster hidden behind socks and underpants. The weapon was small but effective. Efficient from short range with a silencer attached. Beside the gun was a packet of bullets. She picked up the gun and held it in her hand, sighting a pretend target. As she pulled the trigger it gave her a thrill. A slight smile appeared on her face as she opened the packet of bullets and loaded the cartridge.

There were many people, most of them criminals, who had a grudge against Damien. Her name wouldn't even come up if the police were looking for suspects. Not that they'd be trying too hard. Not for a low-life like Damien.

Placing the gun in the holster, she strapped it, put on her brown leather jacket, and zipped it halfway up, high enough to hide the weapon.

Turning to her tracing app, she saw that Damien was at the Kings Cross flat. The next time he was on the move, she'd follow him, wait until he was alone, then shoot. He wouldn't even see it coming.

With the iconic Coke insignia beckoning from the top of the hill, Sebastian and Deon drove up William Street. They found a parking spot and headed towards the heart of the Cross. There was little available garaged parking in this part of the city, which hopefully would increase their chances of finding the van. They turned into Victoria Street and passed a line of grand old terrace houses with plants drooping from their balconies, producing a soothing canopy of verdant green. The massive trees lining the street provided excellent cover from the sun as they wound their way up towards the El Alamein fountain. Whenever they encountered a house with a driveway, Sebastian peered over the fence on the off-chance of finding the white van. Occasionally they'd split up, with one taking the laneway.

It was relatively quiet on the streets, the evanescent Kings Cross in afternoon snooze mode, resting up in preparation for the hectic night ahead. There were a few backpackers clustered in pockets around the takeaway food outlets. When they reached the fountain, they found an outdoor table at a café from where they could watch the main drag.

Deon went to the bathroom and washed most of the ochre from his face and arms. He'd need a shower to remove what remained, but that would have to wait. It mattered little in the present environment, where he didn't attract a second look.

Sebastian scanned the surrounds. The Cross told a tale of rags and riches. There was a group of dour-faced men in Gucci suits, and a colourful young bohemian couple. In the other direction was a homeless lady with her scant bundle of possessions. She was searching through the garbage bins nearby. Pigeons abounded, with the odd indolent seagull dropping in from the coast for the easy pickings.

Sebastian received a text from Kate, saying they were only ten minutes away.

While Joe was at the wheel and Charlie was curled up at her feet, Kate had been dialling and redialling Matt's number. Now and then she would pick up Joe's phone and attempt to contact Sophia.

'Why the fuck won't Sophia pick up?' Joe cursed.

Kate rubbed the nape of his neck. 'Joe… calm down. You won't think straight if you get all worked up.'

'Fuck, Kate. It's going to be like looking for a needle in a haystack trying to find those two fuckers at the Cross.'

Joe fluked a two-hour parking spot close to Darlinghurst Road. Before long, Joe and Kate, with Charlie in tow, arrived at the fountain. Kate had with her a Gregory's street directory and they set about the task of dividing up the area to be searched. Considering the dire circumstances, the group was reasonably upbeat. There was one problem, though. Sebastian's phone had just run out of change.

Joe couldn't resist having a dig. 'I can't believe you haven't charged your phone, Seb! We won't know where in the bloody hell you are.'

'Don't worry, Joe. I'll use a public phone if I need to contact you. I'm not proud.'

'A public phone? Is that a joke? Try finding one of those around here that works.'

Joe's phone sounded. He became excited when he saw it was a message from Sophia.

Meet me at the Strand Hotel... urgent... have info re Matt.

Joe rang her back immediately, but she didn't pick up. 'What the fuck is she playing at?' he said, grinding his teeth in frustration.

'The Strand's only just up the road,' said Sebastian. 'She might have important news.'

'Well, why doesn't she just fucking tell me?'

'Maybe she has somebody with her and can't say too much.' said Sebastian.

'You never like to say much on the phone, Joe,' Kate added.

Joe still didn't want to go, but eventually Sebastian and Kate convinced him they could manage without him. They agreed to meet back at the fountain in an hour.

After Joe left, the remaining three split up. Kate was more than happy to take Charlie with her.

Sebastian set off towards Bayswater Road and soon he was absorbed in the search. He passed two homeless people sitting on a park bench. There was graffiti scrawled on the wall adjoining the park. One line, in large red letters stood out –

The city has eyes.

As he strolled along, Sebastian thought about the large number of surveillance cameras he had seen mounted in proximity to the shops and apartments. And they were just the ones he had noticed. If they had access to all of that footage, the odds of finding Matt would be a lot better. This time he understood Joe's objection to involving the police. Both Matt and Deon would be in serious trouble if the truth came out.

He began to mull over the seriousness of the situation Matt was in. Bates and McDonald were dangerous and, as they already knew from the golf course shootings, they were in possession of a rifle they knew how to use. As did his assailant, and thinking about the man made Sebastian nervous. The attacks might have happened in Newcastle, but he needed to be on the lookout, not just for the white van but also for the four-wheel-drive with Queensland plates.

There was something else that was bothering him. There was the possibility Deon would be, or already had been, drawn into it. After all, he was with Matt when Matt broke into the Little Bay house and stole the money. And the man who shot at him in Newcastle had seen Deon and probably knew who he was.

Sebastian spotted a white van that he thought was a Toyota and became animated. He walked down the laneway where it was parked to have a closer look. He wasn't particularly skilled at identifying motor vehicles, but this time he was right. Unfortunately, the numberplates didn't match the van they were after. He thought back to what Deon had said about it being easy enough to change plates. Then he noticed it had a pest control logo on the side and back panels. Peering in through the rear window, Sebastian saw the chemicals and equipment that confirmed his suspicions.

Ten minutes later, he was considering the impossibility of the task they had set themselves when a man up ahead on the corner caught his attention.

He was the same height as Bates. Sebastian pulled out the photo from his pocket. The photo showed someone with much longer hair. Of course, it was easy enough to get a haircut. The suspect turned and spat in the gutter, giving Sebastian a clearer view of his face. There were definite similarities, so it was a lead worth sussing out. He waited until the man had crossed the road. Cautiously, he began to follow.

If this was Bates, then he sure was cocky. Only once did he check his surrounds, and that was just a casual glance across to the other side of the road. That suited Sebastian just fine, as he was paranoid about being seen. The man turned down a side street and went into a fast-food shop. Sebastian waited across the road, out of view.

Ten minutes later, the man came out carrying a bag of food. Sebastian didn't want to get too close, least the man see him, but now he had the food the man was walking away quickly. Sebastian had to hurry to keep up. By the time he'd reached the corner, the man was nowhere to be seen.

Sebastian was confounded. He couldn't have just vanished. It occurred to him that it was quiet around here at this time of day, once you were off the main drag. Sebastian tried to think logically. If the bloke had gone into a house or down a side gate, he would have surely heard a lock clanging or a door closing. Further along the street there were two blocks of home units, set back from the road. This had to be where the man had gone. Sebastian hurried along the street. As he approached the units, he heard a door close somewhere in the block. He had no idea just where. The entrances to both blocks were at the rear, so he followed the pathway adjacent to the driveway around to the back.

There was no sign of the man. He was about to go, when he caught a glimpse of a white vehicle partially concealed from view by a four-wheel-drive. At that moment he wondered whether he'd located both the vehicles they were after. Approaching the parking lot, he realised the four-wheel-drive was nothing like the one that had run him off the road in Newcastle. However, parked in the space near the entrance to the units on the left was the elusive white Toyota van. This van had the numberplates they were looking for! He stood there, momentarily stunned, not quite believing his luck. Now he had to locate the others as quickly as possible.

According to his calculations, if Kate kept to her planned route, she shouldn't be more than ten minutes away. He jogged up towards Darlinghurst Road and spotted his sister and Charlie in the distance. Kate rang Deon and explained the situation while Sebastian took care of Charlie. While they were waiting for Deon to arrive, Kate made several attempts to contact Joe. In the end, she sent him a text message, informing him of the address where Sebastian had located the white Toyota van. It wasn't long before the three of them were hastily making their way back to Sebastian's car. Charlie was intent on exploring her new environment, and Sebastian had to almost drag the dog along the footpath to keep pace with the other two.

When they arrived back at the car, there was a parking ticket attached to the windscreen of the Commodore. Sebastian was furious; he'd misread the parking regulations.

They drove back to the units, found a parking spot across the road, and decided the best plan of attack was to watch the place for a while. Joe would surely be in contact soon.

A few pedestrians strolled by. A middle-aged couple entered the building, confirming what they had suspected – a key was required to gain entry to the foyer. That wasn't a surprise in a neighbourhood notorious for junkies and break-ins.

They agreed that the best thing to do was to sit tight and wait until Joe arrived.

Kate tried contacting him again, but without success. 'Surely we'll hear from him soon. What the hell is he doing?'

Sebastian told them he wasn't sure which of the units Bates had gone into. Kate applied logic to the situation.

'Doesn't each unit have a designated parking spot? If that's the case, we can work out the unit the van belongs to from where it is parked.'

'That's if they parked in the proper spot, Sis,' said Deon.

Sebastian posed a question. 'Do they seem like the kind of people who would follow the rules?'

'If you don't want to be noticed, you follow the rules,' said Kate.

Deon agreed, but Sebastian wasn't so sure. Charlie began to get restless. Sebastian didn't want him doing his business in the car. There was a small reserve further on up the street, so he decided to take Charlie for a walk.

He had only just stepped away from the car when the door to the foyer opened and a figure appeared. Sebastian ducked for cover behind the vehicles parked in the street.

A woman puffing on a cigarette came out to the front of the block. She cast a desultory eye up and down the street before returning to the foyer. Sebastian didn't have to check the photo in his pocket to know this was Sandra McDonald. The woman tossed her cigarette butt into a nearby garden and propped open the foyer door with a brick. The man Sebastian had been following, and whom he now presumed was Bates, walked up beside her. The two began loading the van.

From Sebastian's position, he could see the entrance to the foyer and a few metres into the parking bay. But it was impossible to make out what they were carrying. From the furtive manner in which the two were going about their business, one got the impression they were doing something dodgy.

When Sebastian caught a glimpse of Bates and McDonald struggling to handle something wrapped in a tarpaulin that was both long and heavy, he was concerned. What, or more to the point, whom were they loading into the back of the van? Sebastian's guts heaved at the thought. Had they already killed Matt? Were they now in the process of dumping his body?

Soon afterwards, the bang of the van door being slammed shut reverberated throughout the space, shaking him from his reverie. His attention was drawn to a window of a ground floor unit, where he saw a curtain move. He didn't know what to make of the shadowy form, but it definitely wasn't McDonald or Bates, who were both in the parking bay.

McDonald was soon back in the frame again, removing the brick and closing the door to the foyer. There was a short lull, followed by the sound of a motor ticking over, and it was only a matter of seconds before the white van was chugging along the driveway.

23

Bundeena

Deon realised it a moment before Kate. The van was coming in their direction.

'Get down!' he screeched.

Kate could only do so much. She was in the passenger seat and the gearstick was preventing her from laying completely flat. She stayed still, watching Deon through the gap in the seats. She wondered what Bates and McDonald would make of him if they saw him. He was dressed in black football shorts and a yellow sports singlet, but it was the remnants of ochre that made him appear as though he was from another world. White stripes were still visible on his face and along his rib cage and limbs, giving him a ghostlike appearance. Crouched down low on the floor of the back seat, his eyes were watching through the window. In his hand was a long hunting stick, which he had grabbed from his bag; the tiger was ready to pounce.

Kate tensed as the vehicle passed within metres of the Commodore. McDonald was too preoccupied ticking off Bates for clipping the gutter to notice anything suspicious.

When the van was further down the street, and Kate felt it was safe to so, she stuck her head out the window, desperate to make contact with Sebastian. He was watching the van and edging his way back towards the car. His thoughts wavered. Should he follow the van or wait for Joe? Surely Joe would arrive shortly.

Deon was haranguing Kate to pursue the van pronto. All of a sudden, he sprung from the back seat of the Commodore and began making his way around the rear of the car. When Kate cottoned on that Deon was heading for the driver's side, she scrambled across from her seat, beating him to it. Deon then backtracked, settling for the passenger seat.

Kate started the motor, looked in the rear-view mirror and saw Sebastian motioning for them to go without him. He was thinking about the face he'd seen in the window of the downstairs unit.

Kate was soon heading down the street in pursuit. They turned onto William Street and Deon spotted Bates and McDonald up ahead.

'You got Joe's number, Deon?'

'Yeah.'

'Call him please.'

Deon did as Kate asked but Joe didn't pick up.

'Kate wondered what Joe was up to. He always answered his phone. Deon attempted to make contact a few more times, but to no avail.

'Can you ring Seb?'

Deon attempted to do so, but then remembered Sebastian's phone was out of charge. Kate let out a loud sigh.

'Joe will be there soon,' said Deon, reassuring her.

This was all new territory for Kate, and Deon was more than willing to apply on-the-job training.

'Right lane,' he called, and Kate indicated as she squeezed across.

Deon urged Kate to drive more aggressively.

'I don't want to get booked,' replied Kate. 'If the police pull us over, we'll lose them for sure.'

'Don't let them get too far ahead,' said Deon, aware that there were numerous side streets the van could take.

'If I get too close, they might see us.'

'Let me drive?'

'No way. You haven't even got a licence.'

The light ahead turned amber and Kate was about to stop.

'Gun it, Kate!'

Kate ran the light, feeling guilty as soon as she'd done it.

Running amber lights was obligatory, they'd decided, if they wanted to stay in contact with Bates and McDonald.

'Ring the police, Deon.'

'And say what?'

'Tell him we think these two have abducted someone.'

'We don't really know if Matt's in the boot. And if Matt's not in the boot, we'll look like absolute idiots and we'll have tipped off his abductors. Joe doesn't want the cops involved. For all we know, Joe might already have Matt.'

'Then why doesn't he answer his phone?'

'Might be out of charge.'

Unlikely, thought Kate. But Deon was right about one thing. Joe wouldn't want the police involved.

The dense city traffic made Kate's job difficult. After stopping and starting for what seemed like an eternity, they were both on edge. It was a welcome relief when the van pulled onto the Eastern Distributor and the traffic began to flow more steadily.

Now they were able to sit back and hide behind larger vehicles, observing Bates and McDonald from a safe distance. Eventually the van turned onto the Princes Highway. From there it continued south past Sutherland before taking a left turn at Farnell Avenue and entering the Royal National Park. They'd talked to Sebastian a number of times and there was still no news on Joe.

Kate's eyes glanced across at the waning sun where a few grey clouds had gathered on the horizon. The day was disappearing fast. A few vehicles already had their headlights on. She began to speculate.

'Maybe they're going to Bundeena or Maianbar.'

'Don't know those places, but there's plenty of bush out here, eh?'

As Kate concentrated on the road, Deon watched the van like a hawk. Now and then his head would dart from side to side to survey the surrounds as he wondered just what Bates and McDonald were up to.

They had been in the National Park for about five minutes or so when they hit a winding section of road and the gap between vehicles began to extend. There were now five vehicles between them and the van, and, with just one designated lane in each direction, it was impossible to overtake with any degree of safety. When they came out of the last turn and onto a straight section of road, they could see the other cars, but the van was no longer visible.

'Turn around.' Deon suggested.

Kate was hesitant. 'They might have sped off ahead.'

'Nah... no way. We'd have seen them. Pretty sure there was a road back there.'

Kate chucked a U-turn and drove back.

After negotiating the second bend, Deon indicated to the spot up ahead.

'Just up there, see?'

The track was barely visible amongst the low-hanging branches. Kate pulled the car over to the side of the road and stopped. They couldn't see the van but that told them little. The dirt road seemed to dip and turn through dense forest and, besides, Bates and McDonald had a couple of minutes start on them.

Kate was exhausted. It occurred to her that she'd barely eaten all day. She propped her arms against the steering wheel and closed her eyes in an attempt to fight off the migraine she could feel coming on.

Neither of them would say what they now both feared. Like Sebastian, they had both observed the van being loaded. Was the purpose of the journey to dispose of Matt's body in the bush?

Deon got out of the car, intent on finding out more. Kate watched on anxiously as Deon put his ear to the breeze and listened for the sound of the van's motor. He then surveyed the dirt road.

'There are fresh tyre tracks in the sand. Come on Kate, let's go,' said Deon pressingly as he hopped back into the car.

'It's too dangerous, Deon. Will you please ring triple 000 and tell the police we think someone has been abducted. And try Joe again. If everything was alright, he would have rung us by now. I had no idea we would end up this far out.'

Kate could tell from his shy countenance that something wasn't right. 'What's wrong, mate?'

'Better you talk to the cops. They won't listen to me.'

Kate glanced across at Deon. Surely, he can't be serious, she thought. But when she reflected on it, she realised she knew little of his situation. 'That's terrible,' she said, the comment sounding somewhat inadequate. But the thought of the police not coming to her aid in an emergency was not something she had ever needed to contemplate.

Kate opened her phone and an expression of annoyance registered on her face. 'Deon... there's no signal.'

'Same thing happens in the mountains,' said Deon, unaffected by the news.

'But I thought you could always get through to 000!' exclaimed Kate, shaking her head.

'Not if there's no tower to connect to.'

Come to think of it, Kate could remember experiencing the same problem around this area before. On that occasion she had been bushwalking near Wattamolla with a group of friends.

'We should go back to Sutherland so we can contact Joe and Seb. We can go to the police station there. Now that we know where they are, and we suspect they are up to no good, we can let the cops take over.'

Deon disagreed and his impatience began to show.

'No way... might be too late if we wait. The cops will fuck around for ages, askin' this and that. What if Matt is all tied up in the back? Why else would they be out in the bush?'

'We won't be of much use to him if we end up tied up as well,' replied Kate, a hint of nervous sarcasm in her tone.

She tapped her fingers on the steering wheel as she thought hard for a few seconds. Not one who usually acquiesced, Deon had her in a bind. She knew he felt partially responsible for Matt's predicament. She also knew that he had no intention of leaving his mate without attempting to rescue him. And maybe they did only have a short time frame in which to save Matt. Although Deon was young, and probably a bit too gung-ho for his own good, he seemed level-headed. She did feel safe with him and, the truth was, if she did refuse to go on, he would undoubtedly go it alone.

And of course, there was Joe and his attitude to the police to take into consideration.

Kate took a few deep breaths, started the motor and set off along the rough but passable dirt road. They had just turned a sharp corner when Deon indicated to Kate that he wanted her to stop.

'Hear that?' he whispered.

In the distance Kate could make out the steady throb of a motor.

'About half a kilometre away, I reckon. Keep going, just a bit further,' said Deon.

Kate found herself again questioning the wisdom of her decision. For the moment she would comply with the insistent Deon. Maybe it was because of Joe's influence, but she was behaving in a way that was foreign and inconsistent with her usual, more cautious character.

After crawling along for fifty metres or so, they came to a steep downhill section where the road had been partially eroded away. It looked barely passable to Kate, so she cut the engine again. The sound they had heard earlier was no longer audible.

'Hey… listen… the motor's stopped. They can't be too far away.'

'Deon, if we could hear them, they could have heard us.'

'You better turn the car around, then.'

Kate looked around to see how much space there was. As if inspired by Deon's fearless attitude, Kate shifted the car into gear and did a nifty three-point turn, leaving the vehicle facing the direction from which they had come. Her skillful manoeuvring drew accolades from Deon.

When Deon had asked her to turn the car around, Kate though he'd had a change of mind and decided it was best to drive back out. But when she began to go forward, he shouted at her.

'Stop!'

'What?' replied Kate, clearly confused.

While she waited for an explanation, Deon reached into the back seat and grabbed his bag containing his hunting stick, a few boomerangs and two clapping sticks.

'I'll meet ya later up on the main road where we came in,' he said.

Kate grabbed his arm. 'You must be joking! They've got guns for godsake. Do you seriously think you stand a chance with a couple of sticks?'

Deon was affronted. 'Hey, Kate... Pemulwuy didn't have guns and he did ok. Fought off them English soldiers using just spears and hunting sticks.'

Kate looked across at Deon. She had no idea who Pemulwuy was, but she did realise that the boy from Bre was undaunted. In stark contrast to her, he seemed to almost relish the challenge.

'You go back up the main road. I'll be fine,' said Deon, as he got out of the car.

'I'm not leaving you out here alone.'

'Don't worry about me.'

'I'm going nowhere,' Kate replied, adamant. 'I'll give you twenty minutes, ok, twenty minutes max, Deon. And don't take any unnecessary risks. Agreed?'

'Ok... but if you hear them coming, take off back down the track fast.'

'You'll need a torch,' Kate added, with consternation, only too well aware that Deon would have happily gone into the bush without one. Kate opened Sebastian's glove box and was relieved to find what she was looking for. She checked that it was in working order, then handed the torch to Deon.

Stern-faced, the boy from Bre whistled lightly to let Kate know what to expect if a signal was required. He then caught her eye and smiled briefly before vanishing into the crepuscular light.

Further on down the track, Sandra McDonald and William Bates had stopped their van where the track petered out. They were on the edge of a valley, parked by the side of the road where there was a small clearing. They were surrounded by a canopy of tall eucalyptus trees which blocked the setting sun. Night was approaching and it was becoming darker by the minute.

McDonald, with a rifle slung over her shoulder, barked out the orders like a sergeant major.

She had Bates loaded to the hilt with a hoe, shovel, bucket and rope. He juggled the gear as he moved, his torch hanging pendulously from his neck, whacking into his body as he shuffled along the dirt track. From the indifferent manner in which the two went about their business, it seemed they were in familiar territory.

They had only progressed ten to fifteen metres when McDonald raised her hands and motioned for Bates to stop.

'Hear that?'

'Just a trail bike, I reckon,' said Bates, unconcerned.

'It ain't a trail bike… it's a car… going by the sound of the engine. After you finish what you're doing, go check it out.'

Bates begrudgingly accepted the task. After dropping off his load, she threw him the rifle and he set off along the track.

After walking halfway up the hill, he could no longer hear the motor. It had probably turned and gone back up to the main road, he thought. Sandra was just being paranoid. Still, better not get back too soon. It would only make Sandra cranky. He found a log nearby and lit up a cigarette. After he had been there for a few minutes, he got to his feet, stamped out what remained of his cigarette, and ambled back up the track to the van.

McDonald had not expected Bates to return so soon. She was literally caught with her pants down in a squat position by the side of the track, relieving herself. She got a shock when she noticed Bates leering at her.

She finished her business quickly and pulled up her trousers.

'You're a filthy pervert, you know that?'

Bates sniggered like a recalcitrant child who had been chastised. He was happy to receive any attention. This reaction further antagonised McDonald.

'How did you get back so quickly?' she yelled.

'They've pissed off, Sandra. Whoever it was is long gone. Probably just kids.'

'For chrissake, can't you do anything properly? You didn't even go up the hill, did you, ya lazy fucker. Go and check it out. Can't you do anything properly?

'Why don't you come with me, Sandra? It's rather romantic out here under the stars.'

Coming from Bates, the line was sickening. He walked towards her with outstretched arms.

McDonald was less than impressed. Her eyes bore into him.

'Come near me and you'll get this shovel across your fucking skull.'

She took a swing in his direction, which had him backtracking at pace.

Sandra cursed inwardly, determined that her days with this one were approaching the final curtain. Thoughts of being fucked by Damien filled her mind. As well as the sex, it would definitely be a positive career move. Damien seemed to wield a lot of power in the organisation.

Bates decided that Sandra was having hormonal issues. Why else would she be behaving like such a bitch? This was his usual analysis when a woman rejected him. Sandra would eventually come around; of that he was confident. Who else would put up with her mood swings? His problem was that he hadn't had sex in over a month, and he was becoming increasingly frustrated.

Deon followed the trail for about fifty metres where he came across a makeshift camping area. There were a few empty beer cans, a cereal packet, and some used teabags. Cigarette butts were strewn about the place, but it looked as though the camp hadn't been occupied for some time.

Up ahead he could hear the dull, intermittent thud of a metal tool whacking into dry, hardened earth. When he got close to the source of the noise, he ascended a hilltop from where he could get a better view. Creeping onto an overhanging boulder, he could see the giant shadow of Sandra McDonald, her figure haunting the night like a spectre, as she raised her arms and whacked a pick into the earth. A powerful torch illuminated the surrounding blackbutts and blue gums, creating the effect of a small amphitheatre.

But why was she digging? Again, the worst-case scenario came to mind; she was digging a grave for Matt. But there was something else that concerned him. He had no idea where Bates was or what he was up to. He certainly didn't want to encounter either of the two unexpectedly. As Kate had impressed on him, it was almost certain they were armed.

In the fading light he could make out the white van. It was parked by the side of the road, not all that far from where McDonald was digging. The vehicle had been turned around and was facing the hill. He thought of Kate. She would have about two minutes on them if they decided to make a quick exit. On the plus side, with McDonald busy digging, it didn't appear as though that was going to happen anytime soon.

He stood for a moment, his eyes scanning the area, looking for signs of life and committing to memory a picture of the landscape ahead of him. He needed to know whether Matt was in the van. It was possible he was still alive, tied up and gagged. Deon refused to contemplate any other scenario. He looked towards the western shy, noting it would soon be dark. Night-time was approaching rapidly, with just a sliver of magenta still visible on the blood red horizon.

Steely eyed, he stealthily made his way down through the hop bush and blady grass, careful not to disturb the abundant birdlife. Once he'd reached the edge of the bush, the van was only metres away. He thought back to the four-wheel-drive and the shooter he had crept up on in the reserve above Matt's place. He'd gotten away with that, but he knew he had been lucky. And this time there were two of them.

He reminded himself of the basics: be quick but tread carefully; don't leave yourself vulnerable for longer than necessary; stay low to the ground.

Just over a minute later, he was approaching the van. He'd planned the route so that when he was in the open, the van was between himself and McDonald digging. Wary that Bill might be inside, he carefully looked in through the passenger side window. There was a solid panel separating the driver's compartment from the main section of the vehicle, making it impossible to see through to the back. There was some good news, though. The van was unlocked and the keys still in the ignition. That wasn't really such a surprise. The two would hardly expect company where they were.

The steady thumping continued, and he edged his way around to the rear of the van, tapping ever so lightly on the side while murmuring Matt's name.

Although Deon was probably less than twenty metres away from McDonald, the vegetation in between was dense, and he gained some comfort from knowing McDonald couldn't see him. He knew his next move would be risky, but if he was to find out whether Matt was in the back, he had no choice.

Listening intently to the rhythm of McDonald's movements, he turned the handle of the rear door to coincide with the thump of the tool hitting the ground. But as he disengaged the lock, it made a much louder sound then he had expected. The sharp metallic sound was magnified by the quietness of the night and an eerie, sudden silence.

Deon froze, as still as a koala stargazing, expecting a torch to be pointed in his direction.

There was a cough, then a pause that seemed to last an eternity, before McDonald continued. Deon, his hand still on the lever, took a deep breath as he slowly opened the door. What a relief it was when it didn't squeak.

In the diminishing light he could see a few bags, a large water canister and a tent, but there was no sign of Matt. He considered the possibility that what he had seen being loaded into the van back at the block of units in Kings Cross was in fact a tent. But if that was the case, why had the two been so cautious? And where was Matt? One thing was certain – the ghostly figure thudding the ground nearby was up to something dodgy. Again, he had the same thought that had been haunting him since they entered the National Park – Matt was already dead, and McDonald and Bates were in the process of disposing of his body. Could Matt be bundled up near McDonald? Just because he hadn't seen him from the rock above, didn't mean he wasn't there.

If they harmed Matt, he was not sure how he would react. His lips curled and his resolve strengthened. His determination knew no bounds as he stealthily slipped back into the bush. He had to find out what McDonald was up to. And there was still the other niggling question. Where the hell was Bates?

Kate had waited for what to her seemed like an eternity. The bush wasn't her favourite place to be at night, even at the best of times. The weather had turned cold, and she wasn't dressed for it. She could start the motor and turn on the air-con, but that might be telegraphing her position and inviting trouble. She played a game to occupy her mind, trying to recall all the lyrics, from start to finish, of her favourite songs.

But she could only fool herself for so long. She had long since given up on religion, but that didn't stop her praying for Deon's return. Now and then she would get angry at him, cursing his gung-ho attitude.

'Why in the hell was he taking so long?' she pleaded out loud.

But time can play tricks on you, particularly when you are on edge. Checking her watch, she couldn't believe that only fifteen minutes had passed. Kate again wondered why they hadn't been able to get through to Joe back at Kings Cross. Just her luck to be stuck in an area without a signal. Despite knowing this, she tried to ring Joe again. She even tried 000. Miracles can happen, she told herself. Then she felt stupid for even trying. As Deon had said, if there's no signal, phones don't work.

She thought back to the last time she'd been in a perilous situation. It was years ago when her children were small. She'd been up in Newcastle, visiting Sebastian, when an eastern low unleashed its fury on the city. They had been driving down Hunter Street. A river of water that reached to the car windows had swept the car away. Things might have been much worse if Sebastian hadn't been there to help her get the children out of the car. They hadn't been able to use their phones because the towers had failed in the conditions. And they hadn't been able to get fuel because the pumps wouldn't work without electricity.

'So much for bloody technology,' she had cursed.

She again considered driving into Sutherland to alert the authorities. But she couldn't bring herself to desert Deon. At that point she began to wonder whether her mind was playing tricks on her. Was that Deon's whistle she had just heard? Perhaps it was a bird that had been disturbed. Unable to contain her curiosity, she got out of the car.

In the distance she could see torchlight. Moments later she could make out an amorphous shape ascending the hill. Deon was back, she thought. Thank God. Her prayers had been answered. Kate wondered what he'd discovered and stepped forward briskly to greet the figure coming out of the grey mist.

Suddenly a powerful bright light was shining directly into her face, temporarily blinding her. Deon was playing tricks on her was her initial thought. But as Kate was about to discover, that was not the case. And it wasn't the glow of enlightenment bearing down upon her either.

Back at Kings Cross, Sebastian was feeling exposed since Deon and Kate had gone. He knew he couldn't just hide behind cars until Joe arrived. There was no other option but to walk up to the small reserve at the end of the street and wait. He could observe the comings and goings from the block of units from there.

Charlie was grateful to have some space. Sebastian was uneasy, not knowing what was going on. He thought back to what he had seen when Bates and McDonald were loading the van. Whatever they were carrying, it wasn't moving. If it was Matt, he was either dead or drugged. If it wasn't Matt, why were the two of them so furtive about what they were doing? Not for the first time, he wished he'd charged his phone. He couldn't even ring Kate and Deon to check how they were getting on.

And where was Joe? Sure, Joe could look after himself, but what was he so preoccupied with? He must have received his text. Whenever he heard a car approaching, Sebastian would become excited, hoping to see Joe's Falcon turning into the street.

Occasionally someone would enter or leave the block of units and

Sebastian would turn his attention that way, worried that he might miss something important.

Sebastian was shaken from his solitude when, from the corner of his eye, he glimpsed a savage, muscular shape hurtling towards him. In his mind, all he could see was a shadowy image of the wolf he knew so intimately from his dreams. Bracing himself for its attack, Sebastian was forced to shield his ears from an earsplitting whistle. He looked up to see the creature scampering off towards a petite, dark-haired woman in a colourful sarong. The woman apologised to Sebastian before attaching a lead to the collar of her large German Shephard.

After the incident, Sebastian was left rattled, and he became impatient. He knew Joe would be asking all sorts of questions once he arrived. And he still wasn't sure whether Matt was inside the unit or in the van. He didn't even know which unit Bates and McDonald had come out of. From the swift manner in which the two had packed the van, there was a good chance they'd come out of one of the ground-floor units.

Sebastian thought about the comment Kate had made about each vehicle having a designated parking position. Although he hadn't agreed with Kate's assessment at the time, there was sense in what she had said. Parking spots were at a premium in this part of town. Bates and McDonald, if they had any sense at all, would in all probability keep to the rules in order to avoid drawing attention to themselves.

Sebastian wondered what Joe would do in his position. He then made a decision that he would soon regret. He decided to do some reconnaissance so he could find out more. Even knowing whether the parking spots were numbered, something he should have checked when he first saw the van, would be useful.

With Charlie on the lead, he strolled along the footpath towards the block of units. He was about to turn down the path adjacent to the driveway when Charlie stopped in her tracks, deciding it was the place to relieve herself. Sebastian felt compromised, existing in some kind of no-man's-land, but he knew he'd cause a commotion if he tried to stop Charlie peeing.

Then he had one of those inexplicable moments. Did he imagine it, or did he really see a shadow near the curtains of that same downstairs window? His intuition told him to go back to the reserve and wait for Joe, but his pride would not permit him to do so. And what would he say to Joe if he allowed himself the coward's way out! Think positive, he said to himself. He soon had himself convinced it was just a nosy neighbour. After all, there was more than one unit on the ground floor.

Charlie finished doing her business, and Sebastian continued along the path and around to the back of the block. The door into the foyer was locked, as expected. He peeped into the foyer but couldn't see in through the opaque glass, so he turned and walked towards the parked cars.

What he saw stopped him in his tracks. Maybe it hadn't been there before. Surely he would have noticed it. He gazed in bewilderment at the four-wheel-drive, with its red roof racks and Queensland plates, at the far end of the parking bay.

He was staring at the vehicle and trying to piece together the puzzle when a voice boomed from behind a concrete pillar.

'Turn around. Leave your hands where they are.'

When Sebastian turned around, he was staring at the barrel of a stubbed-nose 38. After the initial wave of fear had passed, he used a line he had rehearsed. He spoke with relative calm, considering the predicament he was in.

'I'm just out walking the dog. What is this all about?'

Far from placating the gunman, his words seemed to have the opposite effect. With the weapon concealed behind his coat, a man stepped forward and thrust the barrel hard into Sebastian's ribs. Sebastian dropped the lead and Charlie scampered away as though possessed. Sebastian was left curled over, wincing in pain.

The gunman faked a smile and patted Sebastian across the shoulder, before holding him upright as though he was trying to help him.

The man spoke in a temperate voice, incongruent with the fact that he was brandishing a gun.

'Are you alright? Just do as you're told, and you might get out of this alive.'

'No need to overreact, mate,' said Sebastian

The man continued to speak in a placatory tone as he chivvied Sebastian towards the four-wheel-drive. It was days later, when Sebastian thought about what had occurred, that he realised the gunman had put on the friendly act to disguise his real intentions in case another resident or a passer-by realised something sinister was going on.

'Mate… I'm not your mate, old man. You decided to come after me, eh? Well, you've got guts, I'll give ya that. You're bloody stupid, though. You know Frances couldn't really give a fuck about you. You do know that don't ya?'

Sebastian's stomach dropped, as he thought back to the pistol attack. If he'd had any doubts, he knew now he was in serious trouble. It effected his speech. 'You must have me confused with someone else. I don't know who you are talking about.'

The gunman sneered, enjoying seeing Sebastian in a distressed state.

'Tell ya who I'm talking about… Red Fucking Riding Hood. Don't play dumb with me, old man. I think we both know who I mean. Stupid… stupid move. So, where's your Abo mate? He won't save you this time.

Sebastian didn't reply.

'Don't want to tell me? Turn around!' he snapped.

He opened the back door and had a quick look around, before shoving Sebastian into the back of the van. Sebastian felt a sickening numbness as he was struck across the back of the skull with the butt of the weapon. He lay there in the back of the vehicle, drifting in and out of consciousness. It was a horrid sensation to know his life was under threat and feeling utterly powerless to do anything about it.

24

Out of the Darkness

Get that bloody torch out of my eyes, will you.'

As the last two words formed in her mouth, Kate was struck with the depressing realisation that it wasn't Deon playing a game. The torch was lowered, and Kate was greeted by a hideous grin.

'Jees… what 'ave we got here? Must be my lucky day.'

'Get away… get away from me!' Panic-stricken, her voice quivering as she spoke, Kate knew she had to mount a more formidable resistance, or this atavistic creature would run rough shot over her. 'I took a wrong turn… I'm looking for some friends who are out camping. Is this the way to the river?'

'Aww… came to me for directions did ya love? Well, ya come to the right bloke for help. I'll set you right.'

Bates began flicking at Kate's clothing with his rifle. She pushed the weapon away but that just seemed to amuse Bates and a sadistic smile appeared on his face. He jabbed the end of rifle hard into her thigh and Kate cried out in pain as tears welled in her eyes.

'I bet a cute thing like you ain't out here in the bush all alone.'

'Fuck off and leave me alone!' she bellowed frantically, the reality of the dire situation she found herself in becoming increasingly apparent.

So, who's with you, darl? Come on… you can tell me. Don't think you're fooling anyone.'

'I'm all alone. As I told you, I'm looking for friends. Now get away from me!'

Bates grunted something incomprehensible as he turned and scanned the surrounding bush with his torch. 'We'll find you... ya bastard,' he shouted, before turning the spotlight back on Kate.

Her face was contorted, grief-stricken. 'Please... just leave me be,' she pleaded.

'Come on, ya lying bitch. We'll go see what my woman thinks of you.'

Bates slung the rifle over his shoulder and roughly pushed Kate forward. She stumbled and only just managed to maintain her footing. Kate experienced a peculiar feeling of relief. It felt as though she had been given a reprieve. At least McDonald was female, and she wouldn't be alone out in the middle of nowhere at the mercy of Bates.

As they progressed along the dirt road, Bates provided the soundtrack, a hideous clucking noise which had Kate trembling and fighting back tears over the hopelessness of her situation. Occasionally Bates would prod her with the rifle to hurry her along. But it didn't matter how fast she went, he was always close on her tail. She shuddered with each word he uttered.

'You look in pretty good shape for an older woman. You'd be pretty experienced, eh... a lady of the world? Bet you got a few tricks up your sleeve by now. What do ya say love... you and me?'

At that point, Kate realised she couldn't hold on any longer. She surrendered to the struggle and felt the hot trickle of urine run down her leg. Bates didn't even seem to notice. Perhaps he just expected it.

Stay calm and think, she told herself. She could try and run, but he had a gun and a torch. If he didn't shoot, he'd catch her in seconds anyway. Maybe the woman who was with him, and whom she'd glimpsed outside the block of units, would save her. But then she remembered what she and Deon had witnessed. If they did have Matt in the back of the van and were prepared to kill him, would they have any hesitation in doing the same to her?

Kate tried to erase from her thoughts a television show she'd watched recently that focused on a large number of people who had disappeared without a trace. Never to be seen again. Although she knew it was important to remain positive, she got the impression her captor was in familiar territory. There was another way it could play out, though. What if Deon had witnessed her capture and was now in the process of seeking help. Her mind was doing cartwheels. But what if Deon was also captured? Maybe they had coerced him into telling them she was up the road in the car.

Kate became aware of an ominous thudding sound. The thought of somebody digging terrified her. She saw a shimmering light in the distance. Her captor then shone his torch to the side of the road and up ahead was the elusive white van.

Kate was lost in her thoughts, anticipating what would happen, when Bates, catching her unawares, tripped her up, pushed her forward, and wedged her body up against the bonnet of the vehicle. The amalgam of stale odours emanating from Bates made her gag. Barely able to breath, Kate emitted a low guttural growl of desperation.

'Get away from me.'

With one arm pushing hard against her throat, Bates lifted her dress with the other, and Kate gasped in pain as his fingernail dug into her thighs as he tried to separate her legs. It seemed as though nothing could save her now and a weary oppressiveness overwhelmed her. Bates loosened his grip on her throat to grope at her breasts and she managed to slip one arm free. Summoning all her remaining strength she struck out hard, jabbing her elbow into his ribs. The sharp blow caught Bates by surprise, and he screeched in pain, releasing his vice-like grip.

Kate crawled towards the darkness, whimpering, her legs and arms scraping against twigs and loose stones as she went. But just seconds later, the torch was in her face again and Bates was hovering over her, panting with excitement. He grabbed her by the hair.

'You like it rough, eh love?'

Kate could hear ruffled leaves and stones. Somebody was approaching. Bates glanced up unperturbed. A rough-edged voice cut through the air.

'What the fuck is going on?'

Bates put his face to Kate's ear, and she whimpered in anticipation. 'That was just the foreplay, love,' he hissed in a throaty, threatening tone. He turned to greet McDonald. 'Look what the cat dragged in! Found her up there sitting in a car. Waitin' for someone, I reckon.'

Bates lifted Kate by the hair, and she let out a squeal. He shone the torch in her eyes, proudly showing off his prisoner.

'Bit of a looker I hooked, eh Sandra? You jealous?'

McDonald's expression remained blank. She shone the torch outward and did a sweep of the adjacent bush. When she spoke, her tone was terse. 'Where are the keys?'

'Keys to what?'

'The keys to the car the friggin' bitch was in.'

The word "bitch" was fired from McDonald's mouth with such venom that it hit Kate like a thunderbolt. McDonald kicked at the ground in disgust and Bill appeared oddly sheepish as he realised his mistake.

McDonald returned her attention to Kate's dishevelled state. Her knees were bleeding, her hair was ruffled, and her blouse was ripped. When Kate's imploring eyes met her cold gaze, Kate knew McDonald's presence was anything but a panacea for her woes. The chances of receiving sisterly compassion from this woman were zilch.

McDonald again did a sweep of the bush with her torch, studying the surrounds with her calculating, lupine eyes. She grabbed the rifle from Bill. 'You fucking watch her while I get some rope,' she said as she turned and began walking back to the place where she had been digging.

'Don't leave him with me,' pleaded Kate.

A humourless grin appeared on McDonald's face, as she continued on her way.

Bates stood there, tumescent, gawking at their prey, his mind ticking over with possibilities. 'You don't like me. Is that what you are trying to say?' Bates feigned disappointment before his tone became harsh. 'Tell you what sweetie, you can make it easy, or we can do it the hard way.' He then smiled, his voice sickeningly sweet and feigning kindness. 'What do you say, love?'

Kate's power of resistance was depleted. She called out in desperation, pleading to the heavens.

'Please, please… someone help me.'

Bates shook his head, his smile rigid, sadistic.

'Nobody gunna save you out here, love.'

A melodic whistle sounded from somewhere in the bush.

Bates turned his attention from Kate and his demeanour changed. Spinning on his haunches, he adopted a combative stance as he conducted a sweep of the area. While not an expert on winged, bipedal vertebrates, he sure as hell knew that what he had heard wasn't a bird call. Kate's reaction to the sound only reinforced his analysis.

At that moment the night turned. A green tennis ball came rolling out of the darkness towards them, and so odd was its appearance that the two of them just stared at it as though mesmerised. It was followed by an ear-piercing shrill which could have shattered an iceberg. An eerie fluttering noise gathered momentum as the bush came to life with a chorus of swarming birds, the night sky chockful of cockatoos, bats and crows.

A bedazzled Bates shone his torch upward as a family of kangaroos skipped cross the dirt track.

'What the fuck is going on?'

His question was soon answered. A rhythmic swishing sound filled the air fractionally before a hunting stick whacked into Bates from behind. Clutching at his back, Bates instinctively turned to face the direction of the attack as a large rock struck his right knee. Another flew by, missing him by inches. The next one hit him high, splitting open his forehead. He staggered about on his feet in a daze, like a boxer about to go down for the count.

Kate was about to take off into the bush when she heard Deon's distinctive voice.

'Kate… take the van… the keys are in it.'

Kate felt relieved and invigorated by Deon's presence. The van was only metres away and she clambered towards it, her legs feeling like jelly.

Deon came in closer, on his toes and moving with the grace of a warrior, his right arm braced, ready to unleash further attacks. He let out a vicious growl as he hit Bates with a flurry of rocks. Some missed, but enough of the tirade hit the mark to leave Bates spread-eagled on the ground, battered and bruised, whimpering in pain.

When Bates later explained the events of that night, he would claim that three ferocious Koori warriors attacked him. He'd describe in detail their headpieces and painted bodies. He would also swear on his mother's grave that during the maelstrom a shower of spears reigned down from above, pinning him to the spot.

Kate soon had the motor ticking over, but the van had a manual gear shift and she hadn't driven one in years. Frantically, she heaved the gear stick back and forth, but for the life of her she could not propel the vehicle forward. Kate knew McDonald had a rifle and she now wished she'd listened to her instincts and taken off into the bush.

Sitting there inert in the driver's seat, she was a sitting duck.

When McDonald came racing back up to the van and saw Bates in a heap on the ground, she was mystified. What was going on? What was he afraid of? Surely, he hadn't let that woman get the better of him. She knew that Bill wasn't the heroic type, but was he really that pathetic?

'What the fuck! Get up you stupid idiot, get up!' she yelled, turning her attention to the van. McDonald disengaged the safety catch and raised the rifle to her shoulder.

'Get out or I'll shoot,' she screamed, her fearsome shrill sending a tremor through the night air.

As she was about to pull the trigger she hesitated, distracted by movement nearby. Before she knew it, she was smothered in a cloud of dirt and stones, and someone was trying to snatch the weapon from her grasp. She ducked and weaved, clutching on to it with all her might. Giving an almighty heave, she managed to jerk it away from her attacker and began firing blindly into the night.

By then Kate was kangarooing along the rough dirt road in third gear. She managed to crush the van into first and the engine screamed like a banshee. With the back door banging like the clackers, the cacophony of sound was deafening. Kate shrieked in fear, as the bloodcurdling sound of gunfire was added to the mix.

Kate's entire body shuddered with each shot. Having no idea that

McDonald's vision was compromised, Kate was relieved yet puzzled as to why she or the van hadn't been hit.

It didn't take long for McDonald to clear the dirt from her eyes, gradually regaining her sight. Grabbing the torch from the ground, she swung around on her haunches trying to locate her attacker, but she was chasing shadows. The lubricious Deon was gone. McDonald turned her attention back to the van. Cursing and spluttering, the van had already gone over the first incline and was out of her line of sight.

Whatever McDonald was, she was not a quitter. With a burst of enthusiasm, she took off after Kate and the van. Kate was still struggling with the gears and had to traverse the difficult eroded section at the top of the hill where the soft sand could easily bog the vehicle and bring it to a standstill. She put her foot on the accelerator, crossed her fingers and hoped for the best.

McDonald moved slowly, her lack of fitness adding to her burden. By the time she reached the hump, the van had tackled the tricky section of road and turned the corner at the top of the hill. She bellowed into the night as she saw the lights of another vehicle turn on and fall in behind the van. The van and the car were soon distant lights twinkling like stars in the darkness.

Huffing and puffing, McDonald fired off a couple of shots in anger and seriously considered putting another into the arsehole who had gotten her into this mess, and with whom she was now stranded.

Kate reached the main road and pulled over to the side of the track. She stumbled out of the van, clutching onto the body for support as she staggered around to the back. Pulling open the dangling doors with trepidation, she had been half expecting to see Matt's corpse lying there.

What she saw was an assortment of horticulture gear and a tent. But there was no sign of Matt.

Moments later, Deon pulled up behind her.

'You ok, Kate?'

'I'm fine,' she replied, still high on adrenalin. She'd feel the bruising later.

'Was mad, eh? There was heaps of it back there in the bush,' said Deon, excitedly.

'Heaps of what?'

'Gungi... marijuana... couple of hundred plants at least.'

They locked the van and took the keys. They still had no idea where Matt was. Deon thought he must be back at the Kings Cross flat.

They were still unable to get a signal, but that didn't stop Kate insisting Deon keep trying to contact Joe as they drove out of the National Park.

'Do you mind if I put some music on?' asked Deon

'Sure... it might lift our spirits,' Kate replied.

The song playing on JJJ was so familiar to them both that it took a while for reality to sink in. When it did, they both gaped at each other with expressions of incredulousness.

The opals may sparkle out at the Ridge,
But her wails cry out from the Namoi bridge.
Life in the West, Life in the West.

25

The Wolf

The wolf will surely get him tonight.
He has accepted the inevitable.
He detaches himself and observes it closing in.
The wolf turns into Napier Street,
Then something amazing happens.
He doesn't know where the idea comes from,
But he discovers that if he concentrates
He has the ability to prevent the wolf moving forward.
The wolf, although still running, is not getting any closer.
He pushes, urges, conjures, and slowly the wolf begins to retreat backwards.
Powered on by success, he uses every last ounce of his jaded willpower.
He moves it further and further back, all the way to the Harbour Bridge.
He feels ecstatic, jubilant,
As though he has been given a new lease of life.

As Sebastian regained his temporal bearings he could recognise the room, but he had no recollection of how he got back to the Napier Street house.

Someone was shouting nearby, and the words bore into him.

'And how are you, old man? Back with us now? How's the big fucking hero going to look when the cops realise you were with poor little Mattie when he overdosed. Plenty of bad gear around, eh?'

Sebastian moved his body gingerly, and a sharp pain shot up through his shoulder and neck. His vision was blurry as he peered up with incredulity at the chimera hovering over him. Before him stood the gunman, the same person who had abducted him outside the block of units. But his mannerisms were more animalistic than human. The verbal tirade was coming from a creature with the body of a man, but with a wolf's head. The distorted visual effect was similar to what he'd experienced back in his early twenties when he'd taken LSD. This maniac must have injected him with some type of hallucinogenic.

Something else was odd. He was well aware of the dire situation he was in, but he didn't feel the intense fear that he should.

The smooth façade the gunman had adopted earlier in the parking bay had vanished. Every cell of the man's body was infused with aggression. The gunman emitted a throaty self-indulgent laugh. He raised the weapon, aimed it at Sebastian, and went through the motions of firing a shot.

'What have I done to you?' asked Sebastian, 'I don't even know you.'

'Fuck off, you silly fool. Aren't you the hero everyone needs?'

Sebastian's vision began to sharpen. He could make out the outline of Matt in the corner, lying on the mattress he himself had slept on the night before. Matt's arms and legs were tied with rope, and a strip of black gaffer tape covered his mouth. Although he couldn't move, his eyes were open, and he was alive.

The back room looked like a whirlwind had torn through it. Drawers had been pulled out and some of the floorboards ripped up. The piece of plywood covering the manhole clung to the ceiling like an acrobat suspended midair.

Damien noticed Sebastian's inquisitive eyes.

'I bet you know where Joe hides his money. Don't think I couldn't get it out of you. That would be fun if I had enough time. Mattie's probably blown most of it, knowing what a fucking dill he is. Anyway, I'll be getting plenty of my own soon enough, thanks to my dear mother.'

Sebastian stole a furtive glance at the enraged man. At least the face was starting to look human. He could scream out for help, but the neighbours on the right would most likely be out and the old lady on the other side was practically deaf. And even if the neighbours were home and did hear him, would they be able to do anything in time? Besides, after seeing his abductor in action, he knew he would be either bashed again or shot.

Damien walked over to the table where a syringe and vial were visible. He took the cap off the syringe and began preparing the lethal dose.

'You never know what kinda shit they put in the gear these days... bad enough to make Mattie lose it and shoot a silly old bastard like you before he overdoses.'

He turned his attention back to Matt.

'You fucking-well think you can con my mother with stories about your sad life to get what's rightfully mine? You're not really part of the family ya loser, never have been... ya mum dumped you 'cause you were such a burden. Should've drowned you at birth. That's what you deserved. And who the fuck do you think you are, eh... cuttin' in on Uncle George's business? I'll be doin' George a favour, won't I? Getting rid of a prick like you... Did you really think you could get your clammy hands on my... my fucking inheritance? See this gun?'

Damien caressed the weapon with reverence and smirked as the audience in his head applauded at the plan he'd devised. 'It'll soon have Mattie's prints all over it.'

He paused for a moment to bask in his triumph.

'Where's your old man when you need him, eh? Joe the pathetic... Joe the dope- dealing loser. It's what you'd expect really. I can't wait to see his face. I should take some shots on my phone and send them to him. Post it on YouTube. Make a movie, yeah.'

He laughed deliriously. Damien was well and truly off the tracks and approaching the terminus. 'The journos will love this one, eh? Youth worker gets too close to deranged druggie. I can see the headlines. Be on the 7.30 Report. Couldn't have worked it out any better if I'd planned it this way myself.'

Damien puffed vigorously on his cigarette. Clouds of evanescent smoke drifted to the ceiling, clamouring to escape through the small opening in the window at the top of the far wall.

Sebastian heard a noise nearby that he knew well. It was the distinctive squeak of the side gate opening. Damien heard it as well. He put his finger to his lips, pointed the gun at Sebastian, and motioned for him to shut up.

Frances knew from the tracking device that Damien was at Malabar and decided the timing was perfect. She'd checked out the one nearest to his car, but nobody was home. There was certainly no sign of Damien. On her next attempt to locate him, she peered through the side gate and saw the holes in the ground. She turned the handle and discovered the gate was open. Frances walked down the side passage and around to the back of the house. There was a back room separate from the house. Maybe Damien had found the money he had bragged about and was in the back room bagging it.

Hearing no other voice only confirmed what she expected. Damien was alone. Perfect.

Frances had a simple plan. Tell him she had been visiting a friend down the road and had seen his car. He was so trusting of her he'd believe anything. But it didn't matter. While he was trying to make sense of what she was saying, she'd pull out the gun and shoot him.

'Hello, are you out there Damien?'

Sebastian's ears pricked at the sound of a woman's voice. There was something familiar about the tone, but he couldn't place it. Damien didn't answer. He tippy-toed up to the door, unlatched it and waited. Sebastian thought about warning the newcomer, but from the way she'd called Damien's name, the woman wasn't expecting an unfriendly welcome. Frances walked through the passageway and when Damien saw her, he responded as though he was happy to see her. 'Frances. What a surprise! Come in.'

Frances smiled. She wouldn't even need a story. She was about to pull the gun when she heard a shuffling sound emanating from inside the room. It would be best to check, she decided. The last thing she wanted was a witness.

With her hand on the handgun, she walked up the steps, past Damien and into the back room. What a shock she got when she saw Sebastian lying on the ground. For a split second she faltered, and Damien didn't hesitate. He whacked her across the back of the neck with his weapon, although he did break her fall, ensuring she didn't hit the floor too hard. What a gentleman! He then dragged her across to where Sebastian was lying and dumped her by his side.

'Thought it was you trying to track me. Deserve what you get.'

Damien had his priorities – eliminating Matt and getting his hands on his mother's money were always going to take precedence over his feelings for Frances, even if she had put a tracking device on his car.

Her behaviour only confirmed his core belief – trust nobody. He'd decide what to do about Frances after he dealt with the other two.

Frances's appearance on the scene had a strange effect on Sebastian. He wondered whether she knew this was his family home. How weird it felt, to have her lying unconscious by his side. For some reason he couldn't comprehend, her presence on the scene emboldened him to act.

While Damien went to the window to check that Frances was alone, Sebastian looked around the room. There was a thick telephone directory on the floor, just out of reach. Near the doorway was his wallet which must have fallen from his pocket when he was dragged in. Glancing over his left shoulder, he saw an object sitting on the windowsill that was so familiar he had to look twice to convince himself he wasn't imagining it.

The wooden object had a metallic head which, in his drug enhanced state, appeared to be two protruding tusks. There was a pale tint in the appropriate place for a mouth and dabs of iridescent grey paint masquerading as eyes. It looked like a miniature bull with its head hung low as though it was going to charge. It dawned on him that it was the clawhammer he had pulled out of the piano recently when he was clearing out his mother's belongings. Sebastian's visceral response was to grab it instantly and hurl it at this lunatic who wanted to kill him. Commonsense kicked in. Not yet, he told himself. He would be shot before he even got to his feet.

Damien stepped back from the window, seemingly convinced Frances was alone.

Again, he began to fling invectives at Matt.

'What's your favourite band little Mattie? Probably into that hip-hop shit going by your clothes... fucking Eminem or something like that.'

He glared at his half-brother as though expecting a response, regardless of the fact that gaffer tape was still firmly attached to Matt's mouth.

'Some bad black dude, you stupid fucker... a fuckin' sad loser like yaself. Life's so fucking hard and all that shit.' A cold expression came over Damien's face as he slipped a CD into the stereo and pressed the play button, just like he had seen a killer do in a movie recently.

'I was hoping that you'd like Nirvana. Ya like Nirvana Mattie boy? Kind of poetic don't you think, Kurt Cobain and all? Get to love it Mattie because it's the last music you'll ever hear.'

The gloomy strains of *Something in the Way* filled the room. Damien turned towards the stereo to increase the volume.

Frances began to wake up. When she realised it was Sebastian next to her, she got an initial shock. Then she remembered what had happened. She looked across at Matt and up to Damien and began to access the situation.

Sebastian knew this would probably be his only opportunity, and he summoned all of his courage. Sliding to his knees, he was able to grab the hammer from the windowsill before Damien realised he had moved.

He took a short back swing and hurled the hammer at the maniac.

It was a powerful throw, and if it had been straight would have caused some serious damage. But the instant it left his hand, Sebastian knew he had blown it. He'd rushed the throw and hooked it left, missing Damien by about thirty centimetres. It rebounded off the wall, coming to a halt near the stereo.

The music stopped. In what was a bizarre moment, Sebastian and Damien looked at one another as though the other one might know why this had happened. The hammer had dislodged the power chord from the socket. It may have stopped the music, but it didn't stop Damien. The gun was now pointed straight at Sebastian's head. He was going to shoot, music or no music.

Frances couldn't help herself. 'You are such a fuckwit, Damien. What… are you going to shoot me too?'

Damien looked back at Frances as though it was a trick question.

'There's no point in hurting anyone,' Sebastian pleaded, 'Nothing's a problem if you just let us go now.'

'Fuck off,' said Damien.

Sebastian then saw something out of the corner of his eye that gave him hope. He snatched the telephone book from the floor and began ducking and weaving to ensure Damien's attention remained focused on him. For a brief moment Damien seemed amused by Sebastian's antics. Then, with a cruel twist of his lower lip, his finger began closing in on the trigger.

A harsh voice cut through the space. 'Put the gun down Damien… now!'

The words were spoken with absolute authority. In the doorway was a thickset man in a dark stylish suit. Sophia pushed her wheelchair up beside him.

'Damien,' called his mother. 'Do what he says.'

The suit was carrying a gun, but it was still resting in his shoulder holster. He didn't want to have a shoot-out with this one if he could avoid it. Damien might deserve it, but he was still Souriss's nephew. For a moment it seemed as though Damien might succumb to the suit's wishes, but when he adopted a truculent posture, it became evident hostilities were far from over.

'It's none of your fucking business, George.'

He looked from the suit to Sophia with an arrogance that telegraphed his intention. It appeared as though the suit had miscalculated. The gun was still pointed at Sebastian.

Two gunshots rang out in rapid succession. Damien's weapon flew from his hand. The place went eerily quiet as fumes of spent gunpowder drifted through the space.

Damien's startled eyes darted defiantly around the room, struggling to make sense of what had happened. He had managed to get away a shot before he was hit, but who had fired the other one? The suit hadn't. His weapon was still in his holster. Damien's gaze then became fixed on a hooded figure crouched behind Sophia's wheelchair.

When it dawned on him that it was Joe behind the barrel, he became incensed, snarling like a ravenous animal. A bullet to the hand should have been enough but Damien showed no signs of giving up. Judging from Damien's behaviour, it seemed the pain hadn't even registered.

'Step back against the wall,' shouted the suit, resolute.

'Damien, please,' cried Sophia.

The plea from his mother seemed to only rile him further. Damien made a dash for his handgun which was on the floor near his feet. The muffled sound of another shot could be heard. The suit had his Gamo P-23 in his hand but hadn't fired. Damien slid to the ground, incapacitated. A bullet had ripped into his thigh and blood had begun to flow freely. Frances quickly put her weapon back in the holster, as Damien grimaced in pain.

The suit moved with surprising speed and agility, picking up Damien's gun and slamming a pair of handcuffs on him.

Joe hurried over to untie Matt. He removed the gaffer tape and wiped his face clean. Apart from a bloody nose and a few bruises, Matt seemed unscathed.

Father and son embraced. Tears streamed down Joe's cheeks as he realised just how close he had come to losing his son. At that moment every argument and every antagonistic word faded into insignificance. Matt at some later stage would probably suggest ways in which Joe could have handled the situation better, but at that moment he was truly proud of his father. He thanked him sincerely.

Sebastian was still shaking and concerned. There was blood all over his clothing and he had no idea where Damien's shot had gone. He searched his body thinking he may have been hit. Stories came to mind about soldiers who had been mortally wounded in combat yet were blissfully unaware of their perilous state.

'Where did the other bullet go?' asked Sebastian, bracing himself for an answer he did not want to hear.

Frances was aware of Sebastian's unease, but she seemed in no hurry to allay his fear. She waited a few seconds before pointing to a hole in the floor near the piano. Sebastian breathed a sigh of relief. The blood must have been due to the rough treatment he had received earlier.

Joe came over. 'Are you ok, Seb?'

'Just a few bumps,' he replied, putting on a bold front for Frances's benefit, playing down the throbbing pain pulsating through his head, neck and shoulders.

Matt had trouble getting to his feet. His legs were numb, and Joe gave them a vigorous massage.

'You'll be fine, Son. Keep moving your legs. It'll take a while for your circulation to get going again.'

Hunched up in the corner, a subdued and deflated Damien was coming to grips with the fact that he wasn't invincible, his arrogance still intact. 'Get me a fucking doctor!' he demanded.

The suit raised his eyebrows and strolled over to where Damien was sitting. 'Don't swear in front of your mother, Son.' He lifted his hand and backhanded Damien hard across the face, sending him reeling backwards.

Damien was caught by surprise, and he let out a loud sharp yelp. Matt shot his half-brother a contemptuous gaze.

'You haven't changed, have you? You're still such a fucking sook.'

'Settle down Matt,' said Joe, firing a vengeful gaze in Damien's direction. 'He'll get what's due.'

After ensuring Matt was alright, Sophia went into the bathroom and found antiseptic cream and bandages. She avoided Damien's eyes as she assiduously set about wrapping his wounds.

The suit went out to the front of the house where a few residents had gathered. As he walked towards them, he pulled his wallet from the inside pocket of his coat. Flicking it open, he showed them his identification. It was probably a badge from the Mickey Mouse Club but there was no questioning its efficacy. He assured them everything was under control before going back inside and, with Joe's help, doing a cursory clean-up.

Joe's Lone Ranger ringtone sounded on his mobile. It was Kate calling from a service station near Sutherland. Joe turned the speaker on so Sebastian could hear. There would be plenty of stories to tell tonight. After the call ended, Joe approached the suit.

'A couple of Damien's associates are stuck in the National Park. Apparently, the cops are going to provide transport,' he announced gleefully.

The suit's expression didn't alter. 'Fuck 'em.' He intimated to Joe in a stern fashion that he wanted to exchange a few words in private.

Like generals deciding the terms of peace after a battle had ceased, the two conversed in the corner of the room. After a minute or so, the suit pointed at Matt. He spoke in a haunting whisper.

'We still want that five grand back.'

'Where will I find you?' asked Joe.

A sardonic smile appeared on the suit's face. He spoke in a manner that was intended to leave Joe in no doubt as to who was calling the shots. 'Don't worry about that, Joe. We'll find you.'

The suit cast an obligatory glance around the room. 'Let's get out of here.'

Sophia wheeled her chair over to where Matt was sitting. She hugged him with exuberance before whispering a few comforting words into his ear.

The suit attended to Damien with due diligence. Perhaps he was putting on a show for the benefit of the onlookers because Damien no longer posed a threat. He was a defeated and dejected figure as he staggered along the side passageway and out onto the street.

Sophia drove off. The suit put Damien in the back seat. He had a few words with Frances, who casually strolled off along the footpath and around the corner to her car. Sebastian could only shake his head. How could anyone endure such a precarious situation and appear totally unaffected, thought Sebastian.

26

The Morning After

The clock hit ten o'clock. The occasional car could be heard to zoom past, but inside the Napier Street house it was as quiet as a mouse doing yoga. Everybody had slept in, which was not surprising considering the events of the past few days.

Sebastian awoke mindful of a scratching sound nearby. When he attempted to move, he felt the pain and stiffness of yesterday's wounds. Was a rat or a mouse in the wall cavity? That theory was soon dismissed when he heard a muffled growl that appeared to be coming from outside the house.

Getting out of bed, he moved awkwardly across to the window. He realised what was causing the noise a moment before he'd pulled open the curtain and his curious frown transmuted into a joyful beam. In need of a wash and fatigued after a long night on the road, pawing at the side gate was Charlie. They'd driven around Kings Cross searching for her last night. Joe had been right; Charlie had found her own way home. The others would be thrilled.

While Charlie attacked bowls of food and water, Sebastian logged on to his account. There were a few messages requiring his attention, but it was the one from Jenna that he opened first.

Hey Dad... tried to ring you yesterday but you were impossible to catch. Hope you check your email more often than usual because this is important. I overheard Mum talking to Aunty Laura. She was saying she wanted to go back to Amsterdam. But it wasn't like, you know, when she'd get homesick and we'd snap her out of it by doing crazy Dutch impersonations. She wants to go back there to live. And you know Mum once she gets set on something. When will you and Joe get up here?

Miss ya heaps,

Love Jenna.

The news unsettled Sebastian, but it did nothing to lessen his resolve. He wondered what she'd made of the email he'd sent. Maybe telling her he'd be in Cairns in a few days hadn't been a wise idea. Whatever he did, he knew it would be fruitless to badger Astrid with more declarations of love. And to further apologise would just antagonise her. After having endured and survived the ordeals of the past weeks, the world seemed fresh and full of possibilities.

He'd started on a new song, based on an old Chinese proverb.

Who can predict? Who knows what will come?

The winds of change blow.

You can't anticipate every turn,

The winds of change blow.

The winds of change were surely blowing. Sebastian could hear the muffled voices of Joe and Kate deep in conversation in the bedroom nearby. He and Joe would have to leave for Cairns as soon as possible. The sooner the better as far as he was concerned. He'd take leave from work and resign if things went to plan. In spite of his woes with regard to Astrid, he tried to remain positive. It would be fun playing with Joe again. It would also provide the opportunity to hone his musical skills, to do something he loved.

In was mid-morning in Cairns, and Astrid and her cousin Laura were sitting by the water, sipping on takeaway coffee.

'Do you think going back to Amsterdam will solve everything?'

'I'm not saying Holland is perfect. And I've made some good friends in Australia. But I feel that I need a change.'

'Are you going to talk to Seb? You can't avoid him forever.'

'Do you think it's weird that Seb has a job up here, playing music at a resort?'

She's thinking about him and calling him Seb again, thought Laura. Maybe her cousin was having second thoughts.

'Astrid, perhaps it was meant to be. Why don't you give Seb another chance? Forgive him for his sins. I know what I said before, but I think you still love him. You don't seem interested in anybody else and from what I've seen you are miserable without him.'

'You're sounding like Jenna,'

'Well, maybe Jenna has a point. You can still go back to Amsterdam if it doesn't work out. You know Jenna loves it up here in Cairns.'

When Astrid had found out Sebastian was coming to Cairns, she was in two minds. Should she give him a chance and hear what he had to say? Or clear out before he came? She was leaning towards leaving Cairns before he arrived. Jenna could stay in Cairns, if she wanted, and spend time with her father. What happened next sent her into a spin.

Astrid was sitting in Laura's backyard reading a book by the pool when Jenna came rushing out of the back door laughing and pointing at the small speaker she was carrying in an excited state.

'Listen to this, Mum. Can you believe it?'

Astrid recognised Sebastian's wavering mouth harp and the intro to *Amsterdam Lady*. Then she was taken aback by the immediacy of Sebastian's voice.

Lighten the burden on ya, man,
Don't bury your head in the sand.
You get there as fast as you can,
Get a ticket to Amsterdam.

Astrid noticed Sebastian had added a catchy third section, repeating the words "Amsterdam Lady" in a long, mellifluous refrain. The backup parts, in five-part harmony, repeated phrases used in the verses. To her it sounded phenomenal.

On the long drive to Cairns, Sebastian decided his best chance of being reunited with Astrid was to give her space. She could see him anytime. It was her call. But if she did talk with him, and if he was to have any hope of being reunited with her, he knew he had to convince her he was something like the person she'd once loved and wanted to spend her life with. He knew he was getting way ahead of himself, but what if Astrid let him follow her to Holland? The prospect excited him.

As well as recalibrating his connection with Astrid, it might provide the perfect steppingstone to something he had long dreamed of doing. He had been told often enough by people who worked in the industry – his songs would go down really well with European audiences. He thought of a few more lines for his new song, *Winds of Change*.

The new connect, pathways chosen,
The winds of change blow.
You can build a windmill, put up a wall,
You can bend or you can fall.

Now that he had some money behind him, the time might be right to pull together a set or two of originals and give it a go in Europe. Joe would love the idea and Matt, if he wanted, could come and play with them. Jenna as well. A viola would really suit their sound. Maybe Deon might come over for a visit. He would be a hit, with his unique perspective, talent and personality. It wouldn't matter if they didn't make money out of it, as long as they broke even. They would be based in Amsterdam, of course.

Sebastian pictured the apartment overlooking a canal. Sitting in the lounge room he could see Astrid, Jenna and himself. From where they were living, it would be a short bike ride through Vondelpark and into the centre of town.

The End

ACKNOWLEDGEMENTS:
Thank you for reading *Hunting the Wolf.*

Thanks again to Janet for her astute insights and on-going support. Thank you Vicki, for reading my rewrites and providing much needed advice. Thanks Ginny for your invaluable expertise. I'd also like to express my gratitude to Gaye, Steve, Maraya, Jillian, Peter and Jen.

FROM HERE TO THERE courtesy of Barry and Janet Hill.

GLAD (opening part to Amsterdam Lady) courtesy of Vincent Barrett.

ABOUT THE BOOK:
The wolf dreams are based on actual dreams I had as a child in the room (built illegally by my father) at the back of our Malabar house. The room with the piano that saw numerous bands and musicians pass through back in the day. Unfortunately for our neighbours, my two brothers are also musicians.

The characters Sebastian and Joe are a blend of imagination and real people. While I was writing the book, I had a dream where I actually met Joe at a party. It was a vivid dream and Joe was so compelling that I revised his character in the manuscript.

Deon was inspired by some of the many talented teenagers I met working with the First Nations community in Maitland and the Hunter Valley.

I hope you enjoyed the story.

If you have the time, please review the book on Amazon. You can contact Denis at dbrightbooks or denisbbright@gmail.com